Orbital Strain

Russell D. Jones

ISBN: 978-1-942622-27-7

Published by Pynhavyn Press

Cover art by Miblart

For my loving family, Delynn, Duane, Tiffany and Mary, who have always supported my wild dreams.

Chapter 1

"It's bullshit! I can't keep overloading my team's circuits on these delusional projects. Not when we have hundreds of laborers in popsicle-form. We're a button away from relieving our overstressed doctors and analysts. The administrators' expectations are impractical, and nearing inhumane."

Beth whipped her head around at the sound of Liam's raised voice echoing through one of the many mess halls on the Celestus colony and research starship.

Here he goes again... She rolled her eyes but flashed him a smile as she slid her tray along the metal table, bringing it to a gentle stop in front of Devin. Sophie and Alan rounded out the rest of her close friends. Everyone was now in attendance.

Her uninvited cheeriness went ignored as Liam barreled on. "The thing they don't understand about researchers is, we need time outside the lab too. Downtime increases productivity. I wish I could get the admins to explain their rejection of my personnel de-cryo requests." Other crew members in the vicinity, momentarily caught up in the outburst, turned their attention back to their own conversations or meals.

Alan, still in his white bridge uniform, nodded with too much enthusiasm. "I hear what you're saying, Liam."

Liam interjected over the top of him. "The higher-ups always have the debrik court booked out. I swear that's all they ever do."

Beth pressed her lips into a crooked line and locked eyes with Devin. "How long has this been going on?"

"The last ten or so," he replied. "It's just getting going, really."

"Great..."

Unconcerned with their discourteous aside, Liam continued.

1

"They're the laziest bunch on this ship. Why don't we save the resources and just put the lot of *them* back in cryo?" His demeanor softened suddenly as he met Alan's look of disapproval.

"Liam, I can relate to stress from heavy responsibility. The ship doesn't solely fly itself. The automated nav-system always has errors in its orbital corrections." Alan swallowed his last bits of food and went on. "And even with the colonists on hold, we still make planetary cargo runs, and there are the occasional angular requests from astrophysics. Everyone thinks the flight crew isn't carrying their weight out here, but we actually have a lot on our plates. If you want to hear my theory on the cryo delays, I suspect the synthesizers' inability to produce full meal plans is the result of a supply shortage. Maybe the Ortelius admins know they can't feed everyone, so they're leaving most people on ice."

Liam rubbed his chin. "That's an interesting theory."

Sophie, with half-chewed vitamin mash still in her mouth, jumped in. "You have to admit, though, the flight crew has had it pretty easy since we arrived."

Alan held out his hands, palms open. "Look, I'm not defending it. We really don't have *that* much to do since we arrived at Janis IV, but we busted our tails on the way over."

"Oh hell, you were in cryo half the time with the rest of us." Liam jabbed a finger in his face.

Alan casually brushed Liam's hand away. "Yes, and as I've said countless times, I was only awake when I was on duty. So, from my perspective, I was always working."

"Well, I'm going to submit a formal complaint to Ortelius HR. I'm at my wit's end with these unanswered requests, and I can't even get a decent game of debrik in." Liam seemed to notice Beth for the first time. "Beth, back me up on this."

"Whoa, I'm not taking sides. Besides, who needs R&R when we just received new bacterial samples from the colony that need analysis? Those domes aren't going to unseal themselves."

"Exactly! Maybe if we could relax a bit and blow off some steam, we could clear more colonists for excursions." Liam slammed his fist on the table. "Life in those cramped domes has got to be miserable; the least we can do is give them a break from it."

"And your argument is court time will help with that?" Sophie raised an eyebrow.

"If you need exercise, you could always jog from one end of the ship to the other," Beth suggested.

"That's one way to kill some hours," laughed Devin.

"Burnout is a real thing. As a medical officer, it's my duty to look out for the health of everyone on this ship. Last time I checked, I was one of those people." He tapped his chest.

Beth shook her head and smiled at Devin, since Liam had missed their sarcasm. Alan, Liam, and Sophie seemed locked in an epic stare-down of death and didn't react either.

"Come on, Sophie." Beth nudged her with an elbow. "You know someone in Administration, right? Think you could get a line on some court time for Liam and me?"

"I suppose I can try. But if I call in a favor, I want in on the game too. I'm tired of getting my ass handed to me by the pilots and the rest of the security staff. All they do is practice. I need some fresh rookies like you." She waved an open palm at the assembled group.

"I'll have you know, I was the league all-star and captain back in university," Liam warned her.

"Well, then... All-star," Sophie made air quotes, "... if I get us court time, you have yourself a match."

"You do it," Liam jabbed a finger on the table, "and if they ever get the synths up and running, I'll give you my first alcohol allotment."

"Now I'm motivated." Sophie grinned and rubbed her hands together vigorously.

Beth nodded, satisfied. "You should always wait for me to get off-shift to have an argument. I solved it in record time."

"Only until the next one." Devin winked at her.

"Beth, any idea about the next scheduled thaw?" Sophie asked.

"Your guess is as good as mine. Those orders come from way above me. I'll probably know my schedule about the same time you and Alan know yours."

"We need the rest of the research team," Liam complained. "Not several dozen colonists to examine for cryo-ailments on top of everything else. Why do they want more people down there if the planet isn't even fully cleared for anything beyond brief exploratory and sampling expeditions? I heard they're way behind the dome construction schedule. Where are those people going to live?"

"I doubt they'll dump that on us while we're still running these preliminary tests. The first batch of samples from the planet was completely corrupted," Beth said.

"Really? I hadn't heard that," Sophie said.

"Yeah, that's why we're so far behind," Liam added. "Faulty shielding on the extractors. When they left the atmosphere, they got hit by a particularly nasty flare. It irradiated the entire batch."

"What sets you back may propel others forward." Devin shrugged and cocked his head at Alan. "While the robotics team was working on de-radiating the extractors and fixing all the circuits fried in the event, I made some excellent progress on a little pet project I've been working on. I'm actually on the verge of a pretty major breakthrough. And if so, it's going to be absolutely epic."

"Care to share?" Liam asked, sounding annoyed at the change of subject.

"What, with a security officer sitting right here? You know we aren't supposed to share secrets across divisions." Devin smiled and winked at Sophie.

"Don't make me lock you up." Sophie wagged a scolding finger in his direction.

"But seriously, I might have something to share in a few months. It just depends on how many more robots eat circuit-melting radiation."

The group let out a collective chuckle. They knew each other at the Ortelius corporation back on the homeworld and became good friends over the years. When they were all assigned to the Celestus, they celebrated for a week straight.

As the group finished up their meals, a crew member sprinted up to their table. "Dr. Worth, we've been paging you for the last ten minutes. Why haven't you answered?"

Liam shot an annoyed glance at the girl and shrugged. "I don't have my com on because my shift doesn't start for another half hour."

"I'm sorry, Doctor, but you're needed in the medical bay right away. One of the colonists is being brought up from the planet. It's an emergency."

Liam groaned. "Damnit… all right. What in the universe could these colonists get themselves into while locked in those domes? Probably got run over by a cargo loader. What's the condition?"

"They sent no word on that. Only that he's being transferred to sickbay and should arrive in a few minutes. Admin needs all on-duty medical staff prepped and ready, and since you'll be on next—"

"Yes, yes, I'm on my way. Sorry, everyone. Duty calls… as it always does." Liam rose with his tray of half-eaten food supplements and deposited the whole thing in the recycler before exiting with the crew member.

"So, yeah. It's going to be awhile before we transport more colonists down, I'm thinking." Alan joked, attempting to cut the tension, but no one laughed.

A brushed-silver, humanoid, robotic attendant approached the table. "Shall I clear your meals?" it asked in a tinny, though almost-human voice.

"I'm still working," Beth replied.

"I'm finished." Sophie leaned back, allowing the robot to take her tray.

"Me too," Alan agreed, lifting his empty plate toward the attendant.

"I think I'm going to snag a little desert. Anyone want anything?" Devin asked. The others waved the offer away while the robot finished clearing the table. Devin stood and walked over to the food synth kiosk.

"Since we're all off, what do you say about catching a vid in the upper rec hall when you're finished?" Sophie offered.

"I'm in," Alan said.

"Beth?"

She had just put a big bite of vitamin-infused pudding-substance in her mouth and was chewing away. She swallowed the viscous mass with visible effort. "I think I'm headed to Devin's after this, and then I've got to crash out. Liam wasn't kidding about the shifts we've been pulling. The idea of bed is so appealing that I almost skipped out on dinner."

Devin rejoined them. A green mound of gelatin wiggled on a small plate in his hand.

"Look, it's green today." He took a big bite. "Hmm... tastes like yesterday's..." He frowned with mashed lips.

Beth reached across the table and pushed his face back playfully. "You're so weird. It's always the same."

"Well, we'll leave you two to your evening." Sophie said, kicking her legs over the bench and standing. "Message me when you get up. We'll hit the gym if you're up for it,"

"Yeah, I will. I've been avoiding it too much lately." Beth let out a long breath and pursed her lips, feeling guilty.

Sophie and Alan waved and left the hall. Beth finished her meal while Devin devoured his dessert. With one shift ending and another beginning, fresh faces found their way into the commons, some on their way to work and others getting off. The sparse place filling quickly.

Beth yawned and stretched her arms over her head. "We should go."

"You look really exhausted." Devin grabbed her hands and massaged her palms with his thumbs. "Why don't you get some sleep and come by my place after you're up?"

"Nah, I'm ok. I'll come now. I don't want to bail on Sophie at the gym again, and I won't have time for both when I get up. I'll probably be following up on Liam's incoming patient, and that's on top of the normal data cycles I'm running. Besides, I want to see this secret project you've been hiding from me."

"All right, I'll try not to keep you up too long." He leaned over the table and kissed her on the forehead before standing.

She joined him, and together they left the growing crowds.

Chapter 2

Circuit boards cluttered every surface, wires looped across the floors from one side to the other, and wall-mounted monitors streamed data feeds from every direction as Beth surveyed the total disarray in Devin's room.

No wonder he always wants to stay at my place; he couldn't find the bed if he wanted to.

"Oh man, Dev, you've really got to get a handle on this place. How do you even know what you're working on?"

"I know, I know, but trust me, I've got a system." He grinned sheepishly. "Don't worry about it for now; come and look at this." On what was supposed to be a table for dining sat a square enclosure; inside scurried several white mice. Each of them had tiny metal protrusions from their heads.

"What are you doing with all these mice? And what have you done *to* them?" Beth asked, scrutinizing the creatures as they wandered within their tiny world.

"I received these through a requisition from the medical testing lab. I'm not surprised you didn't see the acquisition, and the implants are what I'm about to show you." Devin picked up a tablet, then took an attached cord and inserted the other end into the data-jack located just behind his ear. "From this tablet, I can access the implants. The magic will happen on the monitor there." He pointed to one of the larger screens.

"By all means. I'm really curious." Beth cocked her head and raised her eyebrows skeptically. Cybernetic implants were nothing special. Almost everyone on the ship had a data-jack they could use to interface with the ship's various computer systems and controls in a much more efficient way than with a keyboard. Of course, the old-fashioned way worked fine for everyday tasks, but the amount of data the researchers crunched daily required light speed control and analysis.

The monitor flashed as Devin interfaced with it and brought up the desired program. "Now watch the mice," he said.

"Ok, I'm watching." As she gazed, one of them grew still, convulsed, then flopped over. "Did you do that? One of them just had a seizure. Did you kill it?"

"I did, but it's not dead. Well, in theory. Now check out the screen." Beth shifted her view to a scene on the monitor of a similar enclosure with several mice running around in it, except none of them had the head implants.

"What exactly am I looking at? Where are you keeping these other mice?"

"That's the same mouse, and others like it. You're looking at a completely virtual world. Not unlike any virtual reality we know, but the subjects are completely immersed in it. See that one just now moving?" He pointed at one on the screen. "That was our little guy there in the enclosure. Now he's completely in this digital world."

Beth watched as the mouse Devin indicated got up from a lying position and began sniffing around its artificial surroundings. "Ok, now I understand why you never showed this to me before. You've created a virtual reality for mice. I hate to tell you this, but people have been completely immersed in virtual reality for, oh I don't know, over a century! Don't you remember the big epidemic a few decades ago where a bunch of hackers starved to death because they were so engrossed, they never unplugged? I'll admit I don't remember there being a study of mice in virtual reality, but this doesn't scream groundbreaking to me."

Devin laughed. "You're absolutely right... If that's what this is. What I've done is completely download this creature's mind into this program. It's not in its body anymore at all." Devin pointed to the unmoving rodent in the physical enclosure.

"Wait, what exactly are you saying?"

"I'm saying this mouse's entire consciousness is inside this virtual world."

"How do you know for sure? Are you measuring brain activity?"

"It's actually much simpler than that. And it's also the problem I've run into. I can't get the mouse back into its body. I've tried dozens of test subjects. Their bodies die shortly after the transfer, and yet in the

8

virtual world, they keep going. There's no brain function, no connection anymore. They are in complete control of their new digital body. And they retain all the unique behaviors they had in physical form."

"That's crazy! Are you really serious about this? The implications of such a technology are… are unimaginable! Should you even be showing me this?" Beth's mouth fell open as she held her arms out wide. "Real consciousness transference? How did you ever manage it?"

Devin laughed. "I'm pretty sure you're not going to tell the admins on me. And besides, I'm only halfway there, as I just explained. The real breakthrough will be getting their bodies to stop rejecting their consciousness after I've transferred it. It's a long way off from being safe for humans. Part of the success is the fact that mice have tiny brains. There are a lot fewer neural pathways to screw up."

"This is… incredible. Incredible!" Her mouth worked open and closed as she fought to find the right words.

"I'm pretty excited about it." He smirked, beaming with confidence.

"You should be." All tiredness left Beth's body, replaced with excitement and disbelief.

"Someday, of course, it'll mean anyone can transfer to a program or even an artificially grown life form," Devin said.

"All the implications are tough to imagine right now. I'm so proud of you. Does the rest of your team know anything about this?" Beth reeled at the mind-blowing possibilities.

"Nope, I'm happy to say you're the first to know what I've been working on. The rest of the team has been largely concentrating on developing better cyber replacement-limbs for the accidents that will inevitably happen on the colony. Depending on what medical emergency arises, we might be working with you in implementing some of the newer designs." Devin winked.

"Have you ever tried uploading one of the mice to a robot, like A.R.I.A., over there?" Beth pointed to the humanoid mechanical assistant, which stood motionless in one corner of the room.

"Yes, and thank goodness I didn't test it on a full-sized robot."

Beth's eyes darted to the Artificial Robotic Intelligent Assistant and back to Devin. "Why, what happened?"

"I successfully uploaded a version of the program into a cleaning robot and transferred a mouse into it. The operation was completely successful, except the mouse's senses didn't interface correctly with the artificial detection systems. At least that's my running theory." Devin pulled the bed away from the wall, revealing several smashed-in panels and the remains of a severely damaged cleaning robot, half-wedged through the floor's metal tiles. "The thing basically went crazy and tried to escape the room. It almost succeeded!"

"You've got to be kidding."

"Made a real mess of things, right? I can't call maintenance either. They'd blow an airlock over it, and then the questions would follow the moment they ran diagnostics." Devin shook his head.

"Who knew those little things packed so much punch?"

"You'll never look at them the same again. For now, I've got to just leave it there and file a report when I have this place cleaned up and its program restored. Then, hopefully, I can convince them it just went haywire."

"The real question is, when did you have time for all this?" Beth looked around the room at the clutter of tech strewn about in what had initially appeared entirely random. Now everything looked somewhat in place, with each component connecting to the whole of the culmination of this project. No wonder he didn't want maintenance or anyone else in the room.

"To be fair, I did most of the research back on the homeworld."

Beth nodded. "Huh. Speaking of the homeworld, there will almost certainly be a lot of ethics pushback on something like this. The religious sects won't like it at all."

"No, they won't. But on the plus side, the Ortelius corporation will probably love it. The trick will be getting the credit for it, and making it accessible to everyone, not just the mega-wealthy."

"That would be pretty short-sighted of them," Beth said.

"You know how the upper-class is. Anything they can flaunt before the huddled masses is something they'll pay almost anything for. That's why I'm doing this work on the side. That way, I have a legal right to control how it's used. At least to an extent."

"You're one of the good ones." Beth stood on her tiptoes and kissed Devin, holding her lips to his for a drawn-out moment. When she came back down on her feet, she yawned and stretched her shoulders backward.

"Anyway, we can talk about it more after your shift. I won't be able to touch it for a while. I have a project coming up, and it's going to eat into my personal time pretty hard." Devin shrugged and shook his head.

"Story of our lives. Alan has it good, even if he doesn't want to admit it. But, then again, he isn't inventing a death cure either."

"No ma'am, he is not."

Beth wrapped her arms around Devin's lower back, tucking her head just under his chin. "I'm so excited I don't want to go. I'm going to have trouble sleeping tonight as it is, but I really should try."

"Yeah, it's the responsible thing to do."

"Why don't you come by just before you go in tomorrow, and we'll celebrate properly." Beth gave him a sly glance and a wink.

Devin blushed. "How could I refuse?"

"All right, I'll see you then." She gave him another brief kiss, then turned to the door.

"Hey." Devin grabbed her hand. "We're just two binary stars..."

Beth smiled and sighed. "Caught in an endless orbit. Love you."

"I love you too."

Beth left the room and headed down several corridors to the central lifts, which would take her to the section with her quarters. When she woke, she'd have to follow up on Liam's emergency patient. Hopefully, they'd already be in a recovery room, and she could focus on analyzing the latest bacterial specimens brought up from the colony world.

Chapter 3

"So, what's up with the colonist they brought in?" Sophie asked through heavy breaths as she jogged on a treadmill next to Beth.

Beth adjusted the pace of her machine down to a slower setting. "I don't know yet. Must not be a big deal. I'll get briefed when I go in after this."

"I hope it doesn't put you too far behind on your current projects."

"Hard to say at this point." Beth shrugged and wiped her forehead. "We're not doing anything exceptionally pressing at the moment, anyway. Just routine busy work. So far, all the tests from the few surface-samples have come back predictable. But of course, losing that large shipment of biomaterial to radiation has really set things back. Still, I'd thought we'd find something a little more interesting by now."

"Interesting like what?" Sophie raised an eyebrow toward Beth without slowing her pace.

"Nothing deadly!" She shouted a little louder than she intended. Beth glanced around to see if anyone noticed her unintended outburst. People occupied most of the machines lined up in rows on black, anti-slip, synthetic tiles. Most wore earpieces and remained oblivious in their workout jams. The mirrors lining the walls also contributed to the distraction, as no one cared what anyone else was doing while focusing on themselves.

"I mean, nothing that would impede the colony's progress, at least not much anyway. I don't know... I was just hoping for something unexpected to survive in the environment. So far, the initial landing teams have only collected plant material. Hardly noteworthy. Can you imagine what finding a whole new category of organisms would feel like?" Beth hopped off her machine before stopping it.

"I actually can't imagine. And as fascinating as it sounds, it's all fine until that new organism gets loose aboard the ship. Then it's my problem." Sophie slowed her treadmill to walk.

"Oh, I think a little excitement would be good for you! Your shifts have got to be pretty mundane."

"They are. I'm actually off for the next several days. There's not much for us to do until it's time to oversee the next round of colonists to go planet-side."

"That must be nice." Beth grabbed a towel and headed to the changing room.

"It is until you realize the company filled a ship with several hundred crew members and only enough recreational space for six people at a time," Sophie joked before joining her.

"Maybe you should consider dating." Beth laughed when Sophie rolled her eyes.

"Sure, send the next available hunk my way as soon as you see him."

* * *

Beth finished showering and dressed quickly at the gym. Energy-charged from the run, she felt ready to tackle her long shift in the med labs. The new patient might keep her moving, but there was no guarantee. She would probably sit for the next several hours analyzing data and looking for extracted sample anomalies.

She left the gym and made her way to the lifts that would take her down to the labs.

The moment she entered the medical area, she spotted Liam, who waved and walked up.

"Hey, Liam." Beth returned his greeting.

"Beth, I'm glad you're here."

"What's the status of the colonist?"

"Not much to tell," Liam admitted. "It's a real pain-in-my-ass mystery. He's been unconscious since before arriving onboard. No signs of foreign substances in his blood. No injuries detected. A heightened white blood cell count is all. Though it's not far out of the standard range. If I bang my head against this problem anymore, I'm going to be bedridden instead of bedside."

"Okay, okay. I get it. So, what exactly happened?"

"That's just as frustrating as the rest of it. Apparently, he was discovered in an unconscious state in one of the colony airlocks."

"In an environment suit?" Her eyes widened, and she gave Liam a concerned look.

"We're getting mixed messages. We heard he was fully suited, but there are also reports he had his helmet off. No one can confirm either way."

"Damn. So possible exposure to something? If we'd been able to check those irradiated samples, we'd better understand what he could have been exposed to. The entrances all have pathogen scrubbers, right?"

"Heavy-duty ones. Besides, no one is authorized to venture far from the small area we've tested around the domes. And certainly not without a suit, breathable atmosphere or not."

They discussed while they walked, eventually ending up in the med-lab quarantine section. "We've done some brain scans and are awaiting results. You'll want to do some follow-up blood samples in a couple of hours to see if we we missed anything or if levels have changed. There he is." They stopped in front of a thick pane of glass. Beyond, the colonist laid on a bed in a sterile white room. A robotic, humanoid medical assistant stood beside him in rest mode.

Beth crossed her arms. "All right, I'll take a look at the results of the scan. How's everything else?"

"Fine. I got quite a bit done on my to-do list, despite this unexpected guest. Unfortunately, since we can't find anything, there isn't much we can do for him at the moment. Maybe you'll have better luck."

"Okay, you have a good rest. I'll let you know if I find anything." Beth gave Liam a reassuring pat on the shoulder.

"Don't, please. I'm off shift, and I want it to stay that way. Just tell me he had a malfunction with his oxygenator and passed out from lack of air. No surprises."

"I'll do my best. Catch you later." Beth smiled and waved goodbye. Liam yawned and nodded in return before leaving.

Beth left the quarantine area for her office, a little way down the hall. Once inside, she slipped onto her desk chair and accessed the main computer database after a quick id scan. "Computer, open the quarantine patient's file and show me the results of his brain survey." The file opened on the screen in a nanosecond, but an indicator showed the computer still finishing the analysis. Beth pursed her lips.

Guess I have time for some coffee. Leaving the office and going a few doors down to a small break room, she greeted the colleagues, who sat chatting, on her way to the food synthesizer kiosk built into the far wall. The simple-looking metallic panel ran from floor to ceiling, sticking half an inch out of the wall. She chose coffee and cream from the touchscreen at its center, and in a few seconds, an aperture snapped open, revealing her selection.

When she returned to her office and sat back down, freshly caffeinated, the computer showed the brain scan analysis had completed. She ran a finger across the screen, noting the data. The computer automatically highlighted anything straying out of normal parameters. In this case, it showed a minor impact to the head. However, it wasn't severe and wouldn't likely have caused a loss of consciousness.

It looks like he might have fallen where he was found. That would account for the slight head trauma, but not his current state. Nothing here to indicate he suffered any lack of oxygen. She browsed further down the list, taking her time with each entry.

There's a slight uptick in his co2 levels, but again not beyond the accepted range. Liam was right; this is quite the mystery.

She closed the scan and opened the file on his blood tests, taken when he first arrived and again several hours later. With a couple of taps on the screen, the first one came up. The computer hadn't flagged anything as unusual, but she looked it over anyway.

This isn't getting me anywhere. I'm sure Liam and the other researchers went over all of this already. I doubt they missed anything. "Computer, bring up the results of all the patient's blood tests." She glanced at each of them briefly, looking at just the first few entries. "Run a comparison between the various tests, display any differences."

"Analysis complete." chimed the computer after a few seconds. Beth studied the results.

This is showing a slight decrease in iron throughout the time the patient has been here. Also, vitamins D and C. It's not much, though. White cell count, on the other hand, is up like Liam said. It could be something, or maybe not. "Computer, bring up the patient's blood results from just after he was taken out of cryosleep."

Once again, the results appeared in short order. "Now run another comparison, with these results included, in chronological order," Beth said.

"Analysis complete." It was immediately evident that something wasn't right.

A much more drastic change in the same elements from the time he left for the colony, 'til now. That's definitely something. But what ? Beth stood up and stretched. She took a sip of her coffee. It had gone cold, and she scrunched her face in disgust. She looked at her watch and saw, to her surprise, nearly two hours had passed.

Damn, I'm overdue to take a fresh blood sample.

The patient hadn't moved at all when she arrived back at the quarantine chamber. She gently touched the controls that activated the robot assistant inside the space. The dull-silver, faceless, mechanical humanoid came to life with a brief system check. The tiny jerking movements it made, as part of its self-diagnostics, looked like an awkward jig. It always made Beth chuckle. As human as they tried to make them, robots were still graceless in many ways.

Finally, the robot stilled. "M.E.R.C.Y is active—all systems normal. Awaiting your command, Dr. Adler."

"M.E.R.C.Y, please take a blood sample from the patient and have it analyzed. Broad scan," Beth ordered.

"Acknowledged." The artificial life-form placed its hand on the patient's arm, siphoned out the sample using its built-in extractor, then moved to the side of the room where it deposited the collected vial of blood into a receptacle designed to scan it. The person on the table didn't react to the intrusion.

"Anything else, Dr. Adler?"

"That will be all for the moment, M.E.R.C.Y. Go to standby mode."

"Acknowledged."

Beth went back to her lab and slid onto her desk chair. "Computer, bring up the latest blood test results from the patient when they are completed."

She took her cup back to the break area, dumped the contents down the recycler, and then made a fresh one. She looked over the selections on the kiosk menu, surprised to see some new additions.

Did maintenance finally fix the food synths? Better take advantage before they go down again. She chose a vegetable wrap, and in a few seconds, the aperture revealed the food on the receiving shelf. Taking the plate and a fresh coffee, she went back to the lab.

The wrap didn't last long as she scarfed it before the analysis completed. When the results appeared on the screen, Beth stared at them for several seconds.

This isn't what I expected. The same elements had dropped further. This time, the computer flagged them as being abnormally low. Adrenaline was up, and white cells remained high but steady.

What's the cause?

A crash echoed from elsewhere in the labs. A horrific, high-pitched scream followed as Beth leaped from her chair.

What the...?

She flew through her door, grabbing the frame to help swing her into the hall as she took off at a sprint. Several other researchers came out of their labs and joined the rush to investigate. The sound of loud vomiting and something solid slamming against metal emanated from the quarantine area. A few doctors were already there when Beth arrived. The patient was up, eyes wide and fearful, his fist repeatedly banging on the glass.

"What's going on!" he yelled. "Why am I in here? Let me out!" He had vomited on himself, the glass, and many parts of the room. M.E.R.C.Y lay on the floor, having apparently been knocked over.

Not an easy thing. Beth noted.

"We need you to calm down. We're here to help," Director Richter, head of the medical wing, said to him. "Dr. Adler, you're assigned to this patient, right? What's his diagnosis?"

She barely heard the question. Instead, her mind worked furiously to deduce the cause. Her eyes searched for answers within the container. Hysteria, vomiting, confusion, mineral deficiencies, increased—

"Dr. Adler, did you hear me? What's going on?" The man laid a hand on Beth's arm, bringing her back to reality.

"Oh, I'm sorry, Director. I'm... I'm not sure. I was looking over his blood tests when I heard the commotion. There are some deficiencies, but nothing to explain this."

"Everyone back to your labs." Director Richter ordered. He went to an interface panel on the wall and activated M.E.R.C.Y while the onlookers slowly dispersed. The robot righted itself after a few seconds of jerking self-diagnostics. The patient's shoulders and stomach heaved as he tried to vomit, but he had nothing in his belly to eject. His face scrunched in pain with the dry heaves.

"What's happening to me? Why am I here?" Screams and cries erupted from his throat between empty purging.

"M.E.R.C.Y, administer a sedative," Director Richter said. An injector needle protruded from the robot's palm as it approached the patient, who backed away, his hands held up in front of him.

"No, what are you doing to me? Stop it! Stop! Why—" His back hit the far wall, and with nowhere to go, his face changed from panic and confusion to anger and determination. Baring his teeth, he lurched forward, grabbed M.E.R.C.Y, and shoved. M.E.R.C.Y placed its hand on his arm, jabbing him with the injector in the process. The robot stumbled back as he pushed it. The man didn't continue the assault but shot wide-eyed, tooth-bare, feral looks at those observing through the glass. After a few seconds, the combativeness left him as the drugs took hold.

"M.E.R.C.Y, clean up the patient and the room. Then administer a blood test," Director Richter ordered.

"Hold on a sec, Director Richter." Beth moved in beside him, though her eyes remained on the patient. "I was reviewing the results from a test I just took. We can wait before taking another. I want a sample of that bile, however. He shouldn't have had much in his system to purge."

"Very well, I'll leave you to it, then. I'll be in my lab; let me know what you find. I'm want to know what's going on here." Director Richter left the room while Beth gazed through the window separating her from the patient. M.E.R.C.Y returned him to the bed before retrieving a bile sample and restoring the space.

What would have caused such a reaction? Nothing I've looked at should have... I need to add memory loss to his file, as well as disorientation and hysteria. "M.E.R.C.Y, did you allow yourself to be pushed away by the patient?" Beth asked.

"No, Dr. Adler," the robot replied as she continued her work.

"Isn't that unlikely given your weight and strength?"

"That is correct."

"Hmmm." Beth wondered aloud. She left the quarantine area and headed back to her office. The latest blood test results might have further clues. The problem was, she didn't know what to look for. Taking a seat in front of her computer, she brought up the readouts. The system had highlighted the drastic drop in various elements in the subject and a rise of adrenaline and white blood cells. However, none of it explained the reason for the lack of vitamins. "Computer, have any of the other doctors done a visual inspection of the blood sample?"

"Yes, Dr. Worth analyzed the initial sample."

"Show me his notes." A text document displayed on the screen, along with a video capture from the microscope. Unfortunately, there wasn't much to it. Liam had reported nothing unusual. He listed the elevated white blood cell count and increased adrenaline, but beyond that, it appeared like normal blood. She was quickly running out of ideas. Something had been draining him of several vitamins but didn't show up on any of their scans.

"Show me a microscopic visual of the latest blood test."

"Displaying."

On the screen, a new image of active blood replaced old one. As she gazed at the live image, something looked off. On several of the white cells, she spotted extremely tiny, bulbous growths, like soap bubbles on the side of a tub, clear and almost imperceptible. She reached up with two fingers and drew them apart on the screen, magnifying a section. A distinct picture emerged. Within the bubbles, something moved. It looked like a tiny transparent fish in a bowl. "Oh my stars…"

What are these things? Fascination and horror battled for supremacy in Beth's mind. She pulled up an earlier blood sample and zoomed in on it. The cells appeared free of the tumors.

They must be growing, whatever they are. They weren't visible at all in the earlier sample. Even now, they aren't that easy to spot. The computers haven't even detected them. I'd better call in Liam and the rest of the medical team.

* * *

Half an hour later, a group of six scientists gathered in a meeting room in the medical wing. They sat around an oval table with a real-time feed of the latest blood sample showing on the table's surface. Beth stood at the head and waited for everyone to settle.

"This better be really eye opening, Beth." Liam sat hunched over, his chin resting on his interlaced fingers, supported by his elbows on the table.

Beth scowled at him, shooting a look to match the seriousness she felt. "Thanks for your confidence, *Dr. Worth*." She bit the name at the end to show Liam she didn't appreciate his attitude at the moment. It didn't matter if he'd been sleeping, or she'd pulled him out of his precious rec-time. A foreign entity had infiltrated a human and was doing who-knows-what to his body.

Liam went white and glanced down, clearing his throat, then looked back up. "Sorry, Dr. Adler, I mean. Why have you pulled us all in?"

"I've discovered a foreign body attached to the white cells of our patient. I picked it up in visual examination with the most recent blood sample. However, I've looked over the previous samples taken, and they're all the same. Something is growing on each of them. It still isn't detectable by our most sophisticated scans and was only visible under a microscope after an estimated twenty hours of incubation, based on the time the patient was found in the airlock. Whatever this is, we need to find out how to detect it and how it managed to get past the subject's envirosuit."

"Do we know if he was fully suited?" one doctor said.

19

"We should verify that," Liam said. "The medics who dropped him off said he was found without a helmet."

"We're monitoring his condition for any changes, but we should study this phenomenon and see what develops. Isolate the infection and develop a countermeasure. We must assume the entire colony could have been exposed," Director Richter said.

"The colony is one thing, but what about the ship? Can we trust the crew that transported him here?" Liam asked.

"Quarantine measures were followed during the transfer from the shuttle to our facilities. It's unlikely there was an exposure here. The colony may be another matter," Director Richter said. "I'll bring it to the attention of the other admins immediately. We should make detection our number one priority. What do you have on that front, Dr. Adler?"

"The earliest symptoms are a drop in iron, and vitamins C and D, an increase in adrenaline, as well as a heightened white cell count. We can take blood samples from anyone suspected of exposure, compare them to their post-cryo tests, and adjust the computer's parameters to note more minuscule changes. It's too early to be sure, but I'm theorizing the organism encourages adrenaline output, which it appears to like, while feeding on the other minerals. The white cells are likely the body's reaction to the foreign organism."

"There could be a lot more variables, given only one patient," one researcher mentioned.

"Yes, but this is a good start." Director Richter said. "Dr. Adler, I know you're hours past your scheduled shift. Get some rest. We'll take it from here." He stood and left the room.

The remaining researchers broke into discussions, which varied from fascination to near panic. The discovery of a new entity, parasitic or not, was cause for celebration. Its integration into a human's body, past all defenses, on the other hand... Beth exhaled a breath that felt long held as she exchanged glances with Liam. He pressed his lips tight as his eyebrows rose, making his eyes widen, matching Beth's concern.

Chapter 4

Beth laid awake in her bed, staring at the off-white hexagon tiles on the ceiling. She hadn't slept well for the last four rotations, the same number of days the medical team had been working on the infected patient's issue, with little success. Early on, they'd reduced his meds and allowed him to awaken. Unfortunately, he'd become aggressive each time, refused questions, and tried to break out of the room. Things weren't going well.

She pulled herself from her covers and went to her computer. It wasn't time for her shift, though everyone in the research labs had been assigned to this project now. She had some influence, but that only went so far in the hierarchy of her department. The situation expanded to the point the admins stepped in and now called all the shots. Still, she had plenty of ways to help. Over the last several days, she'd pulled more hours than anyone else, until Director Richter ordered her to get some mandatory rest, something the administrators rarely did. She'd never suffered from burnout. Having a goal and a time-sensitive purpose provided all the motivation she needed. Even if she couldn't return to the lab for several more mandated hours, she had other ways to be productive. Her computer had access to all the research in the medical mainframe for which she was authorized, so she could stay up to date by reading everyone else's findings.

She logged in, pulled up the project, then ran a search for the latest additions. Several files populated the screen. The entry at the top turned out to be a mundane report on the individual's current state. The parasite continued to grow and spread, but not enough to kill its host, appearing now in muscle tissue cells. She hypothesized it had been there all along and only recently became visible under a microscope. She saw how much strength the patient gained in a short time, enough to push a robot around. Blood testing proved to be the only effective way of detecting the intrusion, as still no visual manifestations appeared on the patient.

Her mail chimed, and she opened the message without checking the sender.

<Dear Dr. Adler,

This is Engineering Specialist Eckhart. My supervisor passed on your message to me. I was one of the personnel who found Mr. Sims in the external dome airlock. To answer your inquiry, Mr. Sims is a civilian consultant brought down with the first wave of colony establishment crew. He's an engineer who helped design the air filtration system.

He was fully suited when I found him in the airlock, including his helmet, which you asked about specifically. There was, however, a small tear in the suit near his right ankle. The dome airlock is a dual-chamber system. He had already passed through the first, which is a complete decontamination unit, and was unconscious in the second. He would not have been able to move out of the first unless the sensors cleared him of all foreign matter. I personally worked on this system and can assure you it's far beyond the standard lab bacteria and virus scanners.

My supervisor has authorized me to send the log, which covers his exit from the dome. I hope this answers all your questions. Please send word of his condition as you are able.

Specialist Eckhart>

"I don't care how sophisticated your sensors are. This entity evaded all our early attempts to detect it." Beth shook her head as she spoke the words to the screen. It had taken over three rotations to get this reply, and while she was glad for it, it should have come much sooner. Still, it contained helpful bits of information. The infection had likely gotten in through a rip in the suit near his ankle. It might have torn on a sharp rock or maybe a piece of jagged equipment used in the dome's construction.

What made little sense to her was the suits were supposed to be extremely durable, with several protective layers. On top of that, they were all equipped with containment breach warning systems. For everything to go wrong with his protection, struck her as suspicious.

Next, she opened the packet attached to the message. It wasn't a complete log, as the only name not redacted was Morgan Sims. The information on the record was sparse. Mr. Sims received a service alert for a malfunctioning moisture intake outside the domes. At least, this was the reason cited for his exit. She noted the time between his exit and reentry was only a couple of minutes.

Not much time to fix anything. What also stuck out was the blank officer authorization signature space.

I thought airlock access required an officer's password. I should find out if he had the authorization to let himself out. Even then, wouldn't the door automatically note him as the authorizing officer? She didn't know enough about the surface procedures to be certain, but the lack of accountability around the incident sat in her gut like a bubbling lump of lead.

She forwarded the message to the rest of the research team, noting her observations before firing off a quick question to Specialist Eckhart.

<Thanks for your reply. I just have one more question for the moment. Did Mr. Sims have the authorization to let himself out? I noticed the log didn't include a signature. If not, how would I find out who opened the airlock? Sorry, I guess that's two questions.

Let me know as soon as you can.

Dr. Beth Adler>

While her research dead-ended on the biological front, it took off on the conspiratorial investigation side; something she hadn't expected in the least. Leaning back in her chair, Beth stretched as her nose picked up the sour stink from her pits.

Whew, I need a shower. She let out a slow breath, then pushed herself up from the desk and headed to the bathroom.

Half an hour later, she strolled back into her main room wrapped in a towel while she dried her hair with another. The new message icon flashed on the computer screen with Devin's name.

<Hey, hope you got a little rest. I know they're making you take some time off. I'm meeting the gang in the dining hall for lunch at 14:00 if you feel up to joining.>

That gave her a couple of hours to decide if she was going or not.

I think I'll head down to the quartermasters before meeting them. I want to ask about the suit. She slipped into clean clothes and ran a comb through her hair, letting it hang loose to dry.

The ship's supply and requisition section lay near engineering, just about the farthest place from where she was now. Nearly all crew quarters were located away from the reactor and heart of engineering. Not that radiation leaks were common, but it was nice to know the ship designers had some safety in mind.

Beth dressed and headed to the main lifts that would get her most of the way there. Unfortunately, the supply area was one of many sections she'd never had a reason to visit, and she only had a vague idea of how to get there. So after getting off on the wrong floor, she used the onboard navigation system to work her way down, which took nearly forty-five minutes.

As she stepped through the automatic sliding doors, Beth beheld a massive open space with seemingly endless shelves holding colossal crates. It rivaled the most extensive planet-side warehouse she'd ever seen. She noticed a desk just inside the door where a short line led to an officer who addressed those waiting. Stepping up to the rear, she stood patiently, taking in the area. All about, cargo loaders, driven by numerous robot workers, pulled down large metal containers and moved them to one place or another. They hovered and zipped above, below, and all amongst each other like insects gathering food. The place swarmed with chaotic activity. As she gaped, the entropy coalesced into patterns in the disorder.

I'm glad I'm not a quartermaster. Looks like one wrong move, and this place would grind to a halt.

Eventually, her turn came. The man at the counter glanced up briefly, not pausing as he typed away at his computer. She stepped up and greeted him with a broad smile as his gaze dropped.

"Hi, I'm Dr. Adler from the medical research facility."

"Congratulations. To what do we owe the honor of your visit?" he said without looking up.

She ignored his sarcasm and pressed on. "I just have a question or two."

The guy looked past her at the long line stretching out the door. "No problem, I have all day," he said with a look that managed to be both smug and irritated.

"On the standard-issue envirosuits, what would it take for one to tear?"

"What do you mean?"

"I mean, what could cut a hole in one? A sharp rock or...?"

"Are you serious?"

"Well, yes."

"No." he sounded annoyed, like someone fed up with a child's constant questions. "A sharp rock could not penetrate a standard-issue envirosuit. Is that all?"

"Almost. What could? Anything found on the colonial planet?"

"Rocks ain't going to do it, and there are certainly no vicious creatures down there that could, either." He looked past her and called out, "Next."

"One more question."

"Lady, I'm swamped here. I don't have time for curious doctors from the med labs."

"Just tell me what could puncture one."

"Look, all the suits are a titanium-carbon, nano-fiber weave. They don't tear. The material is produced and assembled using a laser cutter."

"So, it would take a laser to slice one? Anything else, a knife or a bullet?"

"Absolutely not. The ones sent to the colony are all the same material as the void-walk ones, made to withstand micro-meteor impacts, hostile corrosive environments, and extreme heat, cold, and pressure. Nothing less than an industrial cutting laser will put a hole in one."

"And these kinds of lasers, were any of them transferred to the colony?"

"I'm not in the business of discussing colony supply transports with non-supply personnel. Especially doctors."

"Oh, well, thank you, you've been very—"

"Tell me this, though," he interrupted. "What exactly are you working on up in the medical wing that you think an environment suit won't protect from?"

She cleared her throat. "I'm afraid I'm not in the business of discussing medical research with non-medical personnel. Especially quartermasters." Hands resting on her hips, she stared the man directly in the eyes, daring him to object and taking satisfaction in throwing his words back in his face. His dismayed look told her he wasn't used to pushback. She doubted she would get any more helpful information out of him, so she turned on a triumphant heel and left the supply and requisitions area.

After the doors slid shut behind her, the spring fell from her step.

The information she gained was a mystery at best, and something more sinister at its worst. Her mind went right into theory mode.

Is it possible the suit accidentally came into contact with a laser during or before the unfortunate, Mr. Sims, donned it? The people on the surface had worked on various construction projects since they landed. Establishing a foothold on the surface and preparing for the remaining colonists constituted their primary mission.

If the suit was damaged and not noticed or not reported during this construction, it would explain the breach. Or was a shipment of lab suits mistakenly sent down instead of the planet-approved ones?

She had familiarity with the former. They used them regularly in the labs when handling toxic chemicals or bacteria.

But it should've been obvious he was putting on the wrong type of suit, shouldn't it? That also wouldn't explain why the suit's breach protocol didn't set off any alarms. Then again, it could be some kind of sabotage. But to what end? Who would benefit from it? Could Morgan have really pissed someone off that much? None of it made any sense.

Chapter 5

The dining commons bustled with so much activity it took Beth several minutes to discover she'd arrived before her friends. Picking up scattered conversation, she learned the food synths had been offline for hours and only resumed operation ten minutes ago. She leaned against a wall, a tray of vitamin mash in her hands, waiting for a table to free up capable of accommodating the five of them. The day the patient came up from the colony was the last time she had seen anyone. Devin joined her as she finally snagged a free chair.

"What's going on with the crowds today?" Devin asked, sitting next to her.

"Sounds like the synths went down earlier," Beth answered with a shrug. He nodded, then shoved a large bite of processed paste in his mouth.

Alan strolled over, looking somewhat annoyed as he shook his head. "This place is crazy today. Anyway, good to see you both? What's the latest with your patient, Beth?"

"Nice to see you, too, Alan." Beth smiled. "We're making some progress, I think. He's been kept in an unconscious state for the last several days while we run our tests."

Sophie and Liam arrived and greeted the group. Beth nodded back, then continued. "What's difficult is we really don't know what he's contracted or how to deal with it. But the director has all the labs working round the clock on this. All our other research has come to a complete halt."

"This guy is really the talk of the station. Rumors are flying all over. What do you think his chances are?" Sophie asked.

Liam chimed in. "Well, so far, he's no worse than the day he was brought in. There was a bit of an incident when he first woke up, but the sedation keeps him stable. As far as his vitals are concerned, he's perfectly healthy. What's not common knowledge and should not leave this table..." Liam's eyes met Beth's before glancing around at the other members. He lowered his voice, and they all leaned in. "What's not well known is that whatever is infecting him is growing, and we don't know what it is or how to stop it. It's not killing him, best we can tell, but it's digging in."

Beth's lips drew into a thin line as she nodded.

Her worried look must have scared the others, because Liam quickly spoke again. "That said, I'm confident we will isolate the source of trouble and be all the wiser for it."

"I think we have good reasons to be optimistic." The edges of Beth's mouth turned up in a weak smile, meant to reassure everyone, but she felt like it wasn't succeeding, so she took a small bite of food.

"What's not to be optimistic about? The Ortelius corporation has all the resources, the most advanced A.I. computers, and the homeworld's best researchers. If we can't solve this, no one can," Liam bragged.

Devin ran a reassuring hand back and forth across Beth's back. "I'm sure you'll figure it out, honey."

"Well, I've got something potentially interesting that has nothing to do with the colony or strange infections," Sophie said. Everyone crowded in, their raised brows and wide eyes exposing their piqued interest. A juicy story didn't come along often; besides, Sophie rarely shared gossip from the security department. Those gathered waited like drooling animals about to receive a treat for good behavior. She glanced around for nearby eavesdroppers, then licked her lips and pressed them into a serious line.

Liam cleared his throat. "Well, what is it?" His hands shook in frustration.

Sophie laughed. "You're all really desperate for a bit of gossip, aren't ya?"

"Sophie, you're killing us," Beth said.

"All right, all right. I overheard some of the other security members discussing something they discovered while patrolling the astro-exploration section." Sophie paused and looked around at the curious faces.

"And?" Liam asked.

The rest of them must have been thinking the same thing as they stretched forward to hear her words. She seemed to relish leaving them in total suspense. In all likelihood, what she said wouldn't be profound, but they all ached for some fresh news.

Beth gave Sophie her attention but continued taking small bites of food. The discovery of the hole in the suit, and the distinct possibility someone might've purposely sabotaged it, thrashed about in her mind. Still, some other news might be a pleasant distraction.

"Apparently, something is headed this way."

"Like what? A comet?" Devin asked.

"No, they don't know what it is, exactly. Only it's not anything like a big chunk of rock. Security overheard it described as a wave. But something about it has the whole astrophysics department shitting their collective pants. There's something about it they can't identify, and it's headed this way."

"I find that hard to believe," Alan said. "If there were any danger of that kind, navigation staff would all be alerted, and certain procedures would have to be followed."

The rest of the group nodded their agreement, but Sophie shook her head. "Not necessarily. I don't know when it's supposed to be here, but to prevent some kind of mass panic, the admins might not want to announce it so far in advance. They've only alerted security and a few need-to-know departments and might only make a broad announcement when it's closer. Besides, if it turns out to be nothing, or if the physicists are wrong about its trajectory, and it misses us completely, then they would've stirred the pot for no reason. At the very least, I'd bet they're waiting for more information."

"That seems plausible," Devin agreed.

"I'm not so sure." Liam leaned back, letting out a sharp breath. "It's pretty common knowledge around the ship that we brought a colonist onboard with some kind of ailment and he hasn't been released. It's hard to keep something that simple under wraps. I doubt they could keep anything affecting the entire ship a secret."

"But no one outside your department knows exactly what's happening with him." Sophie held out her palms and gave Liam an expectant look before continuing. "The only reason everyone heard about him is it involved multiple departments to bring him here. Not to mention he fell ill on the colony, where communication isn't as strict as it is up here. If there's something out there, flying through space, how would anyone but astrophysics know about it? If it was visible on scans, maybe some of the shuttle and flight crews could have spotted it, but would they have any idea what they were looking at?"

Liam gave a sort of half-shrug, half nod.

"Not likely," Alan answered for him. "We would probably think it's some rare phenomena. The astrophysics department uses much more sophisticated scanning equipment than we have on the bridge or any of the shuttle-craft. If it's something they haven't seen before, that's news."

"Like I said, it might be nothing." Sophie clapped her hands before holding them up and leaning back in her chair.

"That's actually pretty interesting." Beth shifted in her seat to find a more comfortable position. The dining area was designed with turnover in mind. The chairs weren't supposed to help anyone relax. They made people want to leave for softer pastures. She took in a deep breath and let it out slowly.

"That was a pretty big sigh. What's up, Beth?" Devin asked. "Feeling burned out?"

"No, the opposite, actually. But something's been weighing on my mind the last few days. Liam is up on some of this. I actually shouldn't be sharing, but I feel like I need to tell someone."

"Well, if you shouldn't, then I must caution you," Sophie said. "I know we all like sharing rumors and gossip, but there are severe punishments for talking about sensitive data."

"You're not going to turn her in, are you, Sophie?" Liam asked.

"Shit, of course not. I'm just looking out for her best interests."

"I don't think this is considered classified; it has nothing to do with our research, but it does have to do with the patient and what happened to him."

"If you feel comfortable, you know you can trust us," Sophie said, giving Beth a reassuring touch on the arm.

Beth nodded. "Well, the good news is that when I get back to my lab, I'll check on something I think could be a successful counter agent for the patient."

"Feeling good about what you're seeing?" Alan asked.

"Yes. I've already seen some positive results, and with a few tweaks, I may have solved our dilemma."

"That doesn't sound very controversial," Liam said, crossing his arms.

"I wasn't sure I wanted to share the other part because it might be cause for alarm or nothing at all. Regardless, it's been bugging me." Everyone went quiet, so Beth continued. "We learned our patient likely had an exposure incident outside the domes because of a tear in his envirosuit. If you saw my group message, Liam, that much you know.

Just before I came here, I went down to acquisitions and talked with a rather rude quartermaster. It took some work, but I found out those suits are insanely durable. I mean, micrometeoroid durable."

"That's not all that surprising," Liam said. "I think we could've guessed at that."

"Right, but he told me the only thing that could cut one was a specialized laser. He was really adamant about it. Nothing could cause a breach in the fabric except the same lasers used to manufacture it. I asked if they have any on the colony, but he wouldn't answer. If I had a way to see a manifest, then I'd know."

"What does it matter?" Liam asked.

However, Sophie was right with her and spoke when Beth narrowed her eyes at Liam's hardheadedness. "Because if there are no lasers on the colony, it has to be something else, or there's another explanation. It's about eliminating possibilities; you should understand that."

"Of course, I do. It's basic research," Liam said, looking offended.

"What do you hope to find out?" Devin asked.

"Well, I probably won't have any way to prove it one way or another, but given the circumstances, there is a possibility someone purposely sabotaged the suit."

"Why would anyone do that?" Devin asked.

"That's what I can't figure out."

"There's a lot of construction going on down there. It was probably damaged by accident," Alan said.

"I thought that too, but wouldn't someone have noticed and reported it?" Beth questioned. "I mean, what are the chances that someone would just hang it back up after an incident? And then there are the fail-safes. The suit should alert the wearer of any problems, yet both failed."

"I had no idea you were such a detective," Alan grinned.

"She loves a good puzzle." Devin nodded.

"I'm not joking about this." Beth shot an icy gaze across the group.

Sophie let out a slow breath. "You're suggesting something pretty radical. The company handpicked everyone on this ship and on that planet to be here. We all had thorough background checks and psych evaluations. But assuming you're right, and it wasn't a mistake, what motivation would someone have to sabotage a suit?"

"I don't know. Maybe to kill our patient? It's tough to get any answers when he's kept in a sedated state around the clock."

"Perhaps I can petition the director to have him taken off sedatives again so we can ask him directly why he left the domes. It may even help us work toward a cure for his condition. At least that's what I'll tell Director Richter," Liam said.

"Ok, I'll do my part too," Sophie offered. "I can use my security clearance to do some digging into this guy. Anyone on the initial landing crew should be in the active security files. I'll see if anything comes up as out of the ordinary."

"I really appreciate it, guys."

"Well, this has certainly been an interesting meal," Liam said. "Mysterious spatial anomalies and a possible murder attempt. Being a hundred light-years from home has never felt so thrilling."

Liam stood and bid the group farewell. Alan and Sophie left soon after. When they were gone, Beth and Devin met each other's eyes.

"What do you think? Am I out of my mind?" Beth ran a hand through her hair, then brought it around and rubbed her forehead.

"I think you're great at finding things most people would overlook. But to be honest, I hope you're wrong about it."

"Me too."

He leaned over the table and kissed her. "Come by my place when you're off. I've been having some more success with my little side project."

Chapter 6

When Beth walked into the quarantine lab, a surprise waited for her. The patient, Morgan Sims, sat on the bed in the isolation room, looking lucid and talking with a doctor on the other side of the glass. She spotted Liam and made a beeline for him.

"You work fast," she said, coming up behind him.

He turned to her, raising his eyebrows and shrugging. "I had nothing to do with it. He was up when I got here."

"Have you seen the latest test results?"

"There should be some ready shortly. Let's go take a look," Liam suggested.

Beth followed him back to his lab, where he pulled up the most recent blood test results while she leaned over his shoulder and watched the screen. The analysis showed already completed, and Liam opened the digital chart. The data stated Director Richter had ordered precise amounts of the depleted vitamins and elements administered to the patient through his I.V. That way, they could still monitor any drop in the man's levels. Beth eyed the blood data. Vitamins D, C, and Iron stood at all-time lows, while calcium had gone to the moon.

"The chart says he's receiving supplements. Did that not actually happen yet?" she asked.

"I was there when it started. Director Richter has been steadily increasing the dosage," Liam replied.

"Oh, my stars... Bring up the live sample." Beth pointed at the screen.

"Computer, bring up the live test sample and magnify," Liam said. The microscopic picture appeared before them. It was anything but familiar. The taint of infection overran the cells like a crater-pocked planet.

"This is bad…" Beth murmured, putting a hand over her mouth.

"How can this…? I've been looking at the tests all week. His condition had mostly stabilized. I had a solid theory on the symbiotic nature of the organism, given the lack of harm to the subject. This… this is unsustainable." Liam's jaw hung open as he stared at the feed.

Beth grabbed him by the arm and spun him to face her. "We have to go to the director right away."

Liam nodded, then followed Beth out of the lab. A thunderous crash resounded through the medical wing.

"That came from quarantine," Liam said.

Beth saw his eyes grow wide with realization. She stared at him; the same horror reflected at her. "This can't be good."

They rushed through the lab corridors and into the quarantine room, but stopped short just inside the door. Crumpled, M.E.R.C.Y lay motionless on the floor outside the containment area. Glass shards littered the tiles like shells on a beach. Among them, she identified the bloody form of the doctor they'd seen chatting with Mr. Sims earlier.

"Where's the patient?" Liam asked, as if Beth somehow had the answer.

She barely heard him as she sprang into action, hitting the communicator button near the entrance with her fist. "We need security to quarantine. Emergency!" Her voice rumbled with unwavering authority, despite panic on the rise within. From the isolation room, a figure rose like a deadly cobra. The eyes of Morgan Sims blazed with savage fury, like a lion cornered by weaker enemies. Liam and Beth slowly backed out the door, whirled, and sprinted down the hallway. Behind them, footfalls crunched on broken glass.

Other researchers popped their heads out of doors, curious about the commotion.

"What was that sound?" Dr. Janus asked as Beth and Liam came bolting toward her. Her curious look flipped to surprise and confusion at seeing the two other doctors' faces. "What…What's going on?"

"Shut your doors. We have a breach in quarantine," Beth yelled as she and Liam shoved Dr. Janus back into her lab, joined her, then slammed the door behind them. Alarms whooped suddenly, and the overhead lighting turned red as a calm male voice came over the communication system.

"Medical wing emergency lockdown initiated. Please stay where you are and wait for security." It repeated this phrase about five times before stopping, though the ringing alarm and red lighting persisted.

"What happened out there?" Dr. Janus asked.

"The patient broke out. It looks like he threw M.E.R.C.Y through the safety glass," Beth said.

"How is that possible?"

"It shouldn't be," Liam breathed, just above a whisper.

Beth heard the slap of bare feet combined with the scrape of glass fragments grinding, splintering, and embedding themselves into the heavy footfalls. "I think he's coming this way," she whispered, putting a finger to her lips.

Liam opened a drawer in a nearby cabinet and removed several scalpels, offering them around. Beth glanced at the object with uncertainty, her eyes meeting Liam's. He nodded, fear and seriousness frozen on his face. She took the improvised weapon with a sigh and returned his nod.

The footsteps grew louder. Arguing voices joined them, followed by hastened boots clomping, then the electronic buzz of fired stun darts echoed through the labs.

"He's not going down!" someone said.

Beth caught her breath, tensing.

They must be right outside.

The door burst in as the patient crashed to the floor. Metal protrusions stuck out from his skin at odd angles—the result of a dozen darts designed to deliver an incapacitating shock. One should have been enough to take an average person down. Two if they were robust. Beth could see four on his back, alone.

Morgan Sims writhed on the ground, trying to get to his feet. Blood from glass cuts made his footing unstable, and he slipped about wildly, clawing with outstretched fingers and crimson toes.

Outside, the body of a mangled security guard spilled red from eyeless sockets.

He's going to kill us...I have to do something...

With her scalpel in hand, Beth let out a sharp breath and charged the deranged man. She jabbed the tiny blade in his neck. Scarlet gushed from the fresh wound. Frightened, and with adrenaline pumping, she skittered back, leaving the object embedded.

In the doorway, a fully envirosuited soldier appeared, wielding a stun baton. With furious force, he brought it down on Morgan Sims. Blood ran freely, but somehow the scalpel found its way into the patient's hand. He lashed out at the newest attacker. The suit seemed to deflect the blows, but the patient had the security guard back-peddling. Springing from all fours, he jammed the knife between the helmet and the suit of the soldier. The hunter became the prey.

The baton rolled uselessly on the ground, and its former wielder joined it as the patient pummeled the man. Stun probes appeared in Morgan's flesh as unseen guards opened fire. He lifted the fallen guard with unholy strength and hurled him down the hall, out of sight, before speeding off in the opposite direction. Beth heard a sickening crunch as the person who had likely given their life to save them crashed into something hard.

Moments later, several guardsmen rushed by the room. One stopped and glanced in, spotting the three researchers huddled against the back wall.

"Stay here," a female voice reverberated from the suit. Then she took off as well, stun gun raised and firing.

Beth waited almost a minute before disobeying the order, standing and running for the door.

"Where are you going?" Liam asked. His tone wavered on hysteria.

"To my lab. I need to check something."

"How could you possibly be thinking about the research at this moment?" he said, his voice cracking.

"Because the organism, or whatever it might be, is making our patient immensely strong and unbelievably insane. I want to know how it's transmitted, because we all just got a healthy dose of exposure." She turned away and left. Liam said something else, but she ignored it. Her mind remained singularly focused.

This is ok. We're going to be ok. Maybe it can't transmit in this environment. It's much different from the planet's surface.

She reached her lab, locked the door behind her, and took a seat in front of the computer. "Computer, bring up experiment 27J."

"Accessing sample," the computer replied.

In a few seconds, a readout appeared before her, and she browsed it over.

These numbers are looking promising, but they aren't enough. "Show me the live view of 27J." A microscopic image of a blood sample showed on the screen. "Now measure the active agents and compare them to the control sample."

"Working."

"Give me activity within the tumors, as well as size."

It only took a few moments, but time stretched on like eternity itself. She could still hear distant activity despite shutting the door, though not clearly enough to discern anything specific. It could be security battling with Morgan Sims or staff going from room to room looking for those unlucky enough to be in the medical wing at this moment. They could all have been exposed. If security followed the proper procedure, they would sequester everyone in a secure, airtight area. That might include this entire section for the time being.

I can deal with that. Gives me more time for testing, but if security moves us elsewhere... With a ship so massive, Beth wouldn't be surprised if they carted them off to a brig or other holding area somewhere in the depths. Security, fully equipped for quarantine procedures, had shown up quickly and provided some reassurance a plan existed for a containment breach. As far as her onboard training was concerned, any at-risk patients would be placed in the quarantine area that now lay in shambles. The point was, she could have minutes or days left to work on a cure if she was infected.

"Comparison shows reduced activity and size after 27J solution applied. Odds of full reversal are point four percent," the computer said.

It's not great, but it's a positive result, which I'll take. There has to be something this thing doesn't like.

"Computer, begin new experiments labeled 27K, 27L, and 27M."

"Multiple experiments are not recommended at this stage as samples are limited."

"That might not be a problem shortly, override." She pressed her lips tightly together at the thought.

"Working."

She programmed each batch with a different spread of the elements. The trials so far had been with a minimal number of elements to create a repeatable reaction.

I don't have time to do this as methodically as I'd like. Isotope 429 showed promise. I'm going to hit this thing with four times the dosage and throw in some similar reacting elements on top of it.

The door flew opened as two security guards stepped in, having apparently overridden the lock. "Please come with us. There's been an environmental breach. Everyone may have been exposed," one of them said.

Beth didn't look back. This might be her last chance to set these up. She typed furiously, adjusting the levels of each experiment and setting the gestation periods with focused precision. "I need just a minute to finish this."

"Didn't you hear me? You need to come now. This is not a drill." The guard approached, grabbed her shoulder, and spun her chair around. He must have seen all the blood splattering her lab coat from when she stabbed the patient because he pulled his hand away as if touching something scalding and backed up. Beth whipped back around, returning to her station. Only one of the three experiments had started, but she was out of time. The next one was going to be sloppy work, but it didn't matter if it had a chance of showing results. She entered two more additional solutions to the mix.

"This is the one from the other room. She's code black," the guard who had approached her said to his companion.

"Take her," said the other.

She had just enough time to hit enter before being pulled away. A yelp, more of distress than of pain, escaped her lips.

Focus, Beth. "Computer, add isotope 438 and 440 to experiment 27M and begin gestation, thirty-six hours."

"Please specify quantity," the computer replied as the guards hauled her from the lab.

"Point zero, two, five to one of the sample sizes each!" she yelled back, but she couldn't tell if it heard her command. Her attention turned to the security officers dragging her away. "You don't understand. I have to finish what I was doing. I need to know that things are set up."

"No, *you* don't understand." The guard tightened his grip on her arm. "You're a contamination risk. You're covered in infected blood."

"And I'm trying to stop all this! If you'd just let me make sure my tests are running properly, we can all avoid the same fate as Mr. Sims." She countered as she struggled against their grasp.

"She's non-cooperative," the other guard said. Then, suddenly, they released their hold.

Are they letting me go? Shocked, she started back toward her office at a run. "I just need to double-check those doses, and it'll be...." Her whole body tensed up as electricity coursed through every muscle. She barely felt the ground as she crashed into it.

Chapter 7

Beth opened her eyes and rose slowly on her elbows. Darkness drank her vision. Her mind felt sluggish and clouded, like she'd been wrenched out of a dream and her brain tried to merge reality and fantasy. She reached down and felt the surface below her give a little. A bed, too cushy to be used in the medical wing or quarantine, she deduced. Those were much firmer, not designed for long-term rest. This felt more like the one in her room.

I'm in my quarters? That wasn't all a dream. It happened. But why am I here?

"Lights on," she commanded. Nothing. "Computer, respond. Emergency lighting." Darkness remained.

Something's wrong with the room's power. Is the entire section is down? Gravity is still on, so that's something.

When she pushed herself up, her hands sank into the familiar sheath of an environment suit. Quickly running her palms over her body, she felt the suit's snug, encompassing grasp, minus the helmet.

This doesn't make any sense. Why would someone put me in an envirosuit? The contamination? I was completely covered in the patient's blood. If anyone was infected, it would be me. Did they try isolating my body in a sealed suit? It makes some sense, but still… I have to figure out what's going on. And I need to contact Liam and see if he can check on the status of my experiments. If there's been any kind of positive results…

She swung her legs around and set them on the floor, feeling the uneven sensation of loose debris under her boots. She kicked the objects aside so she would have secure footing, then stood. In the pitch black, she took a step forward, knocking something with her boot. Junk was scattered everywhere, it seemed.

Where in the universe am I, the recycler? Her arms reached forward, searching for any freestanding object. Along the floor, she shuffled her feet, pushing small bits about. Finally, her hands found a diagonal surface somewhere in what could be the middle of the room.

Ok, this must be my quarters. Or someone's quarters. Even toppled over, the table is in roughly the same place. At least I should be able to find the door. But why is this place trashed? Did I go crazy and do this?

Moving around the table, she took a step in the direction where standard quarters had their entrances, keeping her arms out in case some other piece of furniture lay unexplainably in her path. In the deepest black infinity, the short distance to the far wall grew to unimaginable proportions. Any moment she expected to find a solid surface, yet it eluded her. She moved forward with caution. Debris and junk threatened her balance with each footfall. She reached down and shoved the more substantial objects out of her way as they appeared. Eventually, her hands stretched out, and it was there, the wall.

About time. Now let's find that door. She slid sideways to her right, but reversed direction when the familiar edging of the egress didn't come. In crossing the room, she must have been off target, that or the table was not in its usual spot—a likely hypothesis given the state of the place.

Soon enough, her fingers pressed against the familiar inset of the door in the quiet dark. She felt along the edge until she found the controls. They didn't respond. "Damn! It's not just the lights." She called out in frustration.

Fine, the hard way it is. She pressed on a small panel slightly below the interface. It popped out enough for her to get her gloved fingers beneath it. In the cove beyond, she felt a handle, which she pulled down with ease. The sound of clicking gears in the wall echoed in the silent room. The exit, however, didn't open.

What the...? She yanked the lever several more times, but the door refused to budge.

"Hey! Hello? Can anyone hear me?" Beth banged her fist on the door repeatedly. It made a dull metallic thud under the gloves. "Anyone? What's going on?" After a minute, she turned her back to the barrier and slunk down, leaning against it.

Okay, let me just think about this. I'm locked in a crew cabin. It's been trashed, and I'm in an envirosuit, but missing the helmet. The power seems to be out, and no one is answering me. Okay. If I'm trapped in here, then I must have been infected. That seems likely. I could have gone crazy, just like Mr. Sims, and demolished my quarters. But I'm fine now for some reason. Maybe

I've been cured? Plausible, but what doesn't make sense is that Morgan Sims had memories when he was awake. The last thing I remember was being shocked by security. Could I have been sedated up until a point I went mad? How do I contact someone? No power means no room coms... The suit!

The idea hit her. She had spent little time in an envirosuit like this one, but recalled they possessed several useful functions. Her experience lay with the simple ones used in the labs to prevent contamination, but this one felt thicker. Probably similar to the one the colonists had found Morgan Sims in. It could go into space as well as protect from radiation and toxic environments.

On her sleeve, she located a small control panel and pressed it. After a few tries, it winked to life. She looked at the bright touchscreen and the controls; a sun in an expansive void. A readout of her vitals flashed a warning, all reading zero detection.

Let's calibrate this thing and see how sophisticated its vital sensors are. She input a few commands for it to do a fresh scan and relay all critical data. After a few seconds, it read 'error', then set vitals to zero.

Okay... That's not good. But since I'm alive, I'm going to say the suit is malfunctioning. Let's hope the com works. She found the communicator icon and pressed it.

"This is Dr. Adler. Can anyone hear me?" She waited several long seconds in silence. "Is anyone able to hear me? Please respond." More time and more silence. She checked the controls. All channels were opened and being broadcast. "Does nothing work anymore?" she griped to no one.

What am I'm missing? Someone has to be listening. She refocused on the screen. Everything appeared on and operational, with all channels open. But there was no way for her to tell if the suit was actually sending out a signal.

I must have damaged it while trashing the room. Then she spotted something she'd overlooked before, a small sun icon. She pressed it, and from the upper right side of her chest, a beam cast glorious light into the dark space.

It took only a brief second for her to realize exactly where she was. She recognized the extra tables lining the walls, the heaps of electronics and cables running about, and the experiment that held the mice now on the floor where the table had been tipped over. Devin's room.

Why am I here? Something is wrong. Did Devin put me in the suit? This makes even less sense.

Shining the light, she gazed around the room more carefully.

Perhaps there would be a clue or something to help her. However, things were out of place, even for Devin's room, and everything felt wrong. A creeping distress wound its way up her spine.

The first things she noticed were the mice. The table had been knocked over, and certainly, they would have had the chance to escape, but they hadn't. She stared in confused disbelief at the enclosure. In the bottom corner, a pile of bones indicated their only remains. Enough for all the mice she'd seen, maybe a couple more by her estimation. They'd all died and decomposed.

She stood up, her back sliding up against the stubborn door. Nothing made sense, but sitting around wouldn't solve anything. As she took a step, her vision blurred and her head swam. Stopping, she closed her eyes for a few seconds, and when they opened, her sight had returned to normal. With growing conviction, she moved through the room, taking in the enigma. Something cracked under her foot. She glanced down and saw a personal tablet. The screen had cracked from her weight, but she picked it up, nonetheless.

Maybe there's a log that makes sense of this whole mess. The device refused to turn on, showing a dead battery. *That's weird.* She knew her suit possessed the capability to power other devices, and attached the tablet to a small port on the wrist. After a few minutes, the screen came on with a passcode entry form.

If this is Devin's, what would the password be? Beth tried her birthday.

<Incorrect Passcode>

Wishful thinking, I suppose, but a bit obvious. She spent a few minutes trying whatever combinations came to mind, but was denied entry at every attempt. Frustrated, she went to toss it aside, but hesitated. She might have an epiphany at some point and try again. With a resigned sigh, she stuck the tablet into a pouch on her belt and glanced around the demolished room for more clues.

What a nightmare. Could the organism have done something like this? She tripped over a vast apparatus on the floor and landed near the bed. A human skeleton in a tattered engineer's uniform rested nearby, its white skull almost shimmering against the black. Beth pushed herself away. The light beaming from her suit swung back and forth wildly as she scooted backward on her butt as fast as possible. It came to a rest on the remains. The eyeless sockets gazed right through her, as if longing to view the distant celestial night beyond the ship.

How...? This... this person couldn't have died here. Why would this skeleton be here? "What the fuck is going on?" As she gazed at the body, two yellow eyes appeared from under the bed. She felt chills ride her spine. Slowly, she shifted her torso toward them, bringing the light around. A cat squinted and blinked at her from its hiding spot.

I think I've seen that cat. Didn't one of the admins have a cat aboard? What's it doing in here?

"Here, kitty, kitty. What are you doing here?" she edged toward it slowly. Suddenly, it turned away and disappeared.

"No, kitty. Where are you going? Come back." Rolling to her side, she shone the light under the bed and saw the gap in-between the panels made by Devin's possessed cleaning robot.

So that's how you got in here. She got up and slid the bed aside. The crevice between the floor and the wall panels wasn't huge, but it was a start. She grabbed at an edge of the damaged plate and pulled. It proved surprisingly easy to rip it away, exposing a bigger hole. She peered down into it and identified a drop of about two feet into a tight crawlspace with thick cables running through it. Among them lay the cleaning robot, where it had come to rest after its own escape.

Well, if I had to be locked up somewhere, maybe Devin convinced security to put me here. But what about the body and the mice? Creepy.

Just as she squeezed down, she had a thought and turned back to the room, giving it another sweep. I'm wearing this suit for a reason.

Maybe I should find the helmet and bring it, just in case.

She found it with a little searching. Next to the helmet sat several small bottles of high-pressure oxygen used for spacewalks and any atmosphere-devoid environments. She attached the containers to their designated spot on her belt. For now, the suit would simply filter the surrounding air, but maybe she would need the oxygen later. It couldn't hurt in any case.

It wouldn't do simply to carry the helmet, so she donned it. When it snapped in place, the readouts from her arm displayed in the peripheral sections of the visor. It all said the same thing, no vital information, no communication verification, four hours of oxygen remaining in the currently attached bottles. Non-hostile environment detected—filter at 100% clarity.

At least the filter is new. All suited up, she slipped down through the crevice and into the crawl space's cramped quarters.

Chapter 8

The cramped maintenance tunnel ran between the ship's outer hull, allowing repair bots access to ship hard subsystems. Lucky for Beth, Devin's room butted right up against one. Most often rooms sat adjacent to other rooms. Unlucky for her, this space was designed for a specific type of repair robot able to easily maneuver through the passage, not a woman in a level three envirosuit. Her only saving grace was the suit's form-fitting design, which clung tight to her body, except for parts of the torso, the helmet, and oxygen bottles attached to the belt.

With a grunt of effort, she inched through a narrow bulkhead lined with cabling. Except for where the single beam from her suit shone, the tunnel lay in pitch blackness. When crawling on all fours, it pointed at the floor. Every once in a while, she would catch two glowing eyes hovering in the shadows of the distant void, like a lighthouse on a rocky shore of uncertainty. Somehow the cat had accessed these tunnels and following it would probably be her best way out.

She shuffled forward on her knees, trailing the only living thing she had seen since waking up. The lack of communication with anyone else, combined with being locked in her boyfriend's room, left her more and more unsettled as she thought about it. It took significant effort to push it to the back of her mind and press onward.

Whenever she advanced, the cat moved away as if mocking her. In the endless black of the tunnel, it felt like a form of torture where she was cursed to push a boulder up a hill for all eternity. Then the cat vanished. Beth looked up, shining her light as far as possible and, for once, the golden eyes didn't look back at her. This was either a good sign or a horrible omen.

Pressing forward, she found herself up against a maintenance hatch stuck part way open, much too small for her to squeeze through, but perfect for the small feline. The control pad next to the door sat lifeless, with a lack of power. She pressed a few buttons anyway, just in case. It didn't surprise her when nothing happened. The manual release proved just as useless. Unlike the one in Devin's room, which seemed purposefully disabled, this one might simply be broken. When she pulled it down, it moved with too much ease, as if severed from the mechanisms it operated.

Beth adjusted her body the best she could, sitting up so that her chest faced the open crack ahead. The light revealed a tunnel, just like the one she'd been crawling down, stretching out to a distant starless night. No eyes glared back at her. The animal had vanished.

Maybe I'm losing it. Maybe there was never a cat. Her mind still felt dreamy and dizzy. Most likely the sedatives still working their way through her system. She rolled over and got a good look at the end of the tunnel. Metal plating caged her in on five sides. It seemed obvious what had to be done. She had to go back the other way.

Just as she started back, a soft 'mew' from above caught her attention. In an opening in the ceiling, the cat gazed down at her curiously. It rubbed its head against the side of the entrance and twitched its tail before disappearing. Once again, the animal showed her out of a dead end.

What a curious creature. She stood up, poking her upper body into the hole. Her top half stretch into a maintenance room of some kind. Turning around in a circle, she shined the light over the space. Metal shelves covered in various parts filled the space, while cables ran along the floors. Lining one wall, several tunnel repair robots sat lifeless in their charging stations. No lights blinked on them to indicate they received power. They were much smaller than the larger humanoid robots like M.E.R.C.Y, which had their own mini reactors and could run for years, if necessary. These needed regular charging if they were to be in use.

How far does this power failure stretch? It must be more than one section of the ship, considering how far I had to crawl. I hope it isn't a problem with the reactor.

Still glancing around the space, she spotted another two hatches on opposite walls leading to different maintenance tunnels. They both lay open and unsealed.

I'm not sure, but I'd think these are sealed most of the time. It seemed logical they'd be shut, unless someone needed to access them for a specific task. Last and most importantly, she spotted the doorway out to the rest of the ship. The cat was nowhere in sight. She heaved herself up and out of the hole, then moved toward the exit.

Time to find someone and get some answers. Something on the floor caught her eye, a taser gun. She recognized it as one of those security had carried. Like the one they'd used on her. It sat by itself on the ground, discarded. She wasn't very familiar with these things, but she'd played several virtual shooter games in her youth. She picked it up, welding it normally, and pressed a button on the side with her thumb. It should have displayed the remaining charges of the weapon. Nothing lit up.

Empty. Was there a fight this far from the labs? It painted a mysterious picture of what could be happening on the ship.

Like the rest of the doors she encountered thus far, the access to this room was unpowered, but unlike the others, the manual release worked as intended. As Beth removed the panel beside the controls and pulled down on the handle within the alcove there, the door slid aside with a series of small mechanical clicks.

Beyond the space stretched a hallway like any other on the ship, sterile gray metallic walls with white edging along the corners and edges of the doors. To her delight and surprise, emergency lighting along the floor pulsed dimly. No one was in sight. Her light crossed a number on the wall. 4-11H.

At least have emergency power. That's something. But where am I? Same level as Devin's quarters, so somewhere near the augments research section. Maybe Devin is there.

The hallway stretched out in both directions. So many parts of the ship had been built in the same way, looking identical to each other, that knowing exactly where she'd emerged proved nearly impossible. After a few seconds peering down each passage, she stepped off to the right.

If there was a major power outage, the crew probably evacuated this section. The lighting blinked off as a rolling blackout hit her area. As she moved ahead in the darkness, she recognized more and more of the location. After a few minutes, she stood in front of Devin's room, where she'd been trapped not all that long ago. An obvious line of welded metal held the door fast. It wasn't a clean job. Even to her inexperienced eyes, it looked sloppy and uneven, like it had been rushed. Why had she been sealed in there? And with such haste? Visions flooded her mind of the infected patient ravaging through the medical wing, flinging objects with unimaginable strength, being stunned over and over by the security force, and still charging them with bestial vigor.

Could she have done the same? Did she pose a threat to the ship and crew, and was locked away? But why Devin's room? She fully believed he had something to do with it, but why? Was he protecting her? Or was he protecting the rest of the ship *from* her? She couldn't look at the door any longer. It wasn't helping anything. Dizziness and confusion washed over her. The drugs in her system made her feel insane. Or was it the virus still? There was going to be a reasonable explanation for all this, no matter how strange it seemed, she reminded herself. She turned away and marched down the hall, but paused.

If I was infected...If I was, or if someone believed I was, and Devin hid me away, then I should be careful about who I run into. Security wasn't so friendly last time we had a disagreement. This section is pretty abandoned, so I'm probably safe, but I should keep a low profile until I have some answers.

She continued down the corridor, away from Devin's room. Ahead, on her right, she saw a large door labeled <Dining Commissary 11b.>

Good. I'm still on deck eleven. I've eaten here before. At least I'm finding my way around. But there could be people inside. She stood beside the wall and engaged the manual door override. It slit part-way open. No sound came from within, and no light escaped through the split in the door. It came as no surprise when she finally looked in the room that it lay abandoned.

She put her hands on either side of the door and pushed it open, walking inside. The light from her suit reflected off the metal tables and cast long shadows over the usually bustling space. Dust drifted in the beam as the freshly disturbed air wafted from her path. The place looked like it hadn't been used in a long while. At the same time, it hadn't been abandoned in an orderly fashion. Trays, cups, silverware, and other objects sat on tables, though most were strewn across the floor.

A sudden sound of aching metal rang out through the entire ship, like two metallic sheets being drug across one another, the twisting of alloys once solid, now warped and mangled. Violent vibrations shook the entire structure. Beth slid to the floor and grabbed a hold of a table, bolted down, in preparation for what might come next. Trays, silverware, and other objects rattled from every surface, clattering on the tiles in a chaotic thrum.

Stars! The ship's ripping apart!

Years ago, she'd been aboard a vessel that had lost power and collided with an asteroid. She would never forget the sound it made as it crumpled part of the ship. The noise was unmistakable. The damage, in whatever form, unraveled the mystery of the power outages. Something had harmed the Celestus, and now it moaned in wounded protest. She hoped that somewhere the crew worked on it. Rescue in this part of the galaxy wouldn't happen, unlike when she'd been stranded in the vessel hit by the asteroid. No civilization nearby, just a near-barren planet and a fledgling colony. No one was coming to help this ship. All emergencies relied entirely on those onboard.

After a little over two minutes, the jarring vibrations subsided until they ceased completely. No hull breaches opened up, nor violent, bone-breaking gyrations rocked her section. She silently thanked the engineers that had built the Celestus. Not knowing the extent of the damage made it difficult to gauge what might be going on, but anything able to rattle the colossal colonial behemoth couldn't be minor.

As Beth got up and surveyed the room again, something caught her eye. Another personal tablet stuck out of a pile of debris. She walked over, scooped it up, and hit the power button.

Everyone must have really been in a hurry if this was just left here. Makes sense if there was a structural emergency. As with the first, the tablet's battery was dead. She plugged it in, and after a few minutes, the gadget flickered on. She selected the personal logs but found them passcode protected. The official logs, however, she accessed.

This must have belonged to a director or someone on the administration board, she guessed. The picture of a woman Beth didn't recognize appeared on the screen. The grainy image suggested the data had been partially corrupted.

"This is officer Davis of the astrological division, official log number 485388..." the screen went blank but the audio continued to roll. "There are growing concerns about the oncoming spatial anomaly. It's still over a day away and already it's affecting several instruments. On the one hand, this is giving us a unique opportunity of discovery and data collection. The origins and makeup of this anomaly has the whole department abuzz. However, there has been talk of moving the ship behind the planet as direct impact with the wave could have unknown consequences. Our initial readings have shown it's not a danger to human life. But, more recent readings are showing the possibility of a more serious event. It's my official opinion that the ship be moved behind the planet and we play it safe. The opportunity to study it will be fleeting given our best chance for data collection will be during the brief time we can sample the wave as it passes by us. However, as exciting as a new discovery is, I feel there are too many unknowable consequences by staying directly in its path. Since this is the first time we've seen a phenomenon such as this, it would be better for the safety of all for caution to win out. I am, of course, the lone dissenting voice of the directors in astrophysics. There's still time before we give our official recommendation to the admins. I'll see if I can persuade Dr. Evers, or Dr. Green to see reason. If not, I just have to hope the ship's captain and his advisors vote for moving us to safety."

The recording ended.

I wonder if they ended up moving? This could shed some light on why this part of the ship is in such a state. Though abandoning an entire section would only happen if there was depressurization, fire, or a quarantine order. The last thought was not a comforting one. She couldn't be the reason everyone was evacuated, could she? Damage caused by the wave seemed more plausible. But still...

The tablet contained two more, older, official logs Beth gave a listen to, but they consisted of more of the same. Concern over the approaching wave and the ramifications of studying the event up close. When she was done, she placed the tablet on a nearby table. She moved straight to the closest exit, eager to find someone and get answers.

If I can get to my lab, that might be best. I'll have better access to the computer systems than in any other department. Then again, Devin should have most of the answers to what in the stars is going on. Since he's not in his quarters, he's either in the augmentation wing or crashing at my place. I'm pretty sure I know the way to Augs and it's nearby.

She opened the next door manually, but with the same caution as before. Events were wrapped in a mystery at the moment, and the last people she wanted to run into were a security detail that might try to throw her back into isolation. Though finding a fellow researcher ranked high on her list, creating a bit of a conundrum.

Beyond the entryway, a dark corridor stretched out. The emergency lighting blinked and flickered. The effect was dizzying and disorientating. She didn't see anyone about, which felt like both a good and bad sign, though not entirely unexpected. The hall curved around until it came to a junction and split in three new directions. She'd never been inside the augmentation wing, but she'd met Devin after his shift just outside on a few occasions.

When was the last time? Not recently. The left passage looked the most familiar, but all the halls blended together due to design and the near blackout of this section. On top of it, her head still didn't feel one-hundred percent. If she wasn't so sure she was awake, then this entire event might be written off as a dream.

She followed the path around until it ended in a sealed blast door. Peering through the small window at its center, blackness stared back at her. None of the lights worked in the area beyond.

So what else is new? Her shoulders slumped. Stepping back, her eyes dropped to the manual release hatch. It sat open. She reached in and gave the handle a firm pull. The door didn't give her access, however. It occurred to her that there may be a problem in the next section. Blast doors were serious business. Or maybe she was in the problem section and beyond was where all the crew was. In any case, she had a good idea that she was on the right path, even if this passageway remained blocked. Many hallways likely led to the augmentation wing.

She backtracked to the intersection and took another left. If she was right, then this would curve around and intersect with a passage bypassing the blocked section. Her instincts proved correct and soon the crossroad in question came into view. A few more lights functioned in the sector, which she took as a good sign. As if in defiance of her positive thinking, they waned and flickered suddenly as the ship moaned again.

How long has it been since the last one? The ship might be in serious trouble. She thought about how badly she needed to get out of this abandoned section. No one was here for a reason. She shouldn't be either. The grinding metal sound didn't last as long this time and as it faded, the lights returned to their normal brightness.

Down the next passage, she saw another blast door sealing the hall. This one was powered and flashed a red light down the hall. When she got close enough, she read the warning.

<Loss of gravity in section.>

Gravity remained normal in her current area, despite the power fluctuations.

So there are multiple problems aboard. I have to hope the crew is on top of things. She didn't know of another path that would get her to augmentation. Staring through the small window in the blast door, she eyed the continuation of the hallway. Like the section she stood in, it was also partially lit. In the center floated something she couldn't quite make out. It was a round lumpy object, obscured in the lines of shadow. As a row of lights oscillated on, she saw it. A clump of robot heads, bound together by the cabling running from their cranial caps like colored spinal cords. Their smooth, blank faces rotated languidly as if in some disturbing display.

What the? It made no sense, but still sent chills down her spine. She turned away, trying to make heads or tails of the scene. Little about this day seemed logical, and she added this to the growing list. Suddenly, it didn't feel worth passing through this section, considering the trophy-like grouping of robotic heads.

Devin might be in the augments lab, but then again, given how difficult it continually proved to get there, that idea seemed less and less likely. She wished desperately she could find him. Any of her friends would do, but she wanted to see his face more than anything. It would be a small amount of reassurance that everything was going to be ok. She considered whether or not she wanted to run into anyone else at all. Her friends could be trusted. She felt good about that. But anyone else? Would they know what had happened in the medical lab with the patient? Maybe it would be best for her to get to her lab without meeting anyone and avoiding those issues altogether.

She turned back the way she came, a little frustrated that once again she'd hit a dead end. In the hall, the cat sat watching her curiously.

Chapter 9

Beth jerked her hands up in surprise at the creature's presence. However, she regained her composure almost immediately, glad that no one was around to see her jump. "Hey, where have you been?" she asked sweetly. The cat responded with vigorous licks to its paw. "Thanks for getting me out of that room, but it looks like this is a dead-end for sure. Do you want to come with me to my lab?" The cat stood up, turned its tail, and strolled in the opposite direction as if in answer. Beth followed.

When she approached the previous intersection, the cat ducked around a corner. Beth hustled after it, but by the time she arrived, the dim corridor hid any sign of the feline. Taking a few moments to glance around, she decided despite it helping her out of a jam before, twice actually, it was headed a different way than she planned to. She knew the general direction of the medical wing and wanted to get there as soon as possible. Figuring out what happened with the virus could be the difference between survival or diving into madness.

Her light flashed down a passage, where another set of blast doors stood out to block progress. However, a green light flashed on them. She approached and looked at the small screen near the indicator.

<Section normality restored>

Thank goodness. Through the tiny window, she glimpsed a round room with many gray-cushioned couches and chairs, as well as a few knee-high tables. Broken cups, pieces of tablets, and other smashed devices littered the floor.

A lot of damage for a loss in gravity.

The manual door override engaged when she pulled the handle, and the door slid slowly aside. A sudden whoosh of air passed from her section into the newly opened one as the pressure equalized. Thankfully, the difference hadn't been enough to indicate full decompression in the following area. But normally, the Celestus kept equal pressure throughout. Concerns ever-mounting, she added malfunctioning pressure detectors to the growing list of problems she'd encountered.

Shifting her gaze around, very little in the room struck her interest. The lounge resembled any of the others throughout the ship. Although, strangely, someone had removed the beverage dispenser from the wall and extracted all the electronics. The housing lay discarded nearby—all signs pointing to a hasty exit.

Why would someone take the parts from this?

Beth scoured the room for any clues. Nothing appeared related to the dispenser, but she found two more personal tablets among the remains of three others, shattered beyond use as if they'd been hurled against a wall. Like the first two, all were completely dead.

Why in the galaxy is every battery dead? It would take weeks for them to drain completely. Have I been unconscious for that long? It doesn't seem possible. And if every tablet is drained, why does this suit have full power? She remembered the suit wasn't exactly functioning correctly. Most likely, the battery read false as well.

She booted up the first tablet by plugging it into her envirosuit. It came to life in a few seconds. Instead of going straight for the logs, she looked for the last date recorded by the processor.

<3/38/909>

That's seventeen days after the lab incident. When was the wave supposed to hit? Sophie said we had several days, but not weeks. Then again, she didn't know exactly.

Beth attempted to access the logs. She saw four entries and started with the oldest one. Both it and the second turned out to be personal; one, a complaint about having a different tablet accidentally put into a dining room recycler by another crew member, resulting in the loss of all the data on it because of a corrupted backup file. The other went on at length about the difficulty of finding free time to use the recreational facilities.

This could almost be Liam's tablet. Beth moved on to the second.

<I've attached my log on the new prototype reality augmentation device since your tablet has gone missing. I sure hope it was fully encoded. This project potentially threatens the livelihood of many on the ship. More so, the techs sent planetside. If they find out what we're working on, they'll be pissed at the very least and rebellious at worst. It could make a lot of their jobs obsolete, as someone with no knowledge of operations could step in and take over. I'm doing you a favor by sending this. If Director Kregs had any idea sensitive information from inside the department was out there for anyone to snatch, you'd be relegated to the virtual babysitter program for the rest of our stay here. Your AI work on the project is brilliant, and I need you on the team. Just make sure you passcode the new device when you get it. -T>

This is fascinating. Beth pulled up the last log and the attachment 'T', whoever that was, had sent this person. A file appeared on-screen. She gave it a quick look over.

<Project A6-401CX. Workplace reality augmentation. Project aim: to create a virtual interface overlay which will allow the most unskilled, uneducated worker to be given step-by-step instructions in real-time on any task. Visual clues will be provided to show each step in the worker's job.

First test: Ship cook. We outfitted Roger with the prototype and gave him access to kitchen facilities on 11b.

Results: With no culinary experience, he was able, through guided instruction and visual indication, to make a meal rivaling any of the replicators designed for that sole purpose. Quite promising.

Second test: Basic piloting. With the permission of Sergeant Sticks, we outfitted Roger with the prototype and uploaded a piloting program. Then, the Sergeant took him out on a routine patrol around a section of the planet near the colony. Roger has no previous flying experience.

Results: According to Sticks, he flew with the skill of a first-year commercial pilot. We had a slight scare when the prototype had him activate weapon systems instead of the landing gear, but the sergeant stepped in and got things under control before any disaster occurred. Obviously, there are still some bugs to be worked out. A mislabeling of the flight controls is likely the issue.

Third Test: Engineering operations. We will conduct this test on

3/43/909. Given the close call on the flight test, we have postponed this test despite the positive results. It will probably involve a hands-off run where we work with a reactor engineer to verify all the controls and systems are labeled correctly in engineering and the reactor core. A bug in the system could prove more detrimental to our efforts than the piloting mishap.>

What followed consisted of a series of prototype schematics. The diagrams showed a pair of gloves worn on bare hands, a set of glasses which would be placed over a wearer's eyes, and a chip attachment for integration into an envirosuit. The instructions showed the bracelet used the suit's visor for the projections.

That's a hell of a project! Handy. I wonder what part of it they had Devin working on? If any.

She considered holding on to the tablet with the prototype blueprints only briefly before deciding they'd be of little use to her. With nothing else to gain, she left the tablets behind. Since she didn't want to risk bumping into crew members who might recognize her, these tablets provided the most effective way to find out what happened. She'd be sure to keep an eye out for more.

Past this room and down a short hall, she came up against another unpowered door. The manual release made quick work of the barrier, and she continued after bracing against another adjustment to the pressure. Beyond, the ship grew dark again. An indicator in her visor warned her of a sudden drop in temperature. Just ahead, a coat of frost covered the walls and floor. She froze at the sight of a single set of footprints crusted into the glaze. A mixture of relief, suspicion, and confusion welled within and kept her from moving forward. Someone had been here since the damage occurred, but did she want to run into them?

Chapter 10

She swung her light over the prints methodically.

I recognize these. Whoever was here also wore an environmental suit. The footprints weren't heading to or from the door she just came through. They originated from somewhere down the hall. She followed them with her illumination up to a medium-sized access panel on the side of the right wall.

This must be a maintenance hatch like the one I crawled through. No way to tell where it might lead.

In search of answers, she considered following the stranger's steps for only a second or two, but ultimately decided getting to her lab still held the best possibility of figuring out what had happened. Passing by the opening, she continued down the frozen hallway. With each step, the frost made a soft crunching sound as she left a similar trail of her own prints.

Farther down, she heard a hissing sound. The curving passage twisted around, and soon she came to the source of the noise. A misty spray spewed forth from a vent in the ceiling, creating a dense wall of gray molecules. Beyond, a brightness back-lit the cloud. Beth couldn't be sure of the substance, however. It didn't look like water, though she supposed it could be anything. The tracks ahead had gone around, avoiding it as well. She felt reasonably confident the envirosuit would protect her from most substances on the ship, but didn't see a reason to test it. Putting her back near one side of the space, just enough not to touch the glistening drips on the surface, she shimmied around the belching vent.

Finally, she reached the end of the section, where a blast door separated her from the rest of the path. She used the manual release, and a great whoosh followed as the doors parted slightly. A sudden warning flashed before her eyes as the suit detected a drastic pressure drop. Beth stumbled back, slipping on the wet, icy floor and landing hard on her butt. Mist sucked rapidly through the open gap. She reached out for anything to hold on to as her body slid along the slick floor. Then, almost as quickly as it began, the suction tapered off. She still received a warning of low pressure, though it appeared stabilized for the moment. Gently, she slid to a stop and let out a groaning sigh.

A hull breach had opened somewhere in the next section. She surmised it couldn't be too large, or it would have wholly evacuated her area of all atmosphere. Though, undeniably, this section expelled air. She grimaced while chewing on the information. She was getting close to the medical wing and her own quarters, yet still encountering structural and internal vessel problems. If the area ahead isn't safe... She rethought her plan as frozen particles wafted past her into the space beyond.

Where else would I go? If I can access the terminal in my lab, it will provide much needed answers. Even better, if she found Devin at her place, he could tell her everything. The chaos, death, and disorder of his room, and her own state when she woke, whipped into her brain. She pushed the memory of the bones to the back of her mind.

They couldn't be his, she told herself firmly. *They couldn't... It wouldn't make any sense. But what was an engineer doing there with me?*

With all her willpower, she regained her feet and pressed onward. It took some effort to separate the doors enough to squeeze between them, but once through, she made it a point to close them behind her and seal off the previous section.

No sense in losing all the air. As the atmosphere thinned, the envirosuit indicated it fed oxygen into her helmet.

Okay, let's get through here asap. Beth had no experience being in zero atmosphere and didn't know how often she would need her oxygen in the future. She took off at a jogging pace. Further ahead, where the hallway once bent, it now corkscrewed, partially caving in on itself. She ducked under the warped and drooping ceiling, moving past it. Beyond lay another intersection of three blast doors.

This is bad. As much as I don't want to run into anyone, it's unsettling to have a hull breach, and no one here patching it. More pressing issues, maybe? The extensive power outage is probably one of them. A reactor complication instead of an isolated section problem? Oh, stars, I hope the non-emergency lights come back on. If the medical wing is still completely unpowered, then I won't get any answers there either. I need a little reassurance someone is working on this disaster.

She tried the manual release on the left-most door, feeling mounting anxiety to pass through the next area and get to her room to see if Devin had holed up there. Or, at the very least, find some kind of clue about her unique quarantine. Her lab wasn't much farther from there. After multiple pulls on the lever, the door hadn't moved. Beth released her grip and looked through the barricaded window to the corridor beyond. The second set of blast doors sat wide open, and she knew full well they should also be automatically shut. Then her light fell upon a great hole in the floor. Beyond it, the twisted metal of the Celestus's mangled hull framed the black void of open space.

She backed away, trembling nerves flashing across her body, and eased towards the entrance, which had stood directly down the hall. When it opened, she ran, barreling through at least five room clusters in a daze. A barrage of pressure adjustments later, she slid to a stop and took in the realities. A crushing feeling landed on her. Damage in every section, no one doing anything about it, and a parasite which may or may not be killing her. She needed to find a different way to get to her room. She needed to hear from her friends. With a gashing hole in the Celestus, open to outer space, was the parasite her primary concern anymore?

Glancing around to see where she'd stopped her panicked dash, she saw a long curving hallway stretching ahead. Down the right wall, at uneven intervals, sat a couple of doors.

Okay, these lead to the main rec area. I doubt anyone is just kicking back at a time like this. The ship gave a groan of metallic pain to confirm her theory.

That's what every available hand must be working on—keeping this boat in one piece. I don't know how much gravity the planet exerts on us, but if we're damaged bad enough, it could tear us in half. She shook the thought away and told herself it couldn't be *that* bad, and the crew was working on it at this very moment. It would explain their absence. Hell, Devin might have suited her up just in case the hull breached where he'd left her. She tried to convince herself the sealed door was also part of his plan, but her subconscious rebelled against the notion, even for her sanity. Someone had sealed her in hard and in a hurry.

Beth dropped to her knees and slumped against the nearest wall. "Get it together, Beth. Get it together. You're a problem solver. This is what you do. Everyone else is doing their jobs at this moment. You're alive for a reason. The lab is only a few sections away, assuming there's not another hull breach or some awful thing in between. Get there!" The self-pep-talk did the job as Beth forced herself to her feet and hastened to the nearest doors.

The rec-room didn't seem important at the moment, but she peeked in on it, especially when her instincts told her to investigate wherever she could. She opened the door manually but cautiously, in case someone lurked inside. The same near-darkness she stood in filled the space ahead. It didn't surprise her. The ship's automatic systems reserved emergency power for non-vital sections of the vessel.

Though there could be additional tablets in the lockers, the time spent looking for them felt like a waste with other mounting problems. Beth swung her light across the court, noting only that the space looked spotless, whereas most other rooms had been trashed. Then she turned back, continuing her trek toward the med labs, passing through two more sets of doors on her way. With everything dark and unpowered, the chance of her being able to access the lab computer looked more and more grim.

At least I haven't run into anyone who might try to detain me. Then again, it could be nice to find someone. She did her best to stay calm. She'd assumed getting some answers from her lab would allow her to make sense of the situation. But that might be out of the question now. The frustration of her predicament constantly assaulted her attempts to stay calm.

What could have happened here? Stars, I hope everyone is okay. Clenching her fists uncontrollably and arching her back, she yelled. "Fuck! Fuck! What the fuck? Ahhh!" Her voice almost sounded foreign to her ears. The words, picked up by her helmet and projected outward, echoed down the blackened pathways.

Chapter 11

The lab lay not too much further, but she'd hit a metaphorical wall. Slumping to the floor, Beth stared at the ceiling through the glass visor of her helmet. The outburst had helped calm her nerves, and she felt a bit better. She'd awoken in a dreamlike state, which faded with every passing minute. Her body certainly took its time purging whatever sedatives kept her under.

Could this be an effect of a cure, or the parasite?

Beth closed her eyes and focused her mind, trying to stay positive. She enjoyed a good mystery, a riddle to solve.

This is just another puzzle, another problem to be worked out. It's just a matter of breaking it down and doing it piece by piece. Going to the lab is still the best plan for now. If Liam is there, if anyone is there, I'll find something out, even if I can't access my computer. At least I won't be alone. She felt so lost and unsure, feelings she rarely experienced. Over and over, she reminded herself of the best course of action, just to keep from completely unraveling.

Feeling more resolved, she sat up, forced herself to her feet, and forged ahead. After a dozen paces, she opened a door leading to the lobby outside the medical wing. She knew her area was one of the larger ones on the vessel. Not only did it house the labs for testing all manner of things found on the planet, but it included all the medical facilities which dealt with infirm crew members.

She entered the room where a receptionist typically directed patients toward the hospital and medical area and checked in those who worked in the labs. Being one of the few doctors doing double duty, Beth rotated shifts between helping patients and assisting in experiments.

With the first step inside, the space felt wrong. Pitch darkness shrouded the usually bright lobby. That differed little from most of the other areas she'd passed through, but this inky atmosphere seemed to drink away the light beaming from her chest-lamp. Chairs that once sat organized lay scattered about, several of them shattered to pieces. On the floor, she glimpsed a thickly crusted spot caused by copious amounts of blood, suggesting someone had bled to death. Drag trails spread out from the dried pool as if something had pulled a person apart, their limbs wrenched in different directions as if drawn and quartered. However, she didn't see any physical parts of the remains.

Beth tried to move into the lab, but her feet refused her brain's order. Fear crept over her like a jealous, maniacal lover, trapping her in place. Finally, she managed to turn her body just enough to shine the light through the glass doors leading to the inner region. Trash and broken medical equipment lay strewn about the hall. Shattered glass reflected tiny beams back at her. One of the blood steaks drew a path from the lobby down into the lab depths.

I shouldn't be here.

This is a terrible place.

No one is alive here.

No one I want to meet will be here.

She trembled as the horrific scene sank in. Her stomach roiled at the carnage as the destruction told a terrible story. Finally, her unwilling feet found the courage to retreat as she took cautious backward steps, always keeping the light on the door. Nothing moved; all remained still as she slunk back into the hall.

The unmistakable sound of metal clanging against metal rang out behind her. Someone had snuck up on her. Her heart rate jumped, and her stomach knotted. No one spoke, no footsteps shuffled. She froze as the ringing echo faded away into the void. No one moved. Silence held everything in the dark, the only light, her own. It still shone brightly into the medical office's lobby, highlighting the slaughter that occurred there. She could only move backward or forward. Should she run or face whoever stood just a breath away? Time to choose. Fear paralyzed her ability to decide, holding her captive with no hope of escape, when suddenly her body moved to action. She whirled around, her chest lamp flashing into the passage, and her fists raised and ready to fight.

Nothing. She glanced all around for anything, anything at all. No new objects lay on the barren floors; no creatures lurked in the fading shadows.

What made that sound?

A slight protrusion from the wall caught her eyes. Near the ceiling on the left wall, a hinged grate hung open, too small for a large person to fit. Had it been that way before? Concentrating on the memory of the hallway, she tried to picture her arrival. If perhaps it had fallen open just now, that would be a relief of some degree. But as she focused, it became as clear as a photograph. The vent had not been open before.

One mystery solved, only to start another. What caused it?

She shot a glance back toward the labs almost by subconscious reaction, before cautiously approaching the spot opposite the grate opening. It was too high to get her light into it effectively, but it was also too restricted for anyone in an envirosuit to hide in. From her vantage point, the duct appeared empty. Self-preservation slammed back into her, and she jerked her body toward the lab entrance again. Blood, shadows, and madness waited for her, though nothing stirred. Paranoia, or maybe survival instinct, kept bringing her attention to the carnage there. Each time, her mind pictured someone standing amongst the slaughter, watching her. It was past time to leave.

Beth backed out of the medical area, her head jerking over her shoulder and back again like a frightened child in a haunted house. Some relief came when she passed through a set of open blast doors and sealed them with the manual control lever. Turning to face the hallway ahead, she took a moment to reevaluate her plans.

Where should I go? My quarters are probably the best place for now. But at this rate, I'm going to have to go to Engineering and see about the reactor. I don't even know where to begin. Hopefully, I can find someone who does. She didn't see the point of worrying about it now. She was close to reaching her quarters from the other side. The thought of finding Devin or anyone there didn't seem likely. No one just hung out in these underpowered sections.

Best I figure is the crew is together in a more functional part of the Celestus. Wherever that might be. She didn't want to think about the reasons why, but they came anyway. It could be as simple as wanting to stay in the powered areas, or in the case of severe damage, maybe even evacuating to the colony on the planet. That didn't seem likely. Not with her current information, at least. The worst-case was more people had developed the same ailments as her patient, Mr. Sims, and had become violent and run amuck. She'd witnessed first-hand the strength and endurance he'd gained. She didn't doubt if more than one got loose, it would've been near impossible for the security forces to contain them.

Could I have been one of those people?

She couldn't imagine herself doing that, becoming an unstoppable, ravaging beast, filled with madness and rage. Still, she knew she was missing at least a couple of weeks of memory, maybe much, much more. Her gut told her it couldn't be, but the evidence showed it to be possible. The idea sent a chill tingling up her spine and along her shoulders and arms.

Down the passageway toward her quarters, another set of unpowered blast doors stopped her. She passed through the first to a small transitional chamber after using the manual release. When the next door didn't open immediately, she closed the rear barrier and tried the front one again. As the handle clicked, it popped open, and the pocket of air surrounding her sucked forward with violent force. Her feet betrayed her as the sudden vacuum picked her body up and slammed it against the crevice between the two sliding sections of the blast doors. The impact sent a shock through her limbs.

When vacuum filled the space, she still hung like a balloon, caught in the crack between the doors, going nowhere. Luckily, the pain felt minimal. Her suit had done its job in protecting her.

No atmosphere and no gravity. Great...but I'm lucky I didn't get sucked into space. Beth did her best to wedge her arms between the doors and shoved them in opposite directions. Enough of a parting gave way for her to squeeze through. She tapped the suit controls on her arm, and two lights, one on either shoulder, came on. They shot straight up, which was perfect for what she planned. Holding onto the door, she set her feet against it. The new beams shined directly down the hallway. She pushed off and sailed weightlessly ahead.

As the hallway curved, she met the wall with all fours and pressed off, looking down at her boots as she did so. Glancing forward, she gasped in horror, and her stomach tumbled to her feet. Dead ahead, the corridor gave way to open space. A gaping hole of mangled hull and contorted metal that once made up the passage now presented nothing but the infinite void. She kicked and squirmed, but her trajectory remained true. The hole loomed, growing bigger as she helplessly approached. Beth cried out, but there was no one to hear it. Not here, not in the vacuum of space.

She exited the ship. Below, the colony planet loomed closer than she remembered it. *Oh, stars! The orbit's decayed!* The thought lasted only a moment, as it was the least of her immediate trouble. She was drifting away from the ship with no means of getting back.

An antenna array appeared before her a short distance to her left. As the ship slowly rotated and came about, she reached out, extending her fingers as far as they would stretch. A thin wire receiver landed in her palm. She gripped it with desperate might and pulled herself in. The force of her directional weight caused the antenna to bend drastically. With little warning, it snapped.

Beth flailed her limbs, hoping to snag anything sticking out into the void. Nothing found her touch. Heat rushed to her ears as she sucked in gulping breaths of rising panic.

"Shit!" *I'm going to die. Stars, I'm going to die.*

An idea struck her. If she could use one of her oxygen bottles as a means of propulsion, then it might get her back to the Celestus. Beth jerked her head around, taking in the fullness of her predicament. For the first time, she noticed the action of grabbing the antenna hadn't been strong enough to stop her momentum, but it was enough to change her course. She now floated back toward the hull. Never in her life had she felt so much relief. Using a series of tucking and releasing maneuvers she saw on a safety vid, Beth reoriented herself to land on her feet.

During the descent, she pulled up the suit controls on her forearm and browsed through the functions. "Damn," she swore. As she feared, her envirosuit provided air and protection from the harshness of space but wasn't designed for spacewalks. Moreover, it lacked one crucial thing, a way to secure its wearer to the ship's hull. She came down boots first, but remnants of her momentum caused her to bounce and spiral off and away. She spun, swinging her arms wildly until her hand latched onto an exhaust port protruding from the surface. With a final bump against the hull, her body came to a rest.

I almost fucking died. Beth took nearly a full five minutes, just gathering herself back up.

I'm ok; I'm ok. I'm still with the ship. I've just got to get back inside. From her vantage point, she glimpsed a significant expanse of the vessel. Its form lay in a blanket of darkness; no lights blinked on its surface; no brightness filtered out the windows. One thing felt clear: the reactor was not on, or something had severed it from the rest of the ship. Nearly everything would be on backup power, or none at all.

I've got to get back inside. This is... She sighed. The hopelessness residing in the lifeless-looking ship threatened to overtake her as well. Was anyone working on restoring the ship's functions? Could she be all alone?

Pushing despair away as best she could and reserving a few moments to collect herself, she shifted her focus to where she might have exited and how she would reenter the Celestus. She didn't immediately see a hole.

I wonder if an airlock would be better? Dismissing the thought because airlocks required power to open from the outside, something in short supply, she continued to examine her surroundings for several minutes.

The idea of being stuck outside of the hull for any longer wrenched at her gut. As a nagging urge prodded her to examine her oxygen and power supply, she instead gathered the strength to ignore the temptation and focus on getting back inside as soon as possible. She couldn't afford to dawdle and risk panicking if she knew she could suffocate at any moment. If she were to survive and make it inside, she needed to stay level-headed and hurry.

Beth scanned the Celestus's surface for a nearby handhold. Luckily, several protrusions, antennas, and sensory arrays rose from the surface. Picking her target, she pushed off. Something about soaring untethered outside the ship exhilarated and terrified her at the same time. It might have been more enjoyable if not for the possibility of a slow death in the vastness of space. She caught the protrusion she'd aimed for and held on for dear life while her body continued around the point in a pivot. Her grip held, and she came to a stop.

Anxiety diminished to slight relief as she held the position for a minute to analyze the next move. From this new spot, she identified the hole she'd emerged from. It resembled a diamond-shaped gash. From her medical knowledge, she thought it looked more like a scrape. As if something had sheared away the metal rather than an explosion blowing a hole in the hull.

This time, she retook aim at a series of rungs running some length of the hull and passing right next to the gash.

Ok, just one more jump, and I'm almost inside. You can do this, Beth. Failure only means dying in some horrible way… no big deal.

She closed her eyes a moment to focus. The utter silence of her surroundings aided in calming her nerves. When her sight resumed, she pushed off, flew for the nearest handle, and caught hold, with her feet coming to rest on the steps below. Expelling a quick sigh of relief, she pulled herself along the outside until she floated right beside the gap. The edge lay just a few feet out of reach.

This next move will be risky. As if the rest of this has been a cinch. She almost hesitated, but her body moved instead. With little thought, she leaped from the rungs, cruising free in the void. She realized her miscalculation the moment her fingers caught the lip of the gash, and her grip slipped. She rolled and reached out, grabbing for anything. Her hand connected with a jagged piece of metal jutting from the damage. It halted her. She didn't waste any time and yanked herself toward the hole with panicked force. The scrap proved brittle and weak. It snapped with the strength of her pull. She spun. The giant planet, much too close, rotated into view as her back turned toward the ship. Then suddenly, she crashed into the wall of the open corridor inside the Celestus. She bounced off, still spinning but farther within the vessel. She was back.

For some minutes, she hung in zero gravity, not moving. *Oh, stars! I almost died... I nearly died out there.* The thought repeated over and over in her mind. Would she have to navigate other places like this? How many other parts of the ship had been blasted or ripped open?

I wish I'd gotten a better look at things out there. But there's no fucking way I'm going back out. Besides, she knew her air remained a finite resource, and it seemed wise to save as much as possible for now.

Using the wall, she directed herself farther down the passage and away from the deadly gap. She remained more cautious about zooming casually through the zero-gravity section. It slowed progress a little, but she arrived at another set of doors after a few minutes. Taking hold of the manual release and placing both feet on the exit, she pulled the lever. No sensation of escaping air passed her.

Is the next section devoid of atmosphere too? This is bad. Was Devin's quarters in the only safe segment of the ship?

Beth moved into an airlock-like area, closing the egress behind her. She sighed in relief at the oncoming force of the wind as she opened the second set of doors, releasing atmosphere into the small room. It seemed reasonable someone had passed the other way at some point, and in doing so, had jettisoned the air from the area where she now stood. She wished she had a way to find out who it had been and what they'd been up to. But at least it proved someone was still aboard.

Feeling relieved at being back in atmosphere, Beth knew the time had come to face some realities. She accessed the controls on her arm and retrieved the oxygen and power levels on the suit. They both read full. That didn't seem right.

This suit is malfunctioning; I know that, so it might be giving me false readings. I know little about these oxygen bottles either. Maybe they're compressed enough to last an extremely long time, but the suit's battery should be at least a little drained. I should be happy about it, but I'd actually feel better if things were somewhat expended.

Unfortunately, she could do nothing about it. Maybe somewhere she'd find another suit to replace this one. But, for now, it had performed well enough to keep her alive. She'd been outside the ship, adrift in the void, and survived. That's all that mattered.

Beth pressed forward down a couple of entrance-lined halls, and after a few minutes, stood in front of her own door. Something stopped her there, an unspoken fear that whatever she discovered would seal her fate. She'd found scattered answers up to this point. Mystery after mystery crept in. For every piece of information she gained, twenty more questions would appear and go unanswered. Behind this door could be some answers she sought, but she wasn't holding up much hope with the power down and the difficulty getting here. Who would possibly be waiting in this room? She felt more likely to find someone's body than any living person. At that moment, it struck her as strange she hadn't come across a single dead body considering the damage to the ship. Other than the one she'd shared her first room with, and that one's bones had been picked clean. It added another puzzle in a long line of unexplainable encounters she'd faced since waking up. However, she'd seen blood and other evidence of death. The lack of bodies seemed like only a formality at this point.

Feeling ready to face any disappointment waiting for her, she accessed the manual release, and the door slid aside. The light from her suit beamed into the room, showing it to be exactly how she'd left it. It felt almost miraculous. Everywhere she explored had been disturbed in some way, often unexplainably. But here was her space, pristine. She stepped inside. "Hello?" She called to the dark. She didn't really expect an answer, and none came. There didn't seem to be anything to find here. It was all just her stuff. If someone had been here, there was no evidence. She almost turned back when something caught her eye, just as the beam passed it—a tablet sitting on the bed.

It must be mine. No, mine was with me at the lab. I left it on the table. Had someone returned it to her? She walked over and picked it up, connecting it to her suit. Taking off her helmet, she stretched out on the bed. Deep relief fell over her, but along with it, a thin lining of melancholy.

What could be happening, and where is everyone? The tablet powered on, and she lifted it to her face. Devin's name popped on the screen.

Chapter 12

Beth's heart pounded, her chafed lips spread across her face, and she sighed; relief welled within to the point she might burst. Although she hadn't found Devin waiting for her, she'd found the next best thing—a message from him. She immediately accessed the most recent log. A password prompt appeared. She tried his room access code, but it didn't work. After wracking her brain for several seconds, she chose the obvious and input her name. The log opened. A video of Devin winked to life on the screen, recorded here, right where she now lay.

"Beth, if you're hearing this, then I bet you're confused. But you're here, and that's something. It's hope for all of us. A lot has happened, and I'm not sure how much you'll remember. First, you'll need to get into the augmentation labs. I've attached an access code for the doors on this tablet. There's a prototype argumentation we've been working on there. I think you'll need it. Depending on the ship's condition, there could be a lot to do, and it may not be easy. I'll explain more about that in a minute. If you haven't been to your lab yet, you need to go there and access your terminal. Beth, you..."

A loud knock emanated from the door, and Devin looked away. "Shit, security is here. They're moving everyone out of this section of the ship. There's been major damage, and some sections have lost power and gravity." Another series of bangs rang out over the speakers, more violent this time, followed by muffled voices. "Beth, I'll be right back." The picture on the screen moved from Devin to the ceiling. She heard him answer the door, followed by a conversation that she couldn't make out. Raised voices echoed over the speaker.

"Just a couple more minutes to gather my things! That's all I ask," Devin said.

She heard more muffled voices.

"You can't!" Devin's raised voice cut in, strained and angry.

Someone else yelled something, sounding like orders. Beth couldn't tell what the subsequent noises were, but the door sliding shut echoed clear to her ears. She knew Devin wasn't coming back to finish his message. Still, she held the tablet, speeding through the picture of the ceiling until the clip ended.

Collapsing back on the bed, she didn't move. She couldn't catch a single break. With everything she'd already been through, Devin couldn't save her. Her biggest hope shattered. She felt broken. Help had been within reach, but stolen away. He'd mentioned the ship's damage, but she already knew about it, knew it all too well.

Beth slammed her fists into the mattress over and over.

What am I going to do? Find Devin and everyone else wherever security has taken them? He was telling me something important, like I had a part to play. Like it was up to me to save everyone? What did he mean? There's still hope—hope for what? That we all survive? Beth let out a scream and held her gloved hands out in front of her, frustration manifesting as her fingers curled into stiff hooks.

She let her arms drop.

I don't think running around haphazardly and handing myself over to security will help Devin or me, or anyone else. He'd wanted her to go to her lab. She'd just been by there. The scene of blood and destruction still burned bright in her memory.

That must have happened after security took him. He wouldn't send me anywhere dangerous, would he? Maybe he'd left more information there for her. It made little sense since he was trying to give her a message on his tablet, but he *had* said to go there. However, the lab ranked near the bottom of the places she wanted to return to. Besides, with that entire section unpowered, her terminal would be useless. She would have to power the whole lab for it to be of any use.

She'd tossed the tablet aside when Devin's message ended, but she retrieved to check the downloads. Typing in the same login password, she found a file containing the Aug lab codes.

This might help eventually, but that area is just as unpowered and inaccessible as my lab. I don't think I have any other choice but to go to Engineering and see what's happening there. Maybe there is a way I can restore power to those places. What were the chances security didn't have that place on lockdown? Bad, most likely. But what other options existed? She would have to go one way or another.

Lying around wouldn't help anyone, herself included. Devin's cryptic message showed that everyone else on the Celestus might need help, and, for whatever reason, circumstances put her, and maybe her alone, in a position to do something. What that something was, she had no idea. She could head to augmentations and grab the device they'd been working on there, but she'd seen the entrance. Manual door releases could only get her so far. Codes didn't work on unpowered computers, lockers, and gates. She anticipated needing to access all the above. After reasoning it out, she had to head to Engineering.

She'd never been there before, but didn't think it lay too far from where she met with the quartermaster. Unfortunately, that entire area sat almost a dozen decks away, and she had yet to explore the many levels below.

Her mind raced as it processed all the things she'd encountered so far. *Stars, I just need a moment to think.* Tapping on her wrist, she powered down her suit. The chest lamp winked off, and she spent several minutes staring at the darkness and contemplating what in the universe she should do. Knowing that Engineering was the most logical play didn't seem to help. Confusion and frustration held her down like a prisoner strapped to a rack. After a while, she couldn't tell if her eyes were open or closed in the void of black.

Her mind wandered to the events leading up to her awakening in Devin's room. If she planned to explore other parts of the vessel, she wanted to be as prepared as possible for any encounters. But what did she know so far?

It started with a civilian, Morgan Sims, having an envirosuit breach while outside the domes. No, it began with someone authorizing him to leave the shelter, which didn't appear on the logs. I don't know what he meant to do planet-side, but it appears someone sabotaged his suit and wanted him to get infected. Next, security transported the patient to the medical labs for quarantine and testing. We discovered a lack of vitamins C and D, as well as iron. The patient also had boosted adrenaline. I didn't see a sample after he got free, but I would surmise it correlates to his increased strength.

He broke out of quarantine and infected some crew members, including me. So, there could have been dozens? Hundreds? Surely not. Though, if I knew how it spread, I might have a better idea of how many could be infected. But, it's safe to say that between security and the ventilation scrubbers, they contained it to this floor. At least, I hope so.

Some days later, a kind of wave, whatever that might be, passed by and presumably caused massive ship-wide damage. Though it's possible, the other infected could do the same, given that Morgan Sims broke out of containment. If his strength was any indication of what others would be like, even five to ten of them could wreak havoc. Would they have destroyed all the robots I saw earlier?

A lot of those answers are at the labs. And the only way I can see to access the information I need is re-power the section. I hope there's an easy switch I can flip in Engineering.

Feeling a bit more resolve than before, Beth forced herself up, put her helmet back on, switched on her light, and left the room toward the nearest lift tube. Luckily, it sat on her side of the ship so she wouldn't have to cross back over through the breached areas.

I don't want to risk venturing outside the vessel if I don't have to.

The lobby around the tubes lay in complete disarray. It looked like something had impacted the hull, denting it in and knocking panels off the wall and ceiling in the process. Wires, lighting fixtures, and warped metal plates littered the floor. Somehow, the structural integrity had held, and the damage hadn't ruptured the whole vicinity. Unfortunately, it had crushed all the lift entrances except one.

She went to the sliding door of the remaining tube and looked for the manual release. Except for the call button on the wall, only smooth metal framed the entry—no access to any inner workings.

How's this supposed to work? She grabbed either side of the two sliding doors that barred her way and pulled. They parted only a few inches before shutting again. "Ugh!" She grunted with effort.

I'm going to need something to wedge in here.

Strewn around her lay several scraps of metal plating that had broken off from whatever caused the damage. She picked up a jagged piece shaped like a triangle and placed it on the ground in front of the lift doors. Then, with all her might, pulled them apart. When a wide enough opening appeared, she pushed the tip of the scrap into the crack with her foot and let go. The metal piece caught, then snapped sideways as the doors closed on it, but it held fast and maintained a small gap.

There must be a trick to this that I don't know, but I've got no other way to get to the lower part of the ship.

She found a couple more usable pieces of debris. She put a broader section on the ground next to the first one and a tapered one, which she wedged in the space between the doors, then pulled on it. The leverage forced them apart even further. She kicked the larger piece in, and it held them open. The gap still wasn't large enough for her to squeeze through, but it was close. She used the chest light on her suit to illuminate down the shaft, hoping for a ladder or some secure way to descend. What she found was as promising as it was disturbing. Another grouping of dismantled robots, tangled together with their internal cabling, floated before her in the tube devoid of gravity. A tingle at the base of her spine ran its way upward, sending chills down her nerves, and she diverted her vision elsewhere in the area.

These tubes must have their own anti-gravity generators. Could that be a safety precaution of some kind? She didn't ponder the discovery long. It would help her get to Engineering, and that's all that mattered.

Repeating the same process as before, she wedged the opening farther apart until it looked wide enough for her to squeeze through. Before entering, she gazed down at the metal scraps holding the pressure of the doors open.

If this snaps closed at the wrong time, it will kill me. Though feeling unsure about traversing the threshold, she stuck one leg out into weightlessness. The sensation of having half her body still solidly on the ground while the other side became buoyant might have been the strangest thing she ever experienced. With as much care as possible, she pushed off with her still-weighted foot and glided forward.

Once past the gap, she held onto the side of the tube. Several pipes and cables ran up and down its length, fading into the darkness on both ends. She activated the shoulder-mounted lights on her suit, inverted her orientation, and peered down the shaft in the direction she wished to go. Scattered robot parts drifted the length of the space. She did her best to ignore the nagging questions about what ravenously dismantled them, and why here.

Taking hold of one of the large cables, she went hand over hand down the tunnel towards the ship's bottom.

Requisitions is only a few floors above the last level the lifts serviced. She assumed Engineering resided at the bottom, nearest the drive engines.

Should I stop by Requisitions on my way? I could get a new suit, and there could be some clues there. Yes, that's a decent idea.

Maybe she'd been in a medically induced sleep for weeks or longer, though she didn't want to consider it. The idea had crept into her thoughts on more than one occasion. After hearing Devin's urgent but cryptic message, she felt a new urgency, a need to figure out this puzzle and help where she could. She knew that meant going back to the labs at some point, but she couldn't get the images of the lobby out of her mind. For now, she would seek answers elsewhere, which started with understanding the power issue.

She traversed slowly along the cylinder-shaped passage, the light from her suit reaching out dozens of feet into the seemingly endless black. She knew the ship was huge, but hadn't considered what it would be like to crawl the length of it. After several minutes of slow going, she decided the time had come to move things along.

Beth grasped the cable, pulling as straight as she could with all her might. She surged forward with a speed that surprised even her. The tunnel flew rapidly past. Far ahead, she spotted the lift approaching quickly, too quickly. Her hands took careful hold of the cables to slow her flight. It didn't work as intended. She was going too fast. Instead, she tumbled out of control down the middle of the passage, far from any handhold.

"Shit!" Tucking herself into a ball, she tried to prepare for impact. Slam! Beth's body crashed into the top of the lift.

Chapter 13

Beth's body shuddered on contact, but it felt strange, like an aching memory, a distant whisper of pain. She bounced and drifted just above the surface, gently grazing a wall.

That should have hurt more. But it didn't. She'd felt it, but the impact should have done some damage. Could she still be under the effects of the sedatives? Did the suit protect her?

I have to admit, despite feeling better, I can't entirely shake this feeling of disconnection and lack of focus. I don't like it, but I haven't liked anything since waking.

Beth moved her limbs and patted herself down, checking for injuries. Nothing felt out of place. She might have some severe bruising later, but that seemed to be the extent of it. A horrible thought crept into her mind.

Security hit Morgan Sims with enough stun pulses to knock a robot out, and he kept going. That crash could have easily broken something, but I feel ok. Does that mean...? She glanced around, trying to distract her mind.

Nothing to be done about it now. She repeated it over and over, like a mantra.

Come on, Beth, focus. You might have just landed right. It's not the parasite. You're not losing your mind.

Over the next few minutes, with eyes closed, Beth concentrated on her breathing and centered her thoughts. When calm finally drifted over her, she resumed scanning the area. She wasn't sure which floor the lift had stopped at, but couldn't see a way to access the carriage from above. A short way back up the tunnel, she spotted an exit, a release lever stuck out beside the door.

Handy.

Upward into the space, she identified several dark alcoves.

Those must be ways to access this tube. She decided the door was her best bet. At least she might figure out where she had ended up. Engineering probably lived farther down, but maybe she could find another way there. She figured it had to be the most extensive area on the ship since it contained the reactor core.

Pushing off the wall, Beth soared toward the door. With a pull of the release, the locks disengaged, and the entrance sprang open. Dim light poured through the gap. She pulled herself out and felt the weight of gravity once more. The emergency lighting held steady in this area. The small sign of functionality sent an excited chill down her limbs. However, other than the illumination, she couldn't identify any other signs of crew activity.

It's nice to see another place with power. I wonder if anyone is holding up here. She stopped at the thought. Would security still be an issue? *As much as I would like to talk to anyone, I should still be wary of who I run into. I suppose if they come after me, I can try to escape back through this lift.*

With no doors or intersections, she walked cautiously down the straight hall, peeking around corners and sticking close to the walls. She clicked off her suit light to conserve energy, but the readout showed a full charge when she checked it.

The passage led to a massive round lobby area where four doors labeled Astrophysics Lab A, Lab B, Lab C, and dormitories stood.

Hmmm, I expected Astrophysics to be near the front of the ship. I knew they were a significant department, but this looks like the only thing on this floor. It must be absolutely massive unless it shares some space with something from a deck below or above.

She approached the entrance labeled Lab A. To her surprise, it was unlocked and accessible.

This could be a good sign. Every other place on this ship has been locked down tight. Someone is probably using these labs.

Inside, she found a series of hallways with doors leading to extensive experiment rooms. Sheets of transparent, synthetic glass wound their way through the gigantic space, sectioning off various areas while still allowing her to view the entire lab. She gazed across desks and lab counters where countless computer screens sat offline. In the far distance, the cosmos twinkled with stars. The view held her rapt attention for several minutes. It reminded her why she accepted this job in the first place, the chance to travel to a distant star and study unknown phenomena. The medical wing was buried in the middle of the ship with no windows to the outside. Seeing the Astrophysics labs made her jaw drop.

Maybe I should go back to school if I survive this. Astrophysics is looking pretty good right now.

She scouted around the room for about twenty minutes. All the terminals received minimal power but enough to boot them. It didn't matter in the end, as Beth found every one of them locked out with bio scanners.

Probably coded to each specific user. It'd be the only way to keep each project secure.

The medical wing and research staff were a much smaller unit. Most of her colleagues collaborated on projects and shared data, though individuals often did their own research. In addition, they shared some field crossover with the biology labs. She didn't know for sure, but assumed the bio researchers also had received samples of the patient's blood after discovering a foreign entity. They could've been working on their version of a cure or been merely dissecting and manipulating the sample in whatever creative ways they could come up with. *Biologists…* She rolled her eyes.

Because of their cross research, the biology labs could be worth checking out. Though, that all depended on who she ran into before then. Her list of places to visit continued to grow.

Despite being powered, none of the computers appeared to be in active use. It seemed reasonable the crew abandoned this place. Beth left and went into Lab B, finding similar openness with glass everywhere. In here, she spotted fewer terminals and more table space with enclosures for setting up experiments. One such chamber looked like it was used to test various amounts of gravity on different substances or organisms. She took her time rummaging through all the experiments.

None of these looks active. What am I even doing here? With a brief investigation, she surmised that no operations currently ran in this space either. And with everything being meticulously clean and sterile, discovering the last time someone used it proved impossible. Like the other lab, bio scanners blocked her access to all computer terminals.

Shaking her head, she turned to the exit.

This is looking like it might have been a complete waste of time. A couple more places to check, though. She left Lab B and went into the final lab, saving the dorms for last. If she found people there, she wanted to have looked through most of the area beforehand.

Lab C was not as open as the previous two labs. A short corridor separated it into different sections. Beth walked into the first and saw what looked more like the ship's bridge than any lab. Several consoles and screens, arranged in rows of raked seating configurations, faced the large windows looking out at the void. She approached and fired one of them up. To her delight, no encryption barred her access. It booted, entered a program, and a hundred or so stars appeared on the viewer. She moved her hand along the touchscreen, and the scene changed. As she zoomed in on one sun, the computer highlighted several small objects near the celestial sphere. *Planets*. A few bits of information about each of them became available. At the bottom of the screen, a question appeared.

<Focus additional scopes?>

She touched it, and a list of serial numbers arose. She tapped the first one. The screen changed and showed a negative thermal image of the star system. Then a few more bits of information materialized. She pressed on different serial numbers. With some, the view adjusted, and for most, extra information popped up: mineral and gas makeup, planetary volume, gravity, density, rate of rotation and revolution, and temperature.

Interesting… this controls the telescopes and other detection instruments for cataloging the immediate region of space. Hm… I'm not sure that's of use to me.

She rose from the terminal and went into the other section. A long hallway split off into several doors. Opening the first one, she saw an empty room, no furniture, or anything, just plain black metallic tiles. She recognized the holo-projector hanging from the ceiling's center and spotted its controls at the far side. Turning it on, her vision filled with a holographic section of the galaxy that encompassed the entire space. The emergency lights dimmed and sputtered. The hologram remained but grew faint.

So, this is why astrophysicists are always in such a good mood. They get to just play in the galaxy all day and night.

She shut off the projector. No sense in continuing the drain on the electricity in this section. She felt thankful to have it and didn't want that to change. The rest of the rooms proved to be the same as the first, all holo-projection areas for in-depth study of the galaxy. An idea occurred to her, and she rushed back to the scope controls. She took a seat at the terminal she and zoomed out. The screen showed a wide section of tiny stars. Turning her attention out the window, she observed the same.

Ok, this is in real-time. I figured as much, but I had to be sure.

With some trial and error, she maneuvered the scopes to show Janis IV, the planet the Celestus currently orbited. A significant amount of information came up over its image, and she began browsing. Most of it proved pretty uninteresting or unhelpful to her goals, but she found what she was looking for after a couple of minutes: the orbital distance between the ship and the planet's surface. It currently sat at one hundred and eighty-eight kilometers.

That seems low, but honestly, I don't know. She accessed a menu, bringing up a history of readings for everything on the current screen, inputting the last date she remembered before losing consciousness. The distance on that day displayed in the center of the screen, nine hundred and seventy-four kilometers. The difference popped into her head immediately.

A drop of seven hundred and eighty-six? This can't…?

She accessed the current date on the computers.

<11/22/912>

That… That can't possibly be right? It's been over two years since we arrived at Janis? This is too much… It's not even possible. I can't be missing two years of memory!

Beth slumped back into the chair, her arms and shoulders falling to dangle loosely at her sides. The realization of that much memory loss shocked her system and threw all her speculation of events into question. If she believed the date on this computer, no one was active on the Astrophysics floor or anywhere else. They were all gone. Maybe some lay in cryostasis, others might be on the planet, but she doubted anyone remained to restore the ship.

If everyone's in cryo, it explains why no one is dealing with the damage to the Celestus. Was that what Devin referred to? Me being the only hope because I'm not in cryo sleep? Oh, stars… But why was I awakened now and put in Devin's room? And by whom?

Chapter 14

Thoughts of her mysterious awakening pulled her mind back to Devin's desecrated space and the skeleton in the engineer's uniform. That one thing suddenly made much more sense. In a sterile environment, decay can take much longer, but if that person had the parasite inside them…

Could it have eaten its host? Maybe rapid decomposition is part of its cycle. It was something she hadn't tested. Nevertheless, it seemed a decent theory, one she couldn't disprove at the moment.

If decomposition has something to do with the parasite, it's one more reason to power up the med labs. Even the biology lab might have what she needed to study it further. But the task felt low on her priority list and she pushed it out of her mind.

However, it brought back the fundamental question: *Whose body was it?* The disturbing scene had confused and frightened her so much that she hadn't bothered to inspect the bones and couldn't even say what sex the person had been.

I'll have to go back there at some point and look. But part of me doesn't want to know. Her worst fear was it could be Devin. He had taken her there, become infected, probably by her, and then died trying to save her life. But with no evidence, all she could do was speculate. Her only clues were that someone sealed her in with another person and that person had died.

A sudden shudder, followed by a metallic groan of a stressed hull, reminded her of other issues existed beside her own personal crisis. She shook her head vigorously and refocused on the terminal.

"Computer, run a graph of the decline of the ship's orbit. Has there been any unnatural decay in our orbit?"

A graph appeared on a screen to her right. The timeline showed a stable orbit from the moment of arrival at the planet. However, a few days after security had knocked her out, a steady line of decline fell directly within the typical orbital decay, without compensation. Near the current date, only a few days past, a sharp delineation dropped drastically.

"Computer, what is this most recent significant change in elevation?"

"Atmospheric drag caused a significant change in orbital decay, resulting in reduced duration of gravitational stability," the feminine, not-quite-human-sounding voice replied.

"How long until the ship enters the atmosphere?"

"The ship is already in the uppermost atmosphere. Due to the air dispersion, drag has not had a catastrophic effect, but it is cumulative. The estimated time of planetary impact is three days, seven hours, fifty-one minutes. The crash site is estimated to be at latitude 24.87 degrees, longitude 67.02 degrees."

Beth swallowed hard as her eyes scanned the screen displaying the computer's horrific admission. "Shit..." She had just over three days to do two things she didn't know the first thing about, figure out why the ship isn't self-correcting its orbit, and do something about it.

Feeling a renewed sense of urgency, she headed toward the dorms. Until now, the best sources of information had been the personal logs left behind, and the living quarters seemed like a decent place to locate more of them. She didn't know the first thing about piloting the ship or what might be involved in Engineering. There could be problems she wasn't aware of requiring days of work. She had little time to waste.

A new nagging sensation of anxiety filled her gut.

No one is coming to rescue me; no one is waiting with all the answers just around the corner. I need to get to Engineering asap and assess what's going on 'cause there's no one else.

Leaving the lab in a hurry, she entered the dormitory. She estimated it took up just over half of this floor, while the labs occupied the other half. Ahead, hallways split off in various directions. On the walls, painted signs and arrows showed Dining Commons, Crew Quarters, and Recreational Hall. She started with the common areas, Dining, and Recreation.

The rec area appeared as she expected it would on any typical day. A clean floor and all equipment safely stowed. Nothing seemed out of place. As a result, she spent little time looking around. Impact with the planet lay a few days away, which gave her some time to look over things. Still, the impending disaster looming on the horizon motivated her to pass up anything that seemed like a waste of time.

The dining commons were closer to what she had encountered everywhere else. Cups, plates, and silverware lay discarded and strewn about the room, as if abandoned in a hurry. After a few minutes of looking about, she found a couple of personal logs. When the first one had enough power to boot up, she played the most recent recording.

"The data! The data! This has been what it's all about. The spatial phenomena gave us so much to contemplate and test. Unfortunately, the servers were so overloaded with incoming information that we actually had to delete a month's worth of star system mapping. That's insane! We were set up to map every star system within ten thousand light-years. More than enough storage space to log and categorize all those millions of stars, and we actually had to delete most of it to accommodate all the data from this wave.

"The Admins initially called it a wave, but I don't even know if that is right. It had properties that appear to be gravitational while being unaffected by the gravitational force of the planet or even the nearest star. According to the earliest analysis, its trajectory didn't change even though it passed within four hundred thousand kilometers of a major gravitational entity. No known object or force is utterly unaffected by that kind of gravity, including rays of light.

"There are particles and forces we detected within the wave that no one has seen before. I just hope the last-minute collectors we set up captured some of them. This will be a lifetime's worth of research. My personal theory is that this is a discharge from the far side of a black hole. The force of which propelled it, the mashup up of particles, and their interactions, point to a highly condensed mass of energy and matter in the process of scattering. If I'm right, the implications are enormous. Perhaps a new form of propulsion could be developed using mini black hole generators. It's science fiction turned into reality!

"The only downside is that it damaged some of our instruments during engulfment. They stopped taking measurements, so there was a lot I think we missed out on. I just hope we can piece things together with what we captured. The rest of the ship seems to have taken it worse from what I hear, so I suppose we are lucky in that. But it means repair crews will prioritize other departments and ship systems over us, per usual... We should be the first to get back up and running. After all, the whole reason we stayed in the wave's path was for us to collect this data. There could be residual, decaying particles we can scan or capture in the wake. What are we missing out on while the crew dithers with everyone else?

"There have been a few rolling blackouts, and apparently, the augmentation wing is entirely without artificial gravity, but they should take advantage of that and use it in their tests. I overheard someone in the rec-room mention multiple departments are having issues with some of their robots as well. If true, it's only going to delay repairs further! I'm going to put in a formal petition in the name of further discovery to the ship's director himself about giving us priority for once."

Stars... sounds like the scientists I worked with back on the homeworld. More interested in getting their names on the top of research papers than making discoveries that might actually help someone. She rewound the recording and listened to the end again.

"... and use it in their tests. I overheard someone in the reg-room mention that multiple departments are having issues with some of their robots as well. If true—"

She cut off the recording.

I've seen several dismantled robots. What issues could he mean? Come to think of it. I don't recall seeing A.R.I.A. in Devin's room. Then again, it was pitch black.

After listening to a few older logs on the tablet, she dropped it and hooked up the second while making her way to the crew's quarters on the floor. Static corruption marred the early part of the final recording with a lack of picture and sound, but she let it play anyway, and after a minute or so, audio broke through the crackle.

"... is a potential disaster. I have a friend who does the repair work requiring spacewalks. He used the phrase, 'I don't know how she didn't tear herself apart.' The wave, while a possible leap forward in astrophysics research, may have killed us all. Several sections have gravitational fluctuations. But apparently, it's not a result of damage to the artificial gravity generators in all cases. Sometimes the gravity just shuts off. That's not supposed to happen. I helped design the gravity generators' layout, and they overlap each other in multiple places to prevent this exact thing. Only a massive loss would cause gravity to fail. And in that instance, we would simply begin a proper rotation of the ship to regain marginal gravity. However, the engines are not functioning. We have intermittent power losses. I went up to some of the other dining commons and started talking to the other scientists. I know we're not supposed to, but this is a genuine emergency. Someone from Engineering suggested they might take the reactor offline. Putting it in low-power mode because of some unknown fluctuations causing dangerous spikes and lulls.

"There have been many injuries. The medical facilities are overfilled. They've been forced to recruit some bio-scientists as medical assistants to help. Others are being put into cryo if it's deemed their bodies can survive the process. This is serious.

"The damage reports I've seen are extensive. Everyone here has been whining about a possible loss of data, but what about the loss of our lives? I don't want to end up as a footnote for some other crew that finds our frozen corpses floating in the dead of space. If we even get that far. A hull breach occurred a full day after the wave passed. A perfectly good section of the hull just blew out into space and took everyone in that area with it. No explanation. It makes me wonder about the structural integrity of all the windows in the labs.

"The bow and top of the ship took the most damage, from what I hear. Our section managed to come through pretty unscathed. Still, with reports of unusual things happening on all decks, it leads me to believe there are lingering effects from the wave. There could be plenty of unseen damage; who knows! I'm going to petition the Admins to evacuate the ship to the planet while the repairs are done. I, for one, don't want to be on this floating death trap while it could spring shut at any moment."

Horrifying. These two worked together? If this guy's right about the extensive damage... I just have to hope the information was exaggerated. If a ship full of engineers can't fix her, what in the stars am I supposed to do? She felt her body temperature rise as blood rushed to her face. It took all her willpower to keep moving. Every step of the way, new obstacles presented themselves as hope fell away.

If it's hopeless, they would've evacuated everyone to the planet. But how would I get there? I don't know the first thing about flying a shuttle. But if I can't do anything about this ship crashing to the planet in three days, then I'm going to need to do something.

While she listened to the log recording, she continued exploring the dormitories, though moving forward felt like a useless endeavor. Beth had never backed down from a challenge, and she wasn't about to start now, but losing two-years' memory and the condition of the ship chipped away at her resolve.

In the Astrophysics dorms, she discovered all the personnel doors sealed tight, each with a bio scanner locking system. Ironically, this place had some of the best security of any wing she'd seen. Though she guessed Administration was, at least, this sophisticated, if not more so. It was much better than her lab's anyway. She hadn't been able to get through a single door. After checking a few dozen of them, she gave up and headed back to the lift tube.

She stuck her head in the tunnel and turned the suit's lights back on. The lift car still made a barrier to any deeper exploration. Looking it over didn't provide any answers to how to gain access, either. She let her gaze move back up the space, noticing the alcoves that occasionally branched off from the main shaft. *Bingo.*

Beth stepped out into the weightlessness of the lift tube and pulled herself along the wall toward the nearest inset. When she reached it, her light showed a short tunnel into one of the other shafts.

This is precisely what I hoped for.

The passage was tight, but not as bad as the one she'd squeezed through to get out of Devin's room. On the other side, she found herself floating in another lift tunnel. Below, she spotted a pile of debris clumped much further down than the lift in the previous shaft. Grabbing a pipe on the wall, she pulled herself toward it. A single exit door lay between her and where the scrap blocked the tunnel.

This is bound to be the same level the lift is stuck at in the other shaft. The urge to look around the floor tempted her, but with different priorities on her mind, she decided against it.

She passed by and continued forward, reaching the debris. It was a collection of what looked like broken sections of the shaft itself. Large beams, panels, shards of glass, all woven together with what must have been a kilometer's worth of cables and wires, jammed the tube.

Maybe I can dig my way through this. She started pulling the pieces away. They sailed one by one back up the tunnel. In short order, she came across several tools.

Someone must have been working in here. They left in a hurry. Just like everyone else, it seems.

As she pulled a large panel away and sent it adrift, a hand reached toward her face.

Chapter 15

Beth screamed and kicked backward, away from the reaching hand. Her legs flailed against the pile, spinning scrap away in the zero gravity. The light from her suit swung in all directions as she tried to distance herself. She couldn't tell what grasped for her as the hand twisted unnaturally in the changing light. Her back bumped against the wall. She reached above her head, clasping for anything. Her fingers found a grouping of pipes, and she began pulling herself back up the shaft. Behind her, a well of darkness swallowed the tunnel. Her lights faced forward and upward. Below, waited mystery and uncertainty.

A long piece of metal pipe drifted in the void. She took it and turned back, swinging as she did. The improvised weapon thudded against something with a metallic thwack. A loose piece of scrap spun off and bounced against the inside of the tunnel. The blow hadn't been hard; with little to brace herself against, it was challenging to bash anything with any force. Still, she readied herself as best she could and pointed her chest light back to the debris.

A panel floated nearby, obscuring most of the pile. It rotated languidly, bringing the debris pile back into view with aching slowness. The hand was there, sticking out limply between two larger pieces of metal.

Did it actually reach for me?

She was sure it had, but now she second-guessed it. Mustering some courage, she crept back down toward the limb, keeping the pipe in one hand.

I wish I had one of those security stun-guns right about now. Maybe I should hit up Requisitions after this. I'm pretty sure it's that door just back up the tunnel a little way.

When she got closer to the arm, it became more apparent that its human features were metallic. This wasn't a person, but a robot assistant model like A.R.I.A., meant to look more like a person but with a smooth, featureless face. Breathing a sigh of relief, she cleared more of the surrounding debris. As the hand and attached arm floated loose, no body came with it. However, after a few more minutes of digging, she found another piece, a headless torso, covered in dents, with one arm and half a leg; most of it crushed beyond operation. She pulled it free to examine closer.

I'm not sure what this is doing here. It's not a maintenance bot; it's a personal assistant.

Unable to gain any useful information from the mangled bot, she let it drift away and went back to clearing out a hole in the debris barrier. She could already see her light peeked through several small openings in the trash pile, sending thin beams further down the dark shaft. Finally, with more effort, she cleared a space large enough to squeeze through. Just underneath the junk, more loosely packed objects littered the length of the lift shaft. She brushed them aside easily in zero gravity as she pulled herself along the wall towards the end.

Less than a minute after reaching the other side of the barrier, she noticed the surrounding debris moving in the same direction she was. Almost imperceptibly slow at first, the objects beside her matched her pace after just a few seconds.

Stars! Gravity is coming back on!

She spun and pointed her chest light back up the way she had come. Sure enough, the entire barrier of scrap slid downward at increasing speed. Beth grabbed the side of the wall and shoved herself forward. Debris and junk bashed her body. She did her best to push it aside as she flew ahead, but it slowed or altered her course every time she did. The door below grew closer, but so did the crushing dam of junk. She grabbed a protrusion on the wall and propelled herself on an altered trajectory. She had to get out of this tunnel before gravity came back on fully. Even at partial force, the weight of the debris would crush her. The fate of the robot rang all too real in her mind.

The manual release protruded from the wall just beside the door. Beth reached out, her hands leading the way like a human torpedo on a crash course.

I only have one shot at this. If she missed the door, then there would be no time to reverse course and come back.

She stretched for the handle, fingers clamping down on it with all the force she could muster. Her momentum pulled at the level, but her angle was poor, and the device moved painstakingly slow as the door cracked open only a crack. Her feet kicked in the air, trying to find something to push off of. There was nothing. With all her strength, she pulled herself around near the wall. Bracing her body, she yanked the handle, and the door fully opened. Smaller debris ricocheted off her suit as larger pieces soared right behind them.

Beth hovered toward the exit, but her trajectory was awkward. The angle from the release handle to the door didn't line up. A colossal support beam crashed into her helmet, flinging her body into the shaft. Her hands flew out and grabbed the edge of the doorway. She pulled and threw herself forward. If there had been any more gravity, it would have never worked. As the mass of debris and garbage fell, she slipped through the gap. A resounding crash echoed up the shaft and spilled into the dark hallway where she lay shaking. Less than a minute later, another collision boomed from the tunnel, more prominent than the first. The lift car joined the rest of the scrap at the bottom of the tube.

Beth lay in the fetal position on the floor. A single beam from her chest lamp cut into the darkness but left jagged shadows as it filtered through her tucked legs. Her whole body convulsed. She wrapped her arms tightly around herself, trying to calm the adrenaline rush. She focused on her breathing, picturing it in her mind as her lungs filled and emptied in decreasing repetition.

I almost died. Everyone is counting on me, and I almost... I... You didn't, Beth. You're alive. It's alright. Everything is ok.

Eventually, she sat up and found a wall with her back. She ran her gloved hands over her helmet, finding a fair-sized dent in the top. Her eyes scanned the glass visor, which appeared undamaged. Still, she pressed on her forearm touchscreen and ran a suit integrity test. A brief sound of escaping air hissed as the oxygen bottle activated. She watched the screen with nervous anticipation.

<Seal Integrity 100%>

Beth slumped her head back against the wall as her arms dropped to her sides.

Ok... ok, lift tubes are officially done. I'll take a void walk before I ever set foot in there again. She now knew the lethal accuracy of the astrophysicist's assertion of unreliable gravity aboard. Fluctuations in gravity while in the dining commons or a lab were one thing. She could handle it if a loose plate fell on her head, but getting caught again in a tube when a lift car came crashing down... She didn't want to think about it. That had been too close. Even if she wanted to risk going back up, there was no easy way to ascend the tunnel unless gravity went back off.

I hope I'm not trapped at the bottom of the ship.

She let a few more minutes go by while she thanked her stars to still be alive before standing to figure out where she'd landed. A small lobby area with the same off-white walls and gray floors surrounded her. In front and behind stood the entrances to the tubes, while the room was open to the side, with passages leading away. She went to the left, which led around one wall. Before her lay a vast open area bathed in darkness, but she spotted a few dim, blinking console lights. She walked down a short flight of stairs to a lower level, where her chest bulb lit the rows of controls. Gages and readouts with labels like core temp, thrust output, and reactor efficiency caught her eyes.

Engineering.

Swinging her beam around the room, she approached what appeared to be the central console, the one with the most lights and buttons. It booted up with a few taps on the keyboard.

<Please Enter Login Information> flashed up on the screen.

Beth shook her head. She tried a few generic login codes with no success.

I've finally made it to Engineering, and I'm locked out of the system? Now I might not even be able to get out of here.

"Shit!" Beth clenched her fists and gritted her teeth. She blew out a sharp breath, then began checking the other terminals around the area. They each had identical login screens. *This is a nightmare!* She had scant options but to search around and see if there was anything else she might access.

On one wall, behind an electric panel, she found a switch labeled "Emergency Lighting," which she activated. In a series of drumming clicks, illumination broke through the shadows in the engineering bay section by section. Having something work for her brought greater relief than Beth expected.

Hurray for small victories. She shut off her suit light to save power.

Maybe there's another suit I can switch to. I really don't like that this thing thinks it has a full battery. There's no way that's true. How many hours have I been using it?

She checked the suit's activation readout. It had been just over thirty-four hours.

Is that when I was first put in the suit? That makes sense, but then who put me there, and where in the blazes are they? Or is it how long I've been awake? I don't feel tired exactly. I've been feeling less foggy, too. But I'm not even hungry. It can't have been that long. Ugh... I need to get a new suit; I don't feel like I can trust the data coming off this one.

Since waking, a lingering fogginess had remained on the fringes of her subconscious. It didn't appear an impediment to her concentration, as it had when she first woke. It was more like a nagging sensation now. Something deep within her that said things are off, things are not quite right. When thoughts of the parasite possibly mutating her cells and causing changes to her physiology invaded her mind, she stamped them right back down. The parasite, and whatever lasting effects it might have, was the least of her concerns at the moment.

Maybe it's the sedatives, but none of that makes sense. I was alone in Devin's room; at least, I had been for some time. There aren't many sedatives I'm aware of that would still be in my system at this point. If I ever get back to my lab, and that's looking like something I'll have to face at some point, I'll need to get a urine sample and analyze it.

The suit she wore took care of all waste. When worn, the user wouldn't be aware of relieving themselves at all. The envirosuit collected, molecularized, and released the waste as harmless particles or stored it in a compressed form until placed in a charging and cleaning station. Beth wasn't sure of the exact process.

I don't know if I want to believe much of what I've seen so far. How much time has passed since the incident? How long have I been awake? Why can't I find anyone aboard? It's looking like a mass abandonment of the Celestus occurred, but if that were true, then why did no one come back? The ship is still here. It hasn't been destroyed or infected as far as I can tell, so what could have happened to everyone?

As she gazed around the colossal engineering area, she spotted several dozen layers of catwalks with open-grating floors lining the cubical room walls. System access points, set at different intervals and on various levels, allowed the crew to monitor the entire ship's status, its power draw, efficiency, gravity, engines, coolant, and what seemed like a hundred other things.

Beth moved to the edge of the platform and took a few minutes to gaze at the reactor core far below. Clear, synthetic glass surrounded its chamber for visual monitoring in case of instrument failure. She didn't know the first thing about reactors, but if she had to guess, this one was in a deficient operating mode. It pulsed with a dimness that reminded her of a dying star, nearly turned to stone. It didn't look healthy.

How long can a reactor operate in a low-power mode?

She didn't know. All the answers to this waited behind a stupid login screen she was helpless to penetrate. She turned away from the viewing area and walked back toward the console array. Her eyes fell on a tablet sitting on a chair.

Well, that's something, at least.

She powered it up and looked at the contents. There was only one log and a single file. None of which was encoded. She fired up the recording, and a picture of a female with mostly gray hair pulled back into a tight bun, brown, weathered eyes, and dressed in an engineering uniform appeared.

Greetings, I'm Chief Engineer Aura, director of all engineering operations for the starship Celestus. If you're listening to this, then things are likely quite serious. But the fact that someone is listening is a ray of hope.

Beth paused the video. *First, Devin says I might be the only hope, and now this officer. Why am I the only one left?*

Chapter 16

Beth held the tablet in front of her face and stared back at Chief Engineer Aura's visage. The woman had expected someone to come by and left this message for them. Against all odds, Beth turned out to be that person.

Why am I the only one alive or awake? Why? She slumped her shoulders, sighed, and shook her head. Despite obstacles she never imagined, she'd made it this far.

I know I need to finish hearing this, so what am I waiting for?

Time wasn't on her side, and she knew it, felt it with each action and hesitation. She ran her gloved hands down the back of the device, still keeping it pressed against her thumbs in front.

I know you feel alone, Beth. Her inner voice spoke. *But there are people trying to help. Chief Engineer Aura is one of them, and Devin is another, even if they aren't beside you. They are helping, and there may be others. Focus up and see what this old gal has for you.*

Beth sighed and started the video again.

"There's been talk of evacuating the ship, and since you're there and I'm not, I expect we did it. Why we haven't come back is a mystery I don't have the answers to. I can't say where I am at this moment or who you might be, but I've left this recording as a way for you to help us all should the worst happen.

"You are likely aware the ship received severe damage because of the spatial anomaly we encountered. Crews have been hard at work assessing and attempting to repair the damage. I can tell you some of it will be nearly impossible without a proper spaceport, but we are doing our best."

The words didn't provide Beth with any encouragement. She was one person, a scientist and a doctor. Not an engineer, let alone a team of them. If the damage was bad enough to need a port, what could she possibly do? Hopelessness sank into her pores like craters capturing rain. Her body slumped farther down as the weight of reality hit her shoulders with the engineer's words.

"The real problem is the power grid and gravity generators throughout the ship have been fluctuating erratically. Our initial assessment was damage directly to the grid or the controllers. While there were some fried components, this does not account for all the problems we're encountering. We'd diagnose a system as operational only to have it malfunction hours later. Because of this unpredictability, we have shut down the core. It will operate in minimal burn mode until we can get a handle on this situation, reducing stress on the entire grid and lowering the chances of a critical core meltdown. We'll continue with emergency power until we're confident the reactor can remain stable.

"Since there's a chance something has happened to me, against regulations, I've included my personal director's logins for all the engineering consoles. You'll find it and any other relevant codes in the document on this tablet. Your first order of business will be to run a diagnostic on the grid and make sure it can sustain the full power of the reactor. Until then, the main console has the control for transferring emergency power to the various decks and sections of the ship. If there are further repairs to be done, you'll need power in those sections. Good luck."

The log froze on the woman's distorted image, and Beth turned it off. A mix of worry and relief brought warmth to her skin. She had the much-needed engineering login info. Still, every personal log she'd come across said the same thing: the ship had been damaged, and no one was sure to the exact extent, only that it was significant.

I don't understand why no one has mentioned the patient or the Medical lab incident.

She still suspected the parasite had something to do with her being sealed in Devin's room. For now, it was the most logical explanation, though she could easily think of many better places to be quarantined.

What isn't apparent is why. If there had been an outbreak, then why is there no mention of it by anyone?

The answers seemed to always lay in some other distant part of the vessel. She'd have to find the Biology department, where they were also studying the parasite.

Maybe they found a counter agent where my team failed. Was the parasite a non-issue by the time the wave hit? None of these account for the passage of time. Whether it has been weeks or years, it doesn't add up.

Beth took a seat and accessed the central engineering console using the login info she found on the director's tablet. Several layers of menus popped up to work through, but luckily, none of it proved overly technical. After a couple of minutes, she discovered how to reroute the power from one section to another. Next to the commands, the screen showed a graph representing the current level of wattage. In its history, it revealed a gradual drain on the ship. Much like the time-lapse in the Astrophysics department, this also displayed a two-year span.

Stunned, Beth slumped back against the chair. She might have ignored the Astrophysics' computer results as a glitch, but seeing the data here drove the reality home all over again.

It really has been over two years... "I don't understand any of this!" She slammed her fist down on the table, holding the console. "Am I losing it? Why am I the only one here? If the ship was abandoned, why was I sealed away? And why in my boyfriend's room? What part did he play? Was he trying to save me from something? Was he trying to save everyone else from me? It's impossible! I couldn't have been in there for two years."

Beth let out a rage-filled scream, shot to her feet, and paced the room to calm her rising panic. She felt like her heart might burst from her ribs if she didn't get a handle on herself.

It's a problem like any other. Just break it down, Beth. Ok... the only explanation for losing time is that I was in stasis. Someone, for some reason, took me out and sealed me in Devin's room. He's the most likely candidate, but I don't know for sure. And I don't understand why he or anyone else would wake me up just to do that.

"Ugh! None of this makes sense!" Her voice echoed out through the speaker in her suit.

Why don't I just add Cryo-Storage to the never-ending list of places I need to investigate? It's like someone wants me to finish a puzzle but stuck every piece in a different part of a maze!

Pushing down her frustration, she looked over the current power distribution, noting the available output only granted emergency lighting and minimal terminal access to four sections of the ship at a time. Current areas with power were Engineering, Astrophysics, Crew Quarters and Mess Hall on deck eighteen, and the Shuttle Bay.

I thought cryo was one of the few places powered at all times. I'm sure of it.

Director Richter mentioned it when we were thawing the first batch of colonists. I know there was a backup generator in the case of complete ship power loss, but how long would it last? Worst case, the tubes are supposed to automatically awaken everyone if there is an extended period of no power. Since I've seen no one, I hope the backup power is still running, or... Her train of thought ended there and she attempted to focus on adjusting the energy distribution.

With a bit of trial and error, she figured out the controls for power allotment and pulled the electricity away from Astrophysics, Crew Quarters, and Mess Hall on deck eighteen. She then transferred power to the biology wing and Cryo-Storage. It would have been convenient if the controls had a map interface, but the screen simply listed the various sections of the ship, which had their own distribution nodes. She wasn't sure why energy was routed to the shuttle bay and considered moving it elsewhere.

Maybe the Medical labs... The image of the bloody lobby and smashed doors washed into her mind. No part of her wanted to return there, but if the Biology labs proved useless, she'd have little choice if she wanted to learn her fate regarding the virus. With a couple of taps on the keyboard, she made the transfer.

Alarms rang immediately. A warning flashed on the screen.

<Power distribution critical failure!>

It flashed over and over. Beth pulled the energy away as quickly as she could. The alarms and warning disappeared.

Right... right, diagnostics first.

It took her a few minutes to find the correct place in the operating system to run a full scan of the power grid, but once unearthed, a list of various levels of diagnostics presented themselves. She opted for a basic stress test. Assuming the reactor came back online, it would only let her know which grids could accept power, either emergency or full. But that seemed the most critical information at the moment. Transferring to a damaged grid could cause fires or electrify every surface in that entire section of the ship.

A countdown appeared, showing the diagnostic would be complete in just a few minutes. After that, she wanted to conduct a deep scan to pinpoint exact problem areas. According to the description on the screen, it would even provide workarounds when available. The deep scan would take several hours, according to the estimate.

I'll definitely run this when I'm finished with Engineering. For now, I think it's most important to identify what sections have terminal access and which might be impossible to navigate.

When the task finished, she noted the inoperable places, including Requisitions, the Medical labs, and several crew-housing sections. Though nearly every level seemed to have suffered some kind of failure, as a whole, most of the ship would operate if given the resources.

Ok, so how do I boot up this reactor? She looked over all the menus. Dozens of things had to do with the reactor: adjusting the temperature, venting, power output, distribution, and various stress tests.

Maybe if I run some of these tests, it'll show me what to do. She accessed the first one and told it to begin. An error message popped up.

<Reactor in low output mode unable to begin test.>

Beth tried several more, all of which resulted in the same error. However, a test labeled *output degradation* started. The status bar indicated only a few minutes until completion, so she waited. Once complete, it showed a gradual drain on the life of the reactor. At this rate, the computer estimated the reactor would lack the output to sustain any systems in fourteen more years. Two years after that, it would be so degraded it could not reignite to full power.

Well, it still has enough juice to be fired back up. The question is, how?

After browsing all the menus and then doing it again, she folded her arms across her chest and sat back in the chair.

What am I missing? How the hell do I start this thing?

Chapter 17

Beth went to all the terminals on the main floor of Engineering, booted them up, and logged in using the director's info. Each could monitor and test a different ship system, life-support, gravity, engine control, etc. In an emergency, an engineer could take over and operate the entire ship from these points. However, none linked to the reactor in any way she found.

Beth stretched her arms, rolling them around backward, then got up and went to the chamber window overlooking the reactor. Catwalks ran around the chamber and up to the dimly pulsating heart of the ship.

Maybe there's a control station nearer to the reactor itself. The re-fire sequence might have to be performed from inside the chamber. She thought about it for a second, then decided it couldn't be.

If I'm in there when that thing fires up, it's going to cook me. No suit could protect me that close to what is essentially a micro star. Not at full power, anyway. No, it has to be here somewhere on the main floor, but where?

Her mind poured over every possibility it could come up with. It occurred to her two separate recordings had mentioned a prototype device in the Augmentation labs, one of which had been Devin's. He had even given her all the access codes. The device was an interface enhancer, which would let an untrained individual operate something they normally couldn't. It might be worth a shot.

Ugh! I don't want to go all the way back up to Augs just to come all the way back here, but what choice do I have? Unconsciously, her hands attempted to rub at her temples, but the helmet turned them away. She slapped her wrists down on her thighs in frustration. Then, with a resigned sigh, she forced herself into action.

First, she went to the central console again and checked the energy distribution. She let out a relieved breath when emergency power transferred successfully from the Biology labs to the Augmentation labs.

"Now to figure out how to get there," she mumbled.

She went back to the lift tube area. Tossing in a piece of scrap metal told her gravity still functioned in the one she'd come down, making it near impossible to ascend. So instead, she went back into Engineering. She'd spotted several tool cabinets in the room when she'd first come in. Opening one, she removed a wedge bar and a device resembling a giant vice.

This will do the trick.

Back at the tubes, she shoved the bar between the doors of one of the other lifts. She avoided the crushed shaft and the one which had the lift car stuck in it. With the third having lost zero-gravity, she only had one choice.

I never thought about this before, but four lifts really seem like way too few for a ship this size. Then again, this is the most I've ever needed to use them. She'd visited Cryo-Storage to help thaw the first and second round of colonists, been on Devin's floor, and had gone to Requisitions the other day, but that was it. Everything she needed was on her deck. Still, at this moment, the lack of options annoyed her to no end.

The metal pry-bar kept the doors apart while she placed the vice between them. She attached a cord from the device to her suit and powered it up. Slowly and methodically, it pushed the doors apart, then locked in place. She wasn't taking any chances and reached around through the doors and pulled the release so they would stay open on their own. In doing so, she discovered a fresh problem. This shaft had gravity as well.

"Fuck!" She cursed her luck.

How the hell am I supposed to get out of Engineering? Maybe there's a maintenance ladder in this one.

She clicked on her suit light and pointed it into the dark tunnel. No ladder came into view, but a thick bundle of loose wiring hung next to the door. It dangled from somewhere far above. Pulling down hard on it, she found it held fast.

Well, I didn't see a way to adjust lift gravity from Engineering, though I'm sure it has to be there somewhere. She thought about going to check, but something in the back of her mind said, push forward. A nagging sense someone left the cable here for this purpose prodded her mind like a repetitive alarm, trying to pull her from a dream. If gravity had been an ongoing problem, then surely someone else could have rigged a way to move up and down the ship's lift tubes.

She stepped inside and stood on the thin catwalk running around the edges of the tube, staying near the door opening. A feeling of lightness fell over her.

Full gravitational pressure isn't active in this tunnel. That should make climbing easier. Taking hold of the cables, she began the ascent. The envirosuit wasn't a fully equipped strength-enhancing apparatus, like something the military would use. Still, it seemed to help, along with the lack of full gravity. After ascending several decks, she still didn't feel overly tired.

The tube went up a frustratingly long way with no exit. The engineering section took up a significant portion of the lower half of the ship, with much of the space housing the engines and the chamber holding the reactor. She stopped at the first exit and stood on the thin catwalk. When she pulled the manual release, the doors sprang open with an ear-piercing whine as they scraped against something metallic. Her light shot through the opening, revealing collapsed beams and debris filling the lift lobby. She could see past it into the room, recognizing it immediately as Requisitions.

Damn, I really want to trade out this suit. Maybe pick up a stun gun or something bigger for when I have to go back to my lab. If I run into someone infected, or even security, should I be armed? Would it matter? She remembered how useless the stun guns were on Morgan Sims.

She'd never been in an envirosuit for this long and wondered when the waste storage molecularizer would be full. Thankfully, the outfit was climate-controlled and didn't make her sweat. Though she had no one to impress. Even so, after a while, it would be nice to peel the thing off and put on something fresh. Maybe she could swing by a gym when she got a chance and just rinse off. The thought passed as quickly as it manifested; too many other immediate problems and mysteries for any respite.

She moved on from the acquisitions level and continued upward, suspecting most of the other places she wanted to go were quite a ways above her.

I could stop by cryo on my way to Augs. It seemed like a reasonable thing to do. She passed another couple of floors, including Astrophysics, then stopped on the Cryo-Storage level. She'd been there before and knew it was another large section occupying several decks. The Celestus contained enough chambers to put the entire crew and the colonists into stasis for the journey here. Everyone had their own capsule, even the rotating flight crew, which staffed the flight deck throughout the journey.

She released the door and looked through the gap. Emergency lighting showed the lift lobby, and beyond it, the entrance to the Cryo-Storage area. Moving into the hall, she stretched her arms and noticed how invigorating moving them felt.

Even with the suit's help, I should be a little tired, right? I suppose I should just be thankful. This is the least of the weird things going on.

Still, it worried her. She'd been covered in a patient's blood and possibly infected with an unknown organism. It would be a miracle if she'd avoided contamination. There was always the chance the parasite had to transfer in a particular way. Conditions on the planet might be ideal, while on the ship, the opposite. Still, considering the evidence, the patient picked it up through a minute compromise in his enviro suit, then it was probable she received the full dose. Without a lab, she had no way of knowing, only suspicions and a constant feeling of unease. After the incident, she had no memory, just the theory security had sedated her for quite some time and then put her into stasis. She wasn't exhibiting any of the patient's symptoms, but the more she thought about it, the more she felt it would be a good idea to test some of her blood when she got the chance.

With the door powered up and her medical access, Beth opened the barrier to Cryo-Storage. Inside, she stepped into a massive open warehouse area. Racks of white, oval stasis capsules, designed to contain a single human each, ran up over fifty meters to the ceiling. To her left, a flight of stairs led up to the control booth. From there, an operator could bring down any chamber to the bottom where it was accessible. She took the stairs two at a time. The computers here would have a log of who was still in stasis, and if she thawed the right person, they might have the answers she was seeking.

Inside the booth, the control console booted up. She was somewhat familiar with the menus and accessed a listing of the personnel in cryo. Engaging the search function, she typed in "Devin Landis."

Chapter 18

<No results>

Beth typed in Devin's name again, carefully pressing each letter on the keyboard.

<No results>

The message glared back at her like a manifestation of all her disappointment.

"Damnit!"

Beth let her body slump. Then, with sudden vigor, she slammed both fists down on the table. "I just want a little help. Is that too much to ask?" Heaving in a few deep breaths, she found her wits and input the rest of her friends' names. Each time, the response came back negative. She tried everyone she could think of in any department, but it was all the same. No results.

There's still the master list of occupants. She'd used it when her team had thawed the first round of colonists. Bringing up the list of currently occupied stasis chambers, she browsed the designations to see if any of the ship's crew were frozen.

This is strange. Most of these tubes have no crew or colonist assignments. But what's this name? Alice Bright. It's listed hundreds of times.

She highlighted the first Alice Bright with a tap on the touch screen. Distantly, in the chamber, a blue light lit up on one capsule.

Ok, let's see who you are. She activated the rotation system. Nothing moved.

<Unable to move stasis chambers under emergency power.>

Well, that's inconvenient. She sighed.

Beth clicked Alice Brights, one after another, seeking their location in the room. After a few minutes, one sitting on the floor finally lit up. She left the booth and jogged down the stairs toward the active stasis capsule. The digital name on the side matched the one in the database. Beth looked through the glass but saw no occupant.

Beth stared through the viewing window, her mind working on what to do next.

Is the name Alice Bright what the system uses for unoccupied chambers? Odd naming convention, but possible. She'd never been at the controls. Her job was receiving and checking in people as they awoke, then transporting them to Medical if a complication arose with their thawing. An idea struck her, and she went back up to the booth.

She highlighted all the Alice Bright names on the screen until she found nearly a dozen on the floor or within her reach. She headed down the stairs, inspected the nearest one, and discovered it also laid empty. Two could be a coincidence, and she decided to examine the capsules until she ran out of options. Her persistence was rewarded, because the next chamber held a young woman.

Well, so much for the empty theory. Beth examined the readouts on the side of the tube.

"Emergency power," flashed back at her, but no information on the woman's vitals. Beth moved on to the other lit chambers. Out of the dozen, individuals occupied eight, none of which she knew or recognized.

She spent several more minutes back in the control booth, going over the information on the console. Having been privy to information about how many were aboard and the schedule for rousing them, felt fortunate. She knew one hundred and thirty-eight were awakened and sent to the planet, and two thousand, two hundred and ninety-nine remained in stasis. At least, before she'd been knocked unconscious. Anything could have changed since then.

Three-hundred-and-forty chambers were designated for the crew, all of which had been awakened after arrival. Someone assigned the empty housings to the name Alice Bright from best she could tell, but some of the occupied ones as well. This meant some of the crew had been placed back into stasis under this name. What didn't add up was why they were put there anonymously and not under their own names.

To top everything off, since the entire deck and ship ran on emergency backup power, she had no way of telling if any of them were alive. Vital readouts required too much energy and were therefore unavailable. As expected, when she tried to thaw the young woman she first came across, the console refused.

<Cannot begin de-stasis operation under emergency power. Please restore.>

There was little else she could do here.

At least I've found some of the crew, but where are the rest of them? I need to get to Augs and hope the prototype thing is still there and working. Getting the reactor back online seems to be the only way to get further answers.

She exited through the lift tube, ascending once again using the loose cables. After climbing for a few minutes, she spotted the bottom of the lift car. Below it, numerous beams had been crudely welded in place with the lines wound around them.

I was right. Someone has been here. This cable was how they descended to the lower part of the ship.

She couldn't tell how long ago the person had put the braces on the lift, but it was a glimmer of hope someone else might be trying to do the same thing she was. Of course, they could've tried and failed anytime between now and two years ago. Still, the thought of any help from survivors bolstered her determination.

Survivors… The word echoed in her mind; it was hard to grasp. In what felt like a matter of days, this colonization expedition had gone from minor setbacks to a life and death situation. Not knowing if those in stasis still lived made her the only confirmed survivor.

Well, there is the cat. She'd forgotten about it until now. *Where did it come from? If it has been two years, how is the cat still alive? It might've been in stasis too, but then why would someone thaw it out? We could have shared the same chamber, but why? It doesn't make any sense.* The cat's presence was another puzzle piece that didn't line up with any other part.

Beth glanced at the area around the bottom of the lift.

I must be around deck fifteen, and I need to be at eleven. If I'm right, the lift car is blocking access to deck fourteen. There's a security station where I could get some supplies. I would really feel a lot better having a weapon, just in case I run into something I don't want to.

Being alone had been simultaneously comforting and disturbing. With each section devoid of life, the chances of running into any opposition or friend diminished. However, the idea of being on this giant ship, orbiting a dead world, all alone, felt overwhelming and terrifying. The bloody mess in the medical labs still kept her on her toes for something lurking in the dark hallways. Then there were the subtle signs of unusual activity after the wave. And what was the fate of her patient? Could he still be skulking around? Surely not after over two years.

What if I run into the person who put these cables here? Will they be friendly? Is there more than one? What if they're infected now? More than once, she felt as if someone watched her activities, and she was part of some lavish experiment where distant observers could view her struggle through this maze. The notion wasn't farfetched enough to dismiss, a fact she hated more than anything.

Beth backtracked down the cables to the entrance on the top-most level she could access. As she pulled the lift doors apart, dim light painted the tunnel in murky gloom.

I didn't power this deck. Maybe I'm not where I think I am?

She peaked her head out into the lobby. A wall blocked her suit's chest light from shining very far, but it proved unnecessary. Beyond the lift entrances, luminescent flowering plants grew in clumps along the floor's edges and crept up the walls to hang from the ceiling.

Was this where the biology lab was? It must be. I should know this since we work with them occasionally. Worked... She let out a sigh.

Dark branches of what looked like tentacles with diamond-shaped leaves clung to every surface. They grew along the walls, floors, and covered most of the ceiling. The dull glow came from bulbous protrusions the size of apples sprouting at random intervals on the plant-mass. The air seemed to move as millions of tiny particles wafted about with the slightest of her movements.

I've never been so glad to be in an enviro suit. Well, there was the time I was sucked out into space. It was pretty handy then, too.

Someone had put her in it for a reason, and every time she considered ditching the suit altogether, something reminded her it had saved her life on at least one occasion.

A thin, crooked path of open floor meandered through the flora-rich hallway leading deeper into the labs.

I'll admit, without power, having the bioluminescence is handy, but it seems hazardous. Maybe someone wanted this, or maybe not. I'd guess it's an unintended biological outbreak. Looks like my lab wasn't the only one with a severe containment problem.

Beth checked her suit's vital readout, which showed power and oxygen holding steady at full. The sensors had to be faulty. She'd been over and over it in her mind since waking up. If it wasn't using oxygen, then it used filtration. Which made sense, but how long was the battery supposed to last? At this rate, she could wander around for another seventy years, and it might still hold strong. Traversing a biohazardous area in a malfunctioning environment suit seemed like an absolutely terrible idea. Beth reminded herself again. It had worked in the vacuum of space, so this was nothing. Still, the notion gave her little comfort.

Another thought occurred to her.

The cables dead-end here, so someone must have used this entrance to come and go. Maybe there's some way nearby to get to the level above. The lift maintenance alcoves seem like an excellent place to start.

She stuck her head back into the shaft and glanced around. A few meters below, she spotted a couple of tunnels leading to the other elevator shafts. Unfortunately, the cables didn't fall very near either of them. She would have to swing herself over.

Beth backed down the shaft by placing her feet on the wall and going hand over hand on the cable until she arrived slightly below the tunnels' level. Then, gripping the lines tightly, she ran along the wall until she went far enough to duck into an alcove.

Crouching in the tight tunnel, she gazed back into the lift-shaft, then her eyes drifted to the lifeline in her hand.

If I let go of these cables, then there's no going back.

Keeping a firm hold, she pulled them along with her as she squeezed down the crawlspace. Nearing the other lift tube, the cables went taut. She pulled and pulled, but they refused to give any more slack. Shifting onto her butt and leaning her back against the tunnel wall, Beth considered her options. The other shaft was a couple of feet away. She just needed to look and see if she could ascend it without compromising her way back.

Beth looped the cable around her feet, ensuring it was secure, then stretched out toward the new shaft. The effort got her head outside enough to look around. The beam of light coming from the upper part of her chest partially illuminated the tube. It was sufficient, though, to see around the area. She felt gravity pull with full force inside the space, and she couldn't spot anything to climb on. Though as far up as her light reached, the tunnel looked clear in its ascension through the ship.

Of course, I have a clear shot and no way to climb.

The cable around her feet shifted suddenly, as if tugged. Beth scrambled to get her hands on it. Too late. The line slapped and whipped as it flew from the alcove. She could hear it hitting against the wall of the other lift shaft.

"Shit!" she yelled. "What am I supposed to do now?"

As if in answer, the ship moaned in metallic protest. From somewhere below in one shaft, she heard a rattle, followed by an echoing crash. She might not slam into the planet for a couple more days, but it felt like the ship wouldn't stay together long enough to impact in one piece. She scooted back the way she'd entered the tunnel.

Maybe the cable isn't too far away? Can I reach it?

She did her best to ignore the nagging feeling the cable hadn't simply slipped but been torn away. At the other opening, she saw the cable swaying lightly against the far wall, almost twenty feet away. She looked around for anything that could get her closer to it. A series of pipes ran parallel to the lift shaft, but took an L-shaped turn just a few feet above and to her right. They were about an arm's length away. She reached out and up, taking hold of it. With little to stabilize them in the alcove, her toes slipped, and her body swung out into the pit.

If I fall, no one will find me. Even if I somehow survive, it would cripple me at the bottom while I wait for the ship to crash into the planet—what a horrible way to go. Coming out here was such a stupid idea. Someone went through the labs, so there must be a way to get past them without involving this lift shaft. I can't take these kinds of stupid risks. Devin and everyone else are counting on me. They still might be in the stasis tubes under the other name with everyone else or even trapped somewhere on the ship. If I fail, everyone dies.

Beth edged along the pipe until she couldn't get any closer to the cables, then swung her body back and forth. The ship groaned and shuddered violently. Beth felt her grip failing. No, it was the pipe coming off the wall. She had no time to think; she had to act. Pushing off with her feet, she flew into the void, spinning around to face the far wall and her target, the cable. Beth felt the sensation of gravity pulling her toward a crushing death. *I'm not going to make it.*

Chapter 19

Beth tumbled down the shaft. Her hands flailed for something, anything, to grab. Air rushed through her outstretched fingers as they swiped at nothing. She clenched her teeth as fear, panic, and self-hatred filled her.

How could I have been so stupid, so careless? Everyone will die and it's my fault.

As hopelessness grew, the cable that had slipped away floated back out into the space as gravity fled the tube. However, weightlessness didn't help as momentum dragged her in the same direction toward a crushing doom. But the line was almost within reach.

If I can only... She reached out with one arm, fingers fully extended, she grazed the cable. It wafted closer, and she latched on with both hands. The sudden stop slammed her body against the side of the tunnel in a whipping motion. The impact, combined with inertia, overpowered her grip, and she slid along the line down the shaft. Beth's feet kicked as her fingers dug in. The metal-plated wall assaulted her body once again as she jerked to a halt.

Beth wrapped herself on the gently swaying cord with arms and legs as if gravity might inexplicably return. Her entire body trembled from pain or adrenaline; she couldn't tell, maybe both. She'd almost died again. Terror and anxiety fought against her will to continue. The ship called out from somewhere distant, a high-pitched whine of metallic anguish.

That sounded worse than anything before. Something's happened. I need to get moving again. She exhaled sharply through clenched teeth and forced herself to ascend back to the bio lab lift entrance.

When she stepped through the entrance, Beth once again basked in the bioluminescent glow emanating off the blue and off-white pods.

However, the light from her suit turned the plants dim and sickly. They melted like ice cream near a reactor, everywhere it touched. Trodding forward along the path, something crunched under her feet. Dead plants lay scattered across the floor. She bent down to examine them and noted the smooth cuts on the stalks. Above, she saw many vines ended abruptly in sheered-off stumps.

Someone cut a path through here. How long ago?

Beth traversed the passage and entered the laboratories. The spread of flora grew even more prominent here. With a glance over the space, she pulled the growth away from several workstations and consoles as she searched for something useful or further evidence of recent activity. On one of the overgrown countertops, she picked up two tablets. The first one refused to charge. Upon closer inspection, she saw tiny roots sticking out from a separated seam.

She tossed it aside and attempted to power the second. It fired up, and she played the last several logs. She found little help in them, primarily personal information. However, it held an extensive chronology that went back farther than the others she had discovered. She started from one of the earliest, "Arrival at colony planet Janis IV."

Beth noted this person actually took the time to label their logs when most people seemed to only label particular ones and let the operating system auto-name the rest using the time and date. However, it also meant most of these entries lacked a date to reference. She picked one called 'planetary sample gathering.' Instead of watching the picture, she just listened while resuming the search for another route off this level.

"Dr. Peterson and I have been assigned to the initial planetary team that will go down to examine 'the Grove,' as the admins have taken to calling it. During a satellite mapping run, the geological researchers discovered a strange area where several life forms are growing. It defies all logic such a place should exist on a planet this barren. We will collect samples and bring them back to run tests. I'm excited to see what we will find."

She let it play on to the next entry but glanced down to see the label, "Fire accident."

"It's only our second day of testing, and there's already been an accident. I think everyone is so excited about the discovery of complex plant life; some people are getting careless. I didn't know Technician Jarret, but apparently, he had an open flame burner heating a test tube and placed a container of plant samples too near it. Well, I wasn't there to see it, but I heard from a colleague the whole thing burst into flames. As in practically exploded and caught the tech on fire. Well, new memos went out within the hour to everyone in Bio about the dangers of the material around high heat.

"Of course, we would have discovered this during our experiments, but we have done little more than categorize the various samples brought up in the first transport. The craziest part is the director didn't have Jarret sent to Medical. I don't know if he died of his injuries too quickly or what, but it doesn't make sense they didn't even try."

How did I not even hear about this? I agree; it makes little sense. All crew injuries are supposed to be reported to Medical. Why not this?

Beth shook her head and reexamined the tablet's recordings, hoping to find something more about this patient or info on the plants themselves. She picked an entry that looked to be several weeks later titled, "discovery and experimentation results."

"It's been several weeks working with a number of the organisms we collected from the planet. We've discovered they all share many DNA sequences and are likely derived from one common ancestor. We've run numerous tests on them, and the data is extraordinary. When mixed with cells from a known organism, it bonds to them, infusing its own DNA to theirs, like a parasite. We started experimenting with some of our cloned mice just a couple of days ago, and we have already received some exciting results, including heightened instincts, improved strength, agility, and stamina.

"The mice we have introduced to the organism have completely dominated the rest of our control mice. We have one test subject with five unaltered in each experiment. Even when given to the runt of the group, it took only a brief time for it to become the alpha."

This is where it all began. Morgan Sims wasn't the start of it. If I had any doubt left his exposure was accidental, it's all gone. Beth let the next log play without a glance at it.

"They continue to evolve, our test subjects. It also appears the organism has infected the control mice. We're not sure how it's passed, but they now exhibit many of the same behaviors seen in the test subjects. We also had a couple of incidents with the first groups. The test subjects attacked and killed the control mice. We aren't sure if this is due to the subject simply having the organism implanted or a more advanced integration of the organism. What is clear is the longer the subject has the organism within its cells, the more DNA it replaces with its own. We expect to see severe mutations in our earliest subjects soon.

As a result, we have isolated most of them. This cell growth and adaptation are like nothing we've ever seen in nature."

Beth glimpsed the next couple of entries and skipped ahead to one labeled "Experiment collapse."

"All the subjects are dead. They all suffered the same fate, rapid cellular degeneration. It doesn't appear to matter if the organism was artificially implanted or spread by its own means. All subjects eventually succumbed to cellular disintegration. This degradation didn't become apparent until visual cues appeared in their cells. Even then, the subjects continued to act 'normally' until it became physically impossible because of their condition's advanced state.

"We are at a loss for how the array of different flora developed with the same DNA sequencing in the Grove, while our subjects all eventually destroyed themselves from within. Our best theory is something present in the planetary atmosphere prohibits cellular collapse. While fascinating, it is also a setback. Though the applications, especially military, are quite extensive. If we find a way to stabilize the organism, it would be a biological enhancement we've never seen before. Faster, stronger soldiers who don't tire quickly are a selling point for the Ortelius corporation. The admins have already made it pretty clear it's what they see coming out of this study and have us working extra shifts trying to crack the code on this thing.

"I heard them discuss other applications with our director, and they're right. It's a potential weapon against the rebel factions back on the homeworld. If we cannot alter it for our soldiers, we could introduce its current form to our enemies to spread, causing them to tear each other apart. Of course, we haven't actually tested it on a human. That's not likely to happen until we send out research back home. Fortunately, some criminals and despots sign up for these kinds of things. However, one admin assured the director a volunteer would be found soon. It sounds crazy that anyone on this expedition would volunteer for self-experimentation at this early stage, when we know so little. I certainly won't sign up. I can't imagine who would. Maybe if we had a way to counteract it before the person's insides turn to jelly, but even then, we are dealing with a very alien organism. For now, it's a likely death sentence to anyone exposed."

Beth stopped the logs and put the tablet down.

So the administrators for the company set this whole thing in motion. They purposefully infected Morgan Sims, and when he went berserk, we were caught completely off guard with no idea what we were dealing with. The bio lab had all this data, from nearly day one, about the effects of this organism, and they led us right into the lion's den. It's almost like they wanted a breakout.

Beth's mind reeled as a ray of understanding and realization lit the situation ablaze. They had just infected the one, but as she knew very well, in any experiment, the more subjects, the better. The administrators had wanted this.

Is it possible the wave screwed up their plans when it damaged the ship? The fact I'm alive tells me either I wasn't infected or somehow cured or stabilized. I need to know.

The bio lab was fully outfitted for any experiment Beth wanted to run, but sterile equipment became nearly impossible to find with the plant matter all over everything. Besides, she knew nothing about these plants. She found no mention of bioluminescence in any of the reports she'd listened to. That would have been a hell of a thing to overlook in this researcher's notes. Still, where else could the flora have come from?

Beth moved on from the overgrown lab space into a connecting hallway similar to the ones on her floor. She passed through several crew quarters, found a few tablets, and charged them up for any useable information. One of them had a very late entry, much later than any of the others she'd picked up. While listening to the audio, she continued through the jungle-scape.

"This is Dr. Min. I'm a researcher in the biology labs on the Celestus. If anyone finds this, I think it will be my last entry. We are royally fucked. Just fucked…"

Chapter 20

Beth stopped and looked down at the screen. A woman in her twenties, with short dark hair and sharp eyes, gazed back at her with panic painted across her face. Beth started the vid again.

"We were getting such valuable data, but I warned them it was dangerous. After the first patient almost escaped and infected others, I told the director it was a bad idea to observe them in an awakened state. This was too dangerous, with too many unknowns to go to human trials. She agreed, and yet we continued anyway. I think orders are coming from the Admins directly or even Ortelius back on the homeworld. They don't give a fuck about us!

"I wish my intuition had been wrong. Things were going fine, and I looked like the overly cautious fool, but then the wave hit. No one could have predicted the chaos that followed. My friend in the Astrophysics department didn't expect it either. She was freaking out, while the rest of her colleagues seemed blinded by the discoveries. Is everyone on this ship insane? I know the recruitment called for 'result-oriented individuals,' but doesn't that describe every scientist? What they meant was 'results-at-any-cost individuals.'

"It may not matter soon. The wave unleashed those things. They infected more crew members. Oh, stars..." The woman looked away from the camera. When she turned back, tears glistened at the corners of her eyes.

"The med lab is utterly trashed. Security has been battling them like it's some kind of zombie infestation. People have suggested some of them got past security and are loose in other parts of the ship. If that's true, then we are done for. This thing jumps hosts too easily. Our immune systems are pathetically easy to fool. Wait, they're making an announcement over the ship-wide com. I need to hear this. I don't

112

know what's going to happen... If someone finds this, it probably means we're all dead."

The image cut out, and the recording ended. Down the hallway, Beth spotted the cat sitting on a clean part of the floor.

"Hey... There you are, Kitty. How did you get down here?" Beth asked, a little surprised to see the creature after so long and so far from where they'd last parted.

The cat looked at her, then tilted its head curiously to the side. As she approached, it casually stood and walked the opposite way. Beth followed.

She passed through a door to someone's quarters, caved inward as if forced open by horrific means. Inside, water dripped from above and pooled in various low places of the room. Beth eyed the clear liquid. *I hope that's water.* Above, she spotted a hole in the ceiling about half the size of an airlock door. The fluid ran in a thin stream out of it. The cat hopped across several pieces of furniture, avoiding the larger pools, jumped up on top of a cupboard, and disappeared up the hole. Beth splashed clumsily after it.

This cat always appears just in time to show me a way forward. What is its deal?

It wasn't easy to climb after the feline. Beyond the larger opening, Beth had to squeeze her body up into a narrow, flat area between the decks. *What is this space? It doesn't look like it's used for maintenance.*

Forced to belly crawl, the lights on her shoulders led the way and gave her an idea of where she was headed. The cat's eyes glowed deeper within the section. It moved effortlessly in the tight area. She watched it jump up into the darkness and vanish. It took Beth a couple of minutes to get to the place she last saw it. Above her, another hole led into a pitch-black room on the deck above.

She stood up and cast her chest-light about and recognized the area as a security station. A large, blackened blast mark scored the hole and the nearest wall. Something had exploded and taken out a section of the room. But it allowed her to get out of the biology deck. With a glance around the space, she searched for the cat. Unsurprisingly, it was nowhere to be seen. Beth spotted a rack of stun weapons against the wall, however.

Here's something I can use. Well, if I run into anyone or anything, I don't want to. Unlikely, but if the organism mutated enough to keep itself alive, like those plants down there, then... She took a rifle off the rack and slung it over her shoulder. There was a belt with attached holster and utility pouches, which she strapped on, then slipped a pistol comfortably inside it. Upon further inspection, she spotted a shelf on the opposite side of the crater labeled "breaching charges," with neat stacks of rectangular items. *Now, these might come in handy.* She took all four and put them in the belt pouches before heading to the exit. The door opened with the manual release, and she entered the rest of the deck. The layout of hallways told her it was likely another research section.

She came out near a dining common and walked through it, looking about for anything out of the ordinary. After a few minutes of finding little of interest, she moved on. Just beyond the commons lay halls of crew quarters. Beth attempted to gain entry to a couple of rooms by tapping on the entry pad, but she stood no chance without power. At this point, she figured more crew logs wouldn't help her get to the augmentation labs. She followed the hall around until it led her to a lab area. Above the doorway, a sign said, "Geo Survey Labs."

Oh, they studied the planet's composition here. Likely found the Grove the biologist mentioned. There might be something helpful here. But it's totally unpowered, so no access. I need to go up another floor or two.

She'd seen nothing resembling an obvious way up, so she entered the lab. The layout appeared different from the others she'd visited. She observed more equipment, large and small contraptions, and fewer traditional experimentation tables. She guessed many of the mechanisms were used to crush and separate various rock and soil samples for easier analysis. Farther in, the ceiling disappeared. With a button press on the suit controls, her shoulder lights flared to life, and she gazed up into a vaulted area. The lab appeared to occupy at least two decks, as did several giant pieces of machinery. On the far side of the room, a set of stairs led to an upper area. As Beth ascended them, she noticed a door, slightly ajar, at the top. She forced it wider.

The room beyond looked like a control center. Various terminals, operation stations, and large monitors occupied the space. She glanced over the consoles and saw most of the labels referenced satellites.

Ah, this is where they control orbital surveying.

In the back of the room, she discovered a large monitor had been pulled off the wall. A tunnel stretched out behind it filled with cables but room enough for a maintenance bot to move and work. Though tight, she could squeeze through as well.

Who would even know to look for this here? I can't imagine where it leads, but the cat hasn't steered me wrong yet.

The hole went on for quite a way before branching out in several directions. One tunnel led upward, so it seemed like the obvious choice. She braced her back against one wall, put her feet on the other, then slowly scooted her way up the passage. A short climb led to another set of divergent tunnels.

She picked a direction at random and went with it. After some time, it bifurcated again.

I'm going to be lost in here forever. Beth glimpsed down both passages. If she could've gone up again, she would have, but it wasn't possible at this junction. The ship shook. Another high-pitched whine echoed through the hull, followed by what could only be an explosion.

"Fuck! I've got to get out of here."

Down one passage, her light passed over the reflection of a thousand tiny sparkles. After gazing at it a moment, she realized frost covered the tunnel in that direction. She turned and started the opposite way.

Wait, wasn't there a place on the same floor as the augmentation labs where coolant or something had leaked?

She altered course and crawled toward the source of the cold. In a few seconds, it became apparent she was going the right way. Scuffle marks, where someone had been, appeared in the frost. Though partially crusted over, Beth saw the surface had been cleaned away at some point. The tunnel led her right to where she wanted, and soon she exited into the very hall she had been in after waking up in Devin's room.

After a quick backtrack, she stood in front of the augmentation lab with its electronically locked door. She entered the code Devin had provided...

<Door Malfunction>

The error message blinked into her frustrated face. She tried the code again and received the same response.

"I don't have time for this!" She slammed her hand on the pad.

Beth pulled out one of the breaching charges from her belt, stuck it to the door, and set the attached timer for thirty seconds. Then taking cover down the hall and around a corner, she waited for what felt too long before a brassy bang rumbled the floor beneath her feet. Beth came back to find a mangled hole where the door had been. After she stepped through the twisted metal maw, she entered the labs and looked for any places they might store the prototype augments. She wasn't disappointed when she glanced around. Dozens of synthetic-glass cases, with different objects displayed in them, occupied the space. They ranged from various robotic body parts to what looked like cybernetic-enhanced clothing and armor. It felt like walking through a museum display of futuristic inventions.

Devin's note described a set of glasses and gloves, along with the accompanying envirosuit enhancement module. So many things filled the cases it was like trying to find an asteroid in a supernova.

I wish Devin had given me more information. It could be anywhere in here.

Beside the cases, which each had their own keypad locks, a ton of augment pieces spread across tables scattered throughout the lab.

Cables ran from consoles to augments on counters, while metal scraps and circuits rested on the floor around the work areas. Screws, bolts, and small tools littered every surface.

This place is a complete mess. Stars, it looks like everything was floating and crashed when gravity came back on. But I've got a feeling this is just how these engineers work. She'd seen Devin's quarters, and the resemblance was staggering.

She stepped carefully around the room, trying not to trip over a cord or piece of discarded equipment. Then she spotted what she came to get, a set of gloves and glasses in one case. She approached and entered Devin's code into the keypad. A red light flashed.

<Incorrect Passcode>

She reentered it.

<Incorrect Passcode>

"What the crap?" She shook her head and stared at the keypad. "Do none of the damn codes work in this place?"

She pulled up Devin's file on her suit's forearm screen and looked over the numbers he'd given her. She had remembered them correctly. Once again, she deliberately put them in a third time.

<Incorrect Passcode. Terminal Lockout. Contact Administrator>

This can't be happening.

She reached into her belt for a breaching charge but changed her mind when she realized it would almost certainly damage or destroy the thing she wanted inside.

How the hell am I going to get in there?

Shifting her gaze around the room, she searched for something to override the keypad. She'd break into it if she had to. That's when she spotted a set of glasses and gloves in another case.

Beth glanced around abashedly, thankful no one was around to see her embarrassment.

Oh, I guess they probably developed multiple kinds of hand and eye enhancements.

As she strode over to the other glass housing, she passed a third case with glasses and gloves. *Why aren't any of these labeled?* With a shrug and a shake of her head, she stopped and entered Devin's passcode.

<Incorrect Passcode>

Beth sighed and went over to the last case. "This better be the one."

<Incorrect Passcode>

The white lights turned red, and an alarm blared.

"What the...?"

Somehow, through the wailing noise, she heard seeping air, then checked her suit. It had detected a hostile environment and switched from filter-mode over to the oxygen supply.

Chemical defenses? Thank the stars for this suit.

From the far wall ahead of her, a tall panel slid aside, and an armored robot stepped out. Though humanoid, it stood about seven feet tall, with a smooth, featureless face and two sonic-concussion cannons where its hands should be.

"Surrender immediately, or be taken with force," the robot's voice boomed across the space.

Chapter 21

Beth whipped the stun rifle from her back as she slid for cover near one case. She caught a glimpse of the robot, scanning back and forth, searching for her.

I don't know how effective stun rounds will be, but here goes.

She hefted the butt of the rifle to her shoulder, took quick aim, and squeezed off three shots; two impacted the robot directly in its broad torso. The mechanical construct jerked its body around to face her. Beth threw herself to the floor as a concussive wave blew over like a rippling wind, shattering a case.

If that thing can shatter synthetic glass, I don't stand a chance. Scrambling up, she took cover behind a set of freestanding cabinets. Beth whipped around the edge of her concealment and fired five more shots at the robot, missing a couple but also striking it as it advanced on her position unabated. Each stun-gun impact did little to impede its movement or affect it in any visible way.

Dropping the useless rifle, Beth retreated farther into the aug labs. Hunched over, she hustled between the cases, tables, and other large objects, then rolled under a low workbench, coming up behind it. Above her, a series of heavy tools hung on a rack. She popped up and hurled a massive wrench through the air. It slammed her assailant in the side of the head. It stopped its advance, wobbled, then fired off another concussive blast. Tools, screws, and half-finished contraptions flew from the work area in a deadly spray of debris. The bench sheltering Beth took the brunt of the trauma as scrap pelted her body. She huddled against the metal base of one case, trying to avoid as much of the sharp rain as possible. The envirosuits were highly durable, but the slightest breach would still compromise the entire outfit.

When the falling items ceased, she grabbed two heavy wrenches off the floor and ran with her head down. The robot wasn't fast, but nothing slowed it in the slightest.

This is insanity! That thing will level the entire lab to catch me.

Her fear and self-preservation struggled against her determination. She needed the prototype to get the reactor core fired up, and it was in this lab somewhere. If she left, she'd only have to come back. The guard wasn't going anywhere. She could deal with it now or deal with it later.

As she moved between cover, she flung another tool at the mechanical bastard. It bounced off its arm, forcing a concussive blast wide and off its mark. So far, she'd kept it from getting a clear shot, but little else. Beth still had the stun pistol on her hip, but considering the rifle's limited usefulness, her mind fought for other options. She had three breaching charges, but would she need them later? Possibly. And setting them off in the wrong place could destroy the augments and gut her mission.

I've just got to find what I came for and get out of here before that thing catches me.

"Surrender. This facility has been locked down. There is no escape. Lay down your arms, and no harm will come to you." The robot's voice sounded surprisingly human.

That's not a tempting offer, especially when I blew the door to this place wide open.

She rejected the request and attempted to move stealthier by keeping as many cases, tables, and chairs between the robot and herself. She thought for sure it must have some kind of thermal optics to track her, but that didn't seem to be the case. With the sheer amount of equipment in this place, Beth found it easy to stay out of the guard's line of sight after just a couple of minutes.

Beth curved her way through different rows of the facility, peering into cases and across workshop surfaces for the items she needed. Elsewhere in the room, she heard the robot thrashing about. Already a maze of significant obstacles, the uninhibited killing machine only made it worse. Beth had bought herself some time by taking a shortcut under some tables, something her attacker was not likely to do. The armored warden patrolled back and forth along the aisles in a predictable pattern. Once she stopped trying to attack it, it hadn't found her again.

Less than five minutes of further looking yielded another case with

119

a glove and eyepiece combination. With a furtive look around for the robot, Beth tapped in the code. The keypad turned green with an audible click. She cringed at the noise, hoping it hadn't given her position away. She opened the case, reached in, and pulled out the gloves, glasses, and a small square chip.

This must be the mobile suit module. She held the circuit gently between her fingers.

From behind, the sharp retort of the concussive rifle firing sounded almost simultaneously with a shattering echo. Synthetic glass crystals peppered her body as the case beside her exploded. She half dove, half fell as another burst impacted the container she'd just taken the items from. The destructive wave picked her up, crashing her body through a synthetic glass table. Instinct kicked in as she clung to the precious objects she'd come for. All she had to do was escape. Disoriented from the blast, she clambered to her feet and took off running, one arm clutching her prize, the other tucked over her head to protect the best it could. The robot found her and pressed in with full violence. Beth cut left and right, putting anything she could between her and her pursuer, not caring where she headed.

Concussion volleys fired repeatedly. The air became a hailstorm of glass shards, flying tools, and deadly force waves. Beth fell to her hands and knees while cradling the retrieved items, then crawled and changed directions, zigging and zagging under tables and around cabinets. She felt the scattered pebbles of shattered synthetic glass under her gloves. Electronic parts, metal scraps, gadgets, and anything not nailed down came raining across the room in a lethal technological torrent. Beth slipped under a table as a wave of objects slammed above her in a tremendous crash.

Abruptly, the table flew away, and she peered upward to see the swinging arm of the robot baring down. "Shit!" She pushed off the balls of her feet with all her might, diving between another table's legs as a blast smashed the floor. The force launched her farther than she'd intended to move. From where she landed, her eyes fell upon the twisted maw of the blown open entrance. Scrambling to her feet, still clutching the items to her chest with one arm, she sprinted with everything she had. The whirring sound of repeated concussive bursts rang in her ears. Chaos erupted like a hurricane come to life as objects spun unpredictably in every direction. Beth ignored the impacts and rhythmic sounds of weapons charging and releasing. She kept running until the hole loomed up before her, then dove through.

I doubt that thing will stop just because I'm out of its jurisdiction.

The priority was to get back to engineering and get things working again, though she yearned to make another attempt at her own lab since it was so close.

No. Stay on task, Beth. She backtracked through the corridors to the frosted hall, then noticed small paw prints in the ice that hadn't been there before.

Is the cat following me?

However, she didn't have time to stop and think about what a feline's motivations might be. She had all the items from the augmentation labs she'd been after. Beth grasped the release lever on her helmet so she could put the glasses on, but hesitated as she glanced at the frozen substance on the floor and walls. She remembered the number of other times her sealed suit had likely saved her. Instead, she checked its integrity seal by running a diagnostic program. Repeated concussion blasts had pummeled her with a torrent of debris. The chance of a small tear seemed all too real.

After a minute, the screen on her forearm flashed green with a message.

<Zero Atmosphere Loss Detected>

Even though the suit hadn't been fully functional, it had thus far performed beyond her expectations. She took the chip and slid it into an upload slot near the forearm screen.

A boot-up sequence appeared in her visor as the program integrated with the suit. Despite impaired vision, Beth continued forward as lines of code blitzed along for several minutes. She half-expected the process to halt with an error because of suit or chip damage, but it continued unabated until, finally, a message displayed.

<Suit Integration Complete. Voice Activation Initiated.>

The message remained in her view for about thirty seconds, then disappeared.

"Do I need the gloves and glasses to operate this module?" Beth asked.

After a split second, a reply came from her suit. "Negative. Suit Module is fully functional."

That's some good news. She didn't need to carry everything with her, so she left the gloves and glasses in the hall.

Beth slipped down the maintenance tunnel and headed toward the lower part of the ship.

An hour later, after retracing her steps, she let go of the cable in the lift-shaft and stepped back into the engineering bay.

"Computer, display information on engineering controls," she said.

In a blink, labels appeared on every piece of equipment in her line of sight. Instinctively, she threw up a hand to block the light. As different contraptions became blocked, the information on them also disappeared. Keeping her visor obscured, Beth rephrased her command. "Ok, uh... display only information on reactor activation." Then she lowered her arm. Everything had disappeared, leaving no labels on anything.

"Are there any reactor controls in engineering?" she asked.

"Current field of view shows reactor activation-related controls are zero."

"Can you direct me to where they are?"

"Negative, this unit isn't equipped with mapping information for this facility."

Ugh, crap! Not helpful.

Beth searched around engineering once again, this time more thoroughly. With a complete lack of relevant experience, knowing what to look for proved an immense challenge. She started a lap around the room but immediately spotted a short staircase that led down to a door with the words *Reactor Core* emblazoned on it.

Well, that was obvious... She descended the stairs, accessed the door, and stepped inside. Just then, her suit's left forearm vibrated with a warning. She peered at the small arm-screen where a red light blinked. Her breath caught as she recognized the flashing radiation warning.

How bad?

"Is background radiation within safe levels?" she asked as nervous tension crept up her spine.

"Detectors are placing radiation levels at well below human lethality and in line with low power reactor core measures," the suit's program replied.

It was a mix of good and bad news. While she'd never entered a reactor room before, she felt confident the radiation detection indicated a leak. Thankfully, she hadn't just received a lethal dose.

Beth paused, her eyes taking in the enormous room. She stood on a catwalk that circled the perimeter. Her gaze dropped to a set of stairs leading to another, and another, as she followed them down to the lower levels of more catwalks. Peripherally, she glimpsed the edges of the reactor core, and she lifted her eyes directly to it. It hung in the center, a massive, transparent, cylindrical housing stretching from the ceiling to the floor. Metal circuits appeared to cap each end. Within it, a circular node hovered, glowing with a faint light.

"Computer, identify controls for reactor ignition."

On her visor, an indicator appeared two catwalks down from where she stood, at the base of the reactor where the synthetic glass ended and the electronics began. Beth jogged across the walkway and down the stairs. A sudden jerk pulled the floor from her feet and sent her tumbling down to the level below. From a prone position, she sat up and patted her body. "Ouch! What the crap was that?"

"Please rephrase."

"I'm not talking to you."

"Please switch off module when not in use to save power."

She ignored the request as the ship rumbled again.

That felt like we hit something. Stars, not now! I need more time. Please hold together, Celestus... As if in answer, the vibrations subsided, but Beth was already on her feet, in motion. Down another floor, she approached a control station where the catwalk ran right up to the reactor.

"Computer, show me how to ignite the reactor."

Indicators on parts of the controls, along with a short set of instructions, appeared in her vision. She read them carefully and followed what they said, only touching the places highlighted within her sight. As she progressed through the tutorial, the indicator changed, and new instructions arrived to direct her to the next step. The entire process labored on for more than an hour as she ran out of guidance. She needed to sprint back up to other parts of the reactor core and even back to the central engineering room to find the next step. Every phase required precise inputs and complex calculations. First, some radiation buildup had to be purged; then, fresh fuel had to be pumped in while temperatures were monitored and adjusted. If the reactor ignited too quickly or too slowly, it could fail completely, either by dying outright or exploding.

This job is for a crew of at least ten! She thought as she hustled up the catwalk stairs for the fifth time.

After several more hours, back up on the main engineering floor, she slumped down in a chair and studied the reactor indicators. Her stomach churned. She didn't know if it was hunger or nerves.

I hope this works. The gauge reflected a steady climb in reactor output. The rate landed on the lower end of what the module recommended. Still, since it had taken her more time to make the necessary adjustments running back and forth between stations, it was the best she could manage. All indicators held within safe parameters and would have to be good enough.

After a few minutes, a bright light surged within the chamber, and all sensors turned green. The ship was back under power. Beth jumped up, all tiredness leaving her. "Yes!" She thrust her arms triumphantly into the air.

Beth placed her hands on her hips and let out a satisfied breath. Finally, something went her way. She approached the energy distribution consoles and glanced over the sensors, noting the reactor showed safe output at eighty-six percent.

Seems good.

While the suit showed her how to use every device in the area, it wouldn't interpret any data. The rest of the core information, temperature, radiation blowoff, coolant levels, containment, appeared within normal ranges as far as she could tell.

A high-pitched whine rang out, followed by a vibration that quickly became a rumble as the sound dropped in tone but increased in volume. Beth latched onto the console in front of her with both hands to keep from being thrown to the floor.

Chapter 22

The disturbance grew in intensity. Tools and machinery rattled, some toppling to the floor with a flurry of tremendous crashes. Then, as quickly as it erupted, the commotion tapered off, leaving an irregular hum which hadn't been there before.

Beth blinked rapidly and slowly released her grip. "What in the universe? That can't be good. Computer, show me how to run a diagnostic on the ship's power grid." An indicator and a set of instructions appeared, hovering over a nearby control panel. The diagnostic process was like the one she'd activated previously, and in a few minutes, she had the program running.

What an incredibly useful augment. I didn't even have to put a chip in my head. Good going, Devin. Beth let out an extended sigh. *Stars...I miss you...*

A pit of sorrow opened in her chest. She missed everyone, but Devin, who never strayed far from her thoughts, most of all. For as many long days and nights as she'd spent alone in her lab, the isolation since waking ranked as something cosmic. She wanted to cry. She felt like she should with all her might, but the tears didn't come. In that moment, it occurred to her, while she'd been distressed for the people on the ship, especially her friends, she'd actually handled this whole situation with more calm than she would have guessed. Sure, she'd had some moments of hopelessness and frustration, but they didn't last. Had the panic, urgency, and mysteriousness of the predicament simply overwhelmed her senses and left no room for emotional outbursts? She couldn't put her finger on it. Like everything else she'd encountered since waking up, an enigma shielded each piece of the puzzle.

The scan ended with a flash of blue light, pulling Beth from her thoughts. She studied the results, noting which areas still functioned.

I swear there had been more stable parts of the ship when I scanned earlier. The feeling nagged at her, but she couldn't do anything about it for the moment. She felt relieved any ship sections still showed operational. Following the instructions, she made the appropriate adjustments to channel the reactor's energy to the stable areas of the ship, able to take full power.

I'm not sure where I'll end up or where there could be crew members hiding out. Hopefully, this will let any survivors know someone is out here. Before leaving engineering, she attempted to do one more analysis on the decaying orbit. The disturbing sounds of stress on the hull and repeating vibrations had finally petered out, but it provided only a small comfort.

"Computer, show me how to see the orbital decay of the ship."

Nothing lit up in her display.

Crap, I probably have to go to the bridge or back to astrophysics.

Taking off at a jog, she reached the lift lobby and attempted to call one of the cars. It was worth a shot, at least. After about a minute of no sound or movement, she sighed and entered the shaft where the climbable cables drooped down. A screech rang out from the tube as air blasted out of the doorway.

"Oh, shit!" Beth scrambled in a half-dive, half-tumble back out of the tunnel. Seconds later, the lift-car crashed into the bottom of the shaft, exploding metal and glass shards out the door.

With a stiff shake of her head, Beth picked herself up off the floor and gazed into the tunnel to assess the situation. The remains of the lift lay in mangled pieces at the bottom of the shaft. She didn't see the cable she'd used to ascend the space anywhere. Sticking her head past the debris, she searched for any other way to climb. Some pipes, lines, and small outcroppings stuck out along the walls but were too few and far between to make scaling possible.

"Stars, this is unbelievable!" She went to the other tubes.

I hope there's a way to get up one of these I missed before. The entry of one lay smashed in, rendering it completely unusable. She checked the remaining two. The first had the car suspended just a little above her head, blocking the whole tunnel. Darkness welled up in the last one as far as her light reached. Like the others, she saw no obvious way of ascending.

There has got to be another way around. I'll even take an airlock at this point.

Going back into the central part of engineering, she searched for something helpful given the current situation; another exit, even a rope might make a difference. After several minutes, nothing new had caught her eye.

I still have some of these breaching charges. I could always try to blow a hole in the side of the ship. "Ugh…" She let out a long sigh. *That's probably the stupidest plan I could come up with. There's got to be something else I can do. I just got the core up and running. I can't be trapped down here!*

In a back section of the massive space, she came across a series of unlabeled cabinets. Inside hung an assortment of tools and gadgets. Some she recognized, some she didn't. On the bottom of one unit, nestled in a large case, sat a shiny, unused cutting laser.

Bingo.

Beth dragged the case back to the elevator shafts, then started pulling scrap from three of the tubes and stacking it inside the forth underneath the car suspended a few meters above her head. Once she could reach the lift easily, she unpacked the laser and, after some trial and error, began cutting away at the bottom. The undercarriage consisted of little more than a thick piece of metal crisscrossed with a few electronics. The work progressed slowly, but after about an hour, she had cut out a hole big enough to squeeze up into the car. Beth pulled herself inside.

The car had not stopped at a floor. It had fallen during the gravity spike like the other ones but came loose from its track and wedged in the tunnel. If she cut through the wall, she would end up right back in engineering. She had to get higher.

After hefting the laser up through the hole, she went to work on the ceiling. The top of the lift held most of the complex interworking mechanisms used to move the unit. Beth did her best to cut around them, but she had to restart her cut twice after discovering too many large devices blocking the way above.

Nearly two hours later, a satisfying feeling washed over her as the last bit of metal fell out of the amoeba-shaped gap. Peeking up into the dark tunnel with her light, she spotted thin catwalks around the door levels starting a dozen meters up. Further examination revealed nothing climbable, so she retreated down and out into the lift lobby. From one of the other tubes, she gathered a bundle of loose cables. Using the laser, she cut a hook shape out of one of the larger metal scraps and punched a hole in it. She threaded the wires through the hole, secured them to the hook, and then headed back up to the top of the lift with her improvised rope and grapple.

It took her several tries to get the hook to latch securely on the catwalk, but Beth didn't let any of the failures dissuade her. She'd just spent hours cutting her way up here and would find a way to the floor above, no matter how long it took. With each toss, she got closer to latching on. Grapple throwing wasn't in her wheelhouse, but the same could be said of any of the skills she'd picked up today. After a near-perfect throw, the hook lodged securely in the open grating. She pulled down on it with two quick yanks. It held fast. Hand over hand, she ascended the tunnel.

At the top, Beth exited out the doors and assessed the level just above engineering. It appeared she'd wound up back in the stasis chamber housing.

I really need to get to the bridge, but let's check on the crew since I'm here. But if they're all dead... Beth pushed the idea away. Still, it nagged at her. What if she alone survived? "Ugh! I can't think about this right now!" But the thoughts assaulted her brain, chipping away at her logic with emotional pangs of failure. Everything she'd done, everything she still needed to do, might amount to nothing. With all her exploration and effort, she and the cat remained the only confirmed survivors.

Chapter 23

Clenching her fists and taking deep rhythmic breaths, Beth left the lift area and entered the massive cryostasis capsule storage facility. Tracks of lighting bathed the space in a welcome radiance, like nothing had gone wrong. She went to the nearest capsule and ran a check on the individual inside. A green indicator light showed solid. He was still alive and in stable stasis. "Oh, my stars...I'm not the only one alive!" The sensation of joy and relief was almost enough to make her leap in the air or collapse in exhausted reprieve. Her body wanted to do both.

Ok, Beth, get a handle on yourself. Focusing again on the many tasks before her, she checked the name. Abram Riley.

This must be one of the colonists. Most of them never left stasis and should be alright. That's a good sign. A really good sign. While I'm here, I should take some samples, just in case I get back to the lab. She'd received a second wind. Her mind felt sharp, as if the lack of sleep and arduous activity did not affect it.

Beth went over to a cluster of storage crates near the wall, opened one, and pulled out three small vials before heading back over to the stasis capsule containing Abram Riley. She inserted one of them into a small circular slot in the side with a click and then entered the control unit's commands to take a blood sample. She had done this many times previously, though only a few times on this ship. After a couple of seconds, the vial popped back out, filled with deep red. The deep, vibrant color stood in stark contrast to the lifelessness of the ship. Seeing it felt like discovering a new band of the rainbow. She pulled the vial out and deposited it safely in a zippered pocket on her chest.

Moving to the next capsule in line, she first checked the name.

Brian Hillock, another colonist. I need one of those Alice Bright people. She glanced over several more chambers until she found one with the matching name, then checked the occupant's vitals. The display showed the person inside had expired.

Shit. There was some stasis failure.

Beth slammed her fist on the chamber and let out a grunt, the finding stealing away her joy. With all she'd done, people had still died. She did not know how many. Her shoulders slumped, and she searched for the next tube labeled Alice Bright, only to find the occupant similarly dead. The next four were also expired. However, after several minutes of hunting, she came across an Alice Bright with stable vitals. Beth put the vial in the chamber and directed the capsule to take the sample, removing the full scarlet container when it finished. Why were so many of them dead? The name could have been a designation for the deceased, which made no sense to her, but she didn't know enough about this department's procedures. Except a living Alice Bright already punched holes in that theory.

I could try thawing this girl, but I can't risk releasing some unstable person on the ship if she has the infection. Anyone who might have some actual answers could also be a liability. "Damnit!" The tablet which had mentioned the infected running amok after the wave flashed fresh in her mind. It meant if she reconstituted anyone, they'd be a risk.

I don't plan on living through that experience myself. Better to look at their blood and know for sure.

The thought train brought her back to the moment she awoke in Devin's room. Sealed inside, with the door barred and a decayed body next to her.

Could I have been one of those people running mad? Could I have been responsible for killing someone? Beth clenched her fists into tight balls and yelled out into the empty expanse. "I hate this! Why the fuck was I in Devin's room?" Her voice echoed back to her in her helmet's audio. It sounded strange and unnatural, bouncing off the various surfaces before reverberating to her ears.

She shook her head back and forth, her hands clenching the sides of the helmet, then she slumped down against the side of the nearest stasis capsule. She had done so much but felt no closer to real answers. Bad things had happened on this ship. She had a better idea now of what they were than when she'd first awakened, but each bit of information felt like disconnected circuits which never seemed to line up. It felt like someone gave her a box labeled 'complete robot,' but when she examined all the parts, they looked nothing like a robot.

Beth sat stationary until calm overtook sorrow and disappointment.

Her vision drifted downward. Scarlet drops stained her fingers. Parts of the vial she'd just filled lay in splattered blots of blood on the floor.

I didn't even feel it break.

Shaking the residue from her hand, she stood and filled her remaining vial from the same Alice Bright chamber. Afterward, she took a couple of minutes exploring the rest of the cryostasis room. It didn't take long for her to discover too many empty chambers to account for the colonists inhabiting the planet. A large part of the crew was still missing.

Maybe I should look through all these until I find Devin. If he's alive, he could be here. The thought felt reasonable. *I want to stay here and find someone with answers. I want Devin more than anything else. But even if I find him, he could carry the infection. Thawing him could kill him outright, or open a bottle I have no way of ever closing again. I need to know what is floating around in everyone's blood.*

She returned to the crate, took another vial, and attempted to fill it from one of the deceased crew members. It took a few tries to find one with non-coagulated blood.

It might be essential to know if they died due to stasis failure or something in their system. She secured the vials in a chest compartment opposite the light on her suit.

No other living thing had made its presence known besides the cat.

How did the cat survive this long? Someone has to be feeding it. A good amount of the ship lay unexplored, but it would have to wait. If someone wanted her to find them, they would have come out of hiding by now.

She looked for a way out. Earlier, she'd climbed past this level using the cables hanging in the lift tube, but with those gone, she would have to figure out another way.

I know there's a giant cargo airlock for loading and unloading multiple stasis chambers at once. If I get outside, then I can bypass most of the levels. I'm not looking forward to another spacewalk, but at this point, my only other option is to blast a hole in the ceiling and see where it gets me. I don't think that's a sustainable solution for reaching the bridge.

Her shoulders slumped as she headed for the cargo lock. Absently, she put her hand up to the suit pocket containing the vials, subconsciously checking she'd sealed it.

A series of supply lockers sat near the entrance to the airlock. Beth looked through them and quickly found what she had been looking for, a pair of gravity boots, and noted several envirosuits hanging there.

Maybe I should change out of this.

She checked her oxygen and power levels. They still read full. She'd been using the suit lights pretty much nonstop, but those likely used minor power. The oxygen also hadn't been used often, just a few exposed places she'd passed through.

Still, shouldn't they be down just a little? Maybe they're designed to last days rather than hours? She had no experience with these things and could only imagine. Still, the question of her suit had been a constant nagging in the back of her mind.

The suit's radiation exposure remained within safe levels, though the reactor room had deteriorated the rad-filters somewhat. Still, the void walk shouldn't expose her to the degree the reactor had.

Since she had already taken the time to install the prototype aug module in the current suit, and it would take extra time and effort she didn't want to spend to change everything over, she decided only to take the gravity boots.

Designed to be used in conjunction with a normal void-walk envirosuit, Beth clipped the gravity boots over her suit's footwear. The enhancements fit snuggly despite her outfit's design for toxic planetary environments or quarantine situations instead of zero-g vacuum activity. With the boots attached, she would stick to the surface as if in normal gravity wherever she walked. The new accessories would draw from the suit's power, but she figured it wouldn't be a problem since it still showed full.

Next to a massive door sat the airlock controls. Beth approached and activated the unlock sequence, opening the gate without issue. Stepping inside, she accessed the inner panel, closed the barrier behind her, and initiated the atmospheric cycle. Her protective wear fluttered as all the air sucked out of the room before the outer doors opened. Beth gazed out into the vastness of the void and immediately felt dizzy.

This is going to be more complicated than I thought. Her previous encounters in the void flooded back as a reminder one wrong move meant drifting helplessly until the planet's gravity pulled her down to a brutal end.

She took hesitant steps to the edge, then gazed across the surface of the ship. Warped sections of the hull stood out like fresh wounds, unhealed and shining in the sunlight. The last time she'd been outside, the damage didn't look this severe.

I should have done some kind of external damage report from engineering. Not that there's much I can do about it, but it would've been good to know what sections are breached. Maybe I can do it from the bridge.

The ship rotated slowly. As it moved, Beth saw part of the planet come into view. It loomed large. Much more than when she'd looked at it from Astrophysics.

How long ago was that? Just a few hours? Almost a day ago? She had trouble keeping track of the hours since waking. The time didn't matter; what mattered was the ship's orbit had dropped dangerously low. She didn't know when they would hit the upper atmosphere, but it couldn't be long. She needed to move now.

Chapter 24

Spacewalks lay far outside Beth's wheelhouse. She steadied herself by gripping either side of the doorway, closed her eyes, sucked in a deep breath, and took a ninety-degree step out onto the surface of the ship. When she opened her eyes, the change in perspective flared her dizziness to new heights. She dropped to her knees, placing her gloved hands flat on the hull. The concept of direction existed in the observer's mind, but all sense of orientation melded into ever-changing chaos in the weightless void.

The Celestus's smooth gray skin loomed before her as she tried to block out the planet and eternal cosmos in her peripheral vision.

I just need something to focus on. "Computer, show me all the airlock entrances in visible range." Beth gingerly raised her head. Three indicators cropped up in her visor, one near and two at the vessel's far end. She took several slow breaths to allow her vision time to adjust to the beacons. The disorientation subsided after a minute.

Beth stood up, wobbled momentarily, then marched forward, barely raising her feet off the magnetic surface.

This close airlock must access acquisitions. A loading dock makes the most sense. But that's too far from where I need to be.

She checked the distant two, hoping their specific locations would show as she got closer. The entire crew was briefed on all entrances when they first boarded, part of a more extensive safety and evacuation orientation for disaster preparedness. She wished she could remember it better. She wished for many things. But wishing accomplished nothing. The planet's looming approach, taking up more of her field of view all the time, spurred her to action.

Beth hustled across the hull, cutting a path around a missing chunk of the ship spanning several decks, with as much speed as she could.

The boot's safety feature wouldn't allow both to release from the surface simultaneously without a manual override. An escape pod drifted by amongst a cloud of debris. Someone might have tried to evacuate the ship using it, or maybe it had blasted clear of the vessel when the wave hit. Either way, no one would be alive inside, and she resisted the urge to look further.

While extensive and inconvenient to her travel, the damaged area didn't appear to go deep into the Celestus. On closer inspection, it looked as if something had peeled the hull away like fingernails ripping the rind from an orange, leaving rough, irregular edges. Wasting precious time, she circumvented the gap and resumed her course for the nearest airlock, honing in on it as if it alone existed in her world. Without warning, the ship vibrated in a growing crescendo, building up from nearly imperceptible shakes to violent gyrations.

Shit, we must be grazing some atmosphere.

Beth attempted to sprint the last couple of yards. The gravity boots, while quite remarkable, impeded any sort of hustle. Unfortunately, their main drawback was their most important safety feature. When she raised one foot, the other would lock to the surface. This made running awkward, if not impossible. When she finally reached the first door, she popped open a small panel for the manual release and pulled it. An error message flashed on a small screen.

<Please Enter Crew ID>

Ugh! I'm sick of the constant errors! Is everything on this ship broken or restricted?

She put in her ID number and pulled the release again.

<Unauthorized>

Damn! What part of the ship is this? She put her visor right against the airlock window and peered through the layers of glass. To her surprise, the inner door lay wide open. Past that, she glimpsed a white hallway with a red line running parallel to it along the wall. She'd been on this deck before, briefly, but knew it immediately. Behind this barrier lay Administration.

I really, really want in here. This is like finding the Celestus mystery equivalent to a cure for cyber-ostracis-syndrome.

The vibrations under her feet evened out, but didn't stop.

Shit, this atmosphere might cut the time I have left to fix the orbit. I don't know if the calculations compensated for it. I had four entire days, which should have been plenty of time. How long ago was that?

Beth glanced back at the approaching planet; its gravitational summons called out impending doom for her and those aboard. As her gaze returned to the hallways of the administration section, she sighed.

I'll come back when I can. If I can't find another way in, I'm sure a good breaching charge will suffice.

Small bits of flame leaching from the horizon of the ship's hull lashed out in her peripherals. "Fuck! We're starting reentry."

Beth forgot all about the mysteries locked within the administration section and took off at an awkward run to the farthest airlock, pulling the release the moment she arrived. To her relief, the lights turned green, oxygen cycled out, and the door slid open. She threw herself inside, closed the exit, and oriented her body to the ship's gravitational arrangement using the large convenient arrows and warning label, 'FLOOR,' painted on the bottom of the room. As the atmosphere finished flooding the chamber, she opened the far exit, only to have all the fresh air sucked out further into the ship. "Shit, there's a breach in here."

A dim hall stretched before her but gave no hint of her location. Beth reached down, deactivated her gravity boots, and ran as feelings of panic and disorientation washed over her. She haphazardly chose a branch of hallway to tear through next. An incredible rumble and horrific grinding vibration echoed up through her legs. The wall beside her disintegrated, ripping out into space with sudden force. She lurched away as flames from the atmospheric entry burst into the new hole in the hull. If the area had contained air, the explosion would have sucked her out. Luckily, the presence of a vacuum saved her life.

Fires raged all around her as reentry ate away at the weakened vessel innards. An alarm rang out in her ears as friction-fueled heat attacked her suit, threatening to melt it from her body and expose her to molten death and absolute zero space. She felt heat penetrating the protective layers as she sprinted forward to escape the destructive torrent. To her left, the walls seared away as the inner part of the ship disintegrated like a parasite devouring its host. She flung herself to the right, still in motion, hoping each step would find the solid floor.

Ahead, she spotted a blast door control panel as the volcanic heat intensified. Focusing, she kept her eye on it as her pace carried her closer and closer. Diving forward, her gloved fist smashed the safety glass and mashed the emergency close button. She hit the floor, and her body went into a roll, then slammed against a curved wall. The door began a slow but steady move down from the ceiling. Beth gave it only the briefest of glances before scrambling to her feet and putting more distance between it and herself. Reentry threatened this entire side of the vessel. From every hull breach, the drag would cook away the insides. If that didn't kill her and everyone in stasis, the planetary impact would finish the job.

Shit, why did I put off getting to the bridge for so long? The slew of clues, questions, and mysteries to investigate devoured the time. Still, the pressing matter had consistently been activating the reactor and preventing the ship from slamming into the planet. Her misconception about that inevitability being days away altered her priorities, but now the procrastination of the immediate situation threatened to kill everyone unknowingly dependent on her.

Ahead, the entrance to a dining common appeared.

I'm in another personnel area. If this is for the flight crew, the bridge must be near. With power restored to this entire section, Beth jerked her head from side to side as she searched for an information console. Each deck had several, typically near the lifts, while others were scattered about to help people navigate the massive ship.

Fortunately, one sat against a far wall. She hopped over a piled-up cluster of tables, undoubtedly gathered during a gravity fluctuation, and landed on the other side without slowing. Her suit showed it remained in oxygen supply mode, meaning no atmosphere filled the area.

The blast door should have closed by now, so there must be other breaches. Beth pushed the problem to the back of her mind. It wouldn't help her to worry about that until after the ship escaped the planet's gravity. The information console booted up with her input, and she accessed the map of the current level. She sighed in relief when the words *Bridge Crew Deck* appeared on the screen. The map showed it just a few turns away and up a separate lift tube.

I never want to deal with the lift shafts ever again. Please let this one be working.

The Celestus rumbled in metallic pain, threatening to throw her from her feet. She took off at a dead sprint to the bridge-access lift, where the doors sat open. She rushed inside and stopped her momentum with her arms as she hit the back wall. Whirling around, she saw only two buttons, labeled bridge and quarters. She jammed her finger on the bridge-level button and prayed it worked. As the doors slid shut painfully slow, Beth felt more anxious than she could remember. Her hands seemed to move of their own accord, writhing together like two fighting octopi, with her nervous energy. When the lift started upward, it brought out a sigh.

Thank the stars. I hate these things!

The doors opened, revealing the bridge laid out before her. Angry orange-red flames licked at the panoramic windows like a tremendous curved hearth. A bright yellow light flashed on one of the computer stations.

"Computer, show me where I can control the ship's flight systems."

"Please specify."

"Damnit!" She clenched her teeth and looked at the various stations with frantic indecision. "Uh... what are my options?"

"Main engine drives, docking thrusters, orbital compensators, combat—"

"Orbital compensators!"

The indicator appeared in her visor over a console in the front, right near the windows. Numerous crew stations with chairs comprised the wide console, but the prototype only pointed to a tiny section.

"Show me how to maneuver the ship back into a stable orbit."

As happened during her engineering escapades, instructions and indicators appeared over the controls. She began going through the directions and imputing commands to adjust the Celestus's path. Suddenly, a message popped up on the screen in front of her.

<Malfunction in Maneuvering Control. Error Code: 2-15BR7>

"Computer, there's a malfunction. How do I bypass and take us into a higher orbit?"

"Analyzing error code... Unable to alter course due to damaged or missing thrusters. Suggest main engine control."

The indicators switched to another area of the console several chairs away. Beth rushed over and adhered to the directions as they appeared. The ship jerked drastically as the primary thrusters rumbled to life with a few inputs. A sudden force threw her off balance, sending her skidding across the floor.

Nightmarish oscillations reverberated through the vessel. Beth grabbed the nearest chair with both hands and pulled herself to her feet. By the time she regained her composure, the flames had vanished from the observation windows. Ahead, one of the many planetary moons grew from a speck to a vast sphere occupying the center of the observation array. She didn't bother asking the prototype how to steer the ship and grabbed what looked most like helm control and jerked it to one side. The vessel veered sideways, like an ancient sailing vessel with a broken rudder.

"Computer, how do I full stop?"

A large button next to her lit up in her visor, and she slammed her hand down on it. Beth's body catapulted forward, crashing onto the controls, then whiplash sent her lurching backward onto the floor. She forced herself back up, shaking her head, and muttering a curse. No unexpected celestial objects grew closer. The ship had stopped. She stared out the side windows at the now more distant planet and figured the Celestus sat at a safe distance from imminent orbital decay. Not wanting to take any chances, she returned to the maneuvering console.

"Computer, show me how to put the ship in a stable orbit using any available thrusters."

She followed the brief set of instructions. Without the planet's closeness, the gravitational forces possessed little influence. After a few minutes of work, she stabilized the Celestus's flight path. With the last command, Beth slumped down in a chair.

Ok, crisis averted. Crisis number one, that is... She blew out a long breath. *Now, for all the other shit I still have to figure out.*

She glanced around the bridge, unsure of what she expected to see. Barreling through in such a mad dash, she'd focused entirely on maneuvering the ship and little else. The yellow blinking light across the room still flashed in a repeated pattern. She'd figured it was a warning about the planet's proximity and had pushed it out of her mind to address that exact matter. But since the ship orbited out of immediate harm, she had second thoughts.

A warning unrelated to the proximity of the planet?

As she made her way over to the console, she spoke to the prototype. "Computer, what is this console here?"

"This light signals the emergency beacon is active."

Emergency beacon?

The simple console possessed only a handful of buttons. Pressing one, she activated the screen, and a message appeared.

<Currently Transmitting Beacon to all Nearby Vessels. Beacon Cannot

be Deactivated Except by Authorized Personnel.>

She accessed a menu function and gazed over the selections. At the top of the shortlist, she selected the option to listen to the recording. A haunting voice rang out.

"To any ship in the area, this is Dr. Beth Adler of the colonial research vessel—"

Beth slammed her hand down on the stop button.

Chapter 25

What the…? It's… It's me? That's my voice. I… I recorded this?

The revelation manifested, pushing her into the workstation chair as if it had a force of its own. Beth had barely heard her own voice, and it changed everything.

I was awake between now and when security drugged me. Beth searched her mind, focusing on the image of her recording the beacon.

The memories must be in here somewhere. She imagined herself standing on the bridge doing it. But, while the act manifested in her thoughts, nothing about the message returned. She'd fabricated the scenario and couldn't remember it, any of it. Her eyes wandered over the oval-shaped room in hopes of recognition. A sizeable curved observation window cut a near-complete band around eighty percent of the wall. Just below, rows of joined consoles with stationary chairs ringed the outside. At the center, near the front, stood three more substantial, blocky seats for the command crew. Behind them, a table-mounted hologram projector for tactical viewing sat lifeless. The beacon station nestled at the rear of the space, near the lift entrance where she'd entered. None of it looked familiar.

Beth's gaze drifted to her gloved hands, clenched together like a shuttle in a docking clamp.

Why am I missing so many memories? The thought repeated over in her mind. After an extended sigh, she reached out and pressed play.

"To any ship in the area, this is Dr. Beth Adler of the Colonial Research Vessel Celestus. We are severely damaged and drifting in orbit. There is an outbreak of unknown classification which has infected many crew members. They have lost all sense of humanity and will attack anyone on sight. Advise only well-armed rescue teams attempt to board. Otherwise, this is a warning to stay away from this ship and its occupants. I am attempting to purge the ship of those infected. If I'm successful, I will delete this message. If you're hearing this, something has gone horribly wrong... To any ship in the area, this is Dr. Beth—"

When the recording repeated, she silenced it. Though brief, the warning impacted her mind like a doomsday meteor. It confirmed a breach of quarantine after the wave, as mentioned on one log, and also hinted she'd avoided infection, at least at the time of the message. If the affliction caused people to become violent and attack anyone, she couldn't have activated this beacon without being cured.

That's something. Still, what became of the afflicted? Did I successfully heal or purge them and not turn off the beacon? It's possible. But how did I get into Devin's room? And why was I barricaded in? I think all the answers lie in the admin section. They called the shots on this whole thing. If any records exist, it's where I'll find them.

With the ship out of the planet's atmosphere, she felt more at ease heading back into the void to attempt entry into the admin's area via the airlock. Blowing out all the atmosphere, along with tablets and other clues, gave her pause, and she mulled over the risk/reward variables.

I guess I can try to get there the traditional way. As she contemplated her options, another idea struck. *Hey, maybe I can contact the colony!*

"Computer, show me communications and how to open a channel to the colony on Janis IV."

She jumped up with renewed vigor and followed the indicator to a nearby console. After a few minutes, she'd opened a channel to the colony's communication array. However, before she could announce herself, a static-infused voice came over the speaker.

"This is outpost one on Janis IV. We have come under attack. Some of our people have gone insane and attacked others. If you can hear this, we need immediate rescue. The last of us are barricading ourselves in warehouse nine. We don't know how long we can hold out. Once we abandon the com-array, further communication will cease. Please send help."

Oh, stars... This is horrible. How long ago was this? They can't communicate, but if I can get there... Devin mentioned being evacuated.

She added it to the never-ending list of mysteries to investigate. If she reached the colony and the colonists had repelled the infected, she would do her part to bring them off the planet.

Everyone she'd found alive aboard the Celestus would rest safely in cryostorage until she ran some blood tests. Still, she hadn't explored large sections of the vessel.

It's time to find anyone else in hiding and tell them I'm here.

"Computer, show me how to access the ship-wide communication system." Following the lit-up indicators and instructions, she opened a channel on all frequencies. She wanted to make sure anyone on the ship could hear her message, so she set it to broadcast on the various speakers around the vessel and private com channels. "This is Dr. Beth Adler to anyone still alive on the Celestus. I've secured the bridge and found no evidence of remaining infected. If you require rescue, I'm encoding my envirosuit's personal transmitter ID with this message. Please let me know where you are and how I can help."

Ok, before I go on another spacewalk or locate transport to the planet, I should stick around in case someone contacts me. After about thirty minutes and no contact, Beth, unsurprised but still disappointed, glanced out the wide window at the distant planet before leaving the bridge and traveling to the crew quarters, where she hoped to find a way to Administration. She spent the better part of an hour searching the navigation-crew section halls, finding little. Though she picked up a couple of tablets in the search, however, they contained older entries that didn't provide useful information.

Eventually, she stood in front of the mangled lift accessing the administrative level. They had their own entrance, which the administrators accessed from the flight crew section, though not anymore. The wave had wreaked havoc on the Celestus's gravity generators and any systems relying on them, including the lifts. Most had crashed to their bottom floors, and the administrators shared the same fate. Beth shook her head, marveling at the utter failure of technology. *What kind of safety mechanisms were built into these things? How did they all fail so epically?*

She tried pushing the sliding doors aside for a better look within. However, they refused to open more than a couple of inches. Inside, she glimpsed a lift-car teaming with robot limbs. Blacken and scored to match the walls, something exploded inside, destroying the lift and its artificial occupants. She'd never figured out the deal with the robots, but having only discovered them in pieces sent a chill up her spine.

She let the door snap shut and stood back, knowing she had one option left for gaining entry; blow a hole in the ship's side.

What's another breach at this point?

Beth found a nearby airlock, in a section unexposed to space, using the map kiosk in the dining commons. After a short trek, she activated her boots, exited the Celestus, and walked along the hull to the outer entrance leading to the administration area.

This is likely a private docking station for top-level people to check-in directly with the company leadership.

"Bastards," she whispered. For the most part, the ship operated without bureaucratic intervention. The captain and officers oversaw the vessel's daily command, and department directors ran the individual research wings. However, all decisions ultimately went through the administrators. They conducted everything, even if they didn't choose to noticeably intervene often. In this case, Beth sensed their fingerprints all over this mess. Every part of the ship she'd explored led to as many questions as answers. It was time to cross things off her list.

She planted a breaching charge on the door and retreated along the surface, taking cover behind a rise in the hull. The explosive blew silently, sending shining particles spinning out into the cosmos. A massive vacuum of atmosphere followed. The force sucked the hefty chunk of warped door out into oblivion. Already in motion, Beth sprinted toward the new opening. She could close the inner barrier and save some objects from ejection into space if she was fast enough. At the edge of the gaping hole, she knelt, gazing into the vessel's interior. Air and small debris rushed past her at an alarming rate. With all her might, she reached down, grabbed a safety bar, and pulled herself inside the airlock chamber. Although she had to fight against the pull of the vacuum, gaining entry came easier than she expected. She felt like the suit augmented her strength. She had no other explanation.

With the gravity boots assisting, she crawled along the ground, pushing her way forward. Several chairs and office supplies flew past her as she pulled herself in close to the side of the airlock. The objects and debris banged against her helmet and shoulders. They threatened her grip and tried to wrench her into open space with each impact. Beth mustered her strength to resist the oncoming wind and battering scrap. She forged ahead, grabbing hold of anything she could. The footwear kept her toes against the floor and pushed her forward. Her hands wrapped around the inner doorframe, and with a massive heave, she thrust herself inside. Fleeing air forced her back against the wall. She threw her hands up as an office chair bashed into her body, knocking her toward the gaping exit.

Chapter 26

The boots alone held Beth's mass in the corridor as the chair flipped past her and out to the void. Her calves and thighs strained while her muscles fought to keep her torso out of the doorway. Her balled fist shot out and pounded the emergency close button near the entrance. The barrier slammed shut with a squeak of air.

Beth slumped down on one knee, the gravity boots keeping one foot locked down. That had been a bad idea. She had almost flown into the void, destined to float helplessly until her air ran out. It wasn't even the first time. She should've known to avoid such risks.

An hour had passed with no one attempting to contact her directly after sending the ship-wide message. She was truly the only one awake, and the fate of everyone in the cryo chambers intertwined with hers. *I can't be so careless.* If she'd waited for all the air to escape, she'd have gained easy access. Saving a few tablets hadn't been worth losing everything and everyone.

Deactivating the boots, she collapsed into a sitting position, her back pressed against a wall.

Beth, you made it. You made it. I'm in. It's fine. I'm fine. She allowed herself several minutes to catch her breath and recover her wits. However, in the back of her mind, a nagging urgency festered. It wanted her to investigate the condition of those colonists trapped on the planet. Still, she'd seen evidence of missing time, likely spent in stasis. Or was it all part of her lost memories? With no timestamp, she had no way to tell if the message first broadcasted two days or two years ago. Something in her gut said everyone planet-side had already died. Still, the remote chance to find survivors, her friends, or Devin forced her up, urging her forward.

The administrative rooms turned out exactly as she might have expected. A few open doors led to lavish executive suites where all the self-important people aboard would spend most of their time. She found a recreational area at least as large as the ones shared by most of the crew and a dining hall with wood furnishings and cushioned seating—nothing like the endless metal and plastic that served for everyone else.

No wonder they rarely invite anyone up here; there would've been a mutiny.

The cost of space on a ship was high and prohibitive. The amount of room and luxury the company awarded to the handful of people who sat on the administrative board staggered Beth. As she searched the area, it also struck her how everything appeared extremely ordered and clean. The rest of the ship lay in total disarray, as loss of gravity, hull breaches, combat, and who knows what else had scarred every other section in one way or another. Somehow, this deck looked almost brand new, with no explanation.

Beth didn't linger long in any of these places. She hunted for tablets left safely behind closed doors or in secure cabinets, but so far found nothing. When the crew evacuated, they dropped things where they were when the alarms went off. But nothing appeared carelessly discarded here.

She found her way past the living quarters and into a large conference room. Giant monitors lined the walls, displaying a 360-degree view of space outside the ship. She saw the planet, moons, and a band of stars filling out the galaxy, every direction she glanced, like the room itself hung in the cosmos. The scene took her breath away. A table with twelve chairs sat in the middle of the room, with a hologram projector protruding from the table's center.

Probably for sending and receiving messages from the homeworld. She looked around for the controls, found them at the head of the table, and turned on the projector. One message remained in the memory, and she played it. A scrambled image of a person she didn't recognize appeared. The deteriorated quality made the person look almost inhuman, and the audio crackled with constant static to the point she couldn't understand anything.

"Computer, display how to clean and playback the last message."

Her suit revealed what she needed to do, and she went through the procedure. It turned out the message wasn't degraded, but partially deleted. She couldn't tell what might have preserved it, but maybe the wave had done something positive for once.

When she finished all the steps provided, she again played the recording.

"... set it in a stable orbit. We've already dispatched a team to infiltrate and take back the Celestus and retain the samples, even with you away. They will also retrieve your shuttle and stasis capsules at Point Alpha. Good luck to you all. See you in eight years." Beth tried playing more, but the small segment remained the only available part. However, she found the transmission date, 3/24/909, the same day Morgan Sims broke out.

That's not much to go on. Though it seems clear, the admins abandoned ship. If I had any idea where Point Alpha was, I'd be tempted to nuke it.

Standing up, she entered a door at the back of the space and found herself in a control room surrounded by workstations. "Computer, tell me what all these consoles do."

Several descriptions appeared in her vision. Most functions related to monitoring communications on the ship and gathering information on the various reports from each scientific division, though one device stuck out. The augment labeled it *'tablet hacker.'* Upon further examination, she discovered it could bypass the passcode on anyone's tablet, or so the description claimed.

Stars! It's an unconscionable violation of everyone's privacy. It struck her as an ironic reaction as she plugged in the unit she'd clipped to her belt back in Devin's room. A tablet menu appeared on a monitor above the hacker, identical to the one on the device itself. Beth saw several stored video logs and played the first one.

The disheveled image of a person appeared. She recognized her immediately.

It's me! Stars, I look horrible.

Chapter 27

5/13/909. "This is Dr. Beth Adler. I'm making this record in case I don't survive the outbreak on the Celestus. As far as I can tell, I'm the only one left not in stasis. The outbreak began when a colonist on Janis IV developed symptoms, and we brought him aboard in quarantine for treatment. At first, we didn't know what had happened to him, but it soon became apparent a foreign entity had infiltrated his body where it quickly flourished. While we worked on treatment, the administrators ordered him off the sedatives, and he escaped. I believe the Celestus admins arranged for the patient's initial infection and orchestrated what was to come. The entity increased its host's strength, resilience, and survival instinct while causing neurological abnormalities leading to madness. When the patient attacked the medical staff and security, it infected several crew members, including me. I was sedated, along with the others.

"I was, however, able to synthesize something of a cure before being quarantined. Its effects turned out to only be temporary, however. The Celestus then encountered a spatial wave of unknown origin and composition. It caused significant damage to the ship, including the medical facilities securing all the newly infected. Upon escaping, they ran amok and pillaged every section I've seen. The infected attacked the rest of the crew, contaminating or killing them. Some may have reached the escape pods and shuttles in the docking bay, as several are jettisoned. If so, they'd have gone to the planet. Some close friends gave me a dose of my temporary cure before I caused anyone harm. So far, the infected don't bother those already infected, but as our experiments showed, it may be only transitory. Even though I've received a cure, the infection is still dormant in my body, so I remain a danger to anyone I come across. I hope my friends escaped, but I have

148

no way of knowing what happened to them, other than a recording on a tablet they left for me."

The log ended, and Beth waited to play the next one.

The treatment is only temporary? So I'm still infected? Why don't I remember any of this?

She played the next one.

5/14/909. "After the wave, I awoke in my room. Somehow, my friends got me there. There are infected all over this deck, but they pay little attention to me. I've explored this level and determined the ship is in critical condition. There are power fluctuations and gravity spikes. It almost crushed me under my own weight during one flair-up. The lifts aren't working, so it's challenging to get to the other decks. Good news is I think most of the initial infected never got off this deck. The bad news is if someone got infected without knowing it and reached a different section, the parasite likely spread there anew. The incubation period is several days, so there's time to get ahead of this, I think.

"As the message left by my friends suggested, the cure is only temporary. I can actually feel it wearing off. It's a strange sensation. I see things that can't possibly be there, and I lose my patience and get angry for no reason. Which isn't like me at all. Luckily, the medical labs are still semi-functional despite being ravaged by the wave and the infected. Whoever finds this needs to be aware of the signs the treatment is wearing off. I've had the computer synthesize as much of the cure as possible. I've got a supply on me if I start feeling not myself. My best plan at this point is to explore the rest of the ship and see if anyone uninfected is out there who can help me subdue the others. Then maybe we can get a handle on these power fluctuations."

5/16/909: "I managed to get down to the cryostasis storage deck. It's given me an idea. I will attempt to inject the chronically infected with the cure and see if it brings them around enough to get into cryostasis. That way, it will suspend them in their current state while I attempt to find another solution. I can get here using the lift tubes, which are currently without gravity. Even if I have to sedate them, I need all of them on ice."

5/18/909: "My plan has been working. I've cleared the medical deck and some of the other easily accessible sections of all personnel. It defies logic, but I think the thing infecting all of them is catching on I'm not its friend. I had to fight a couple of them off and ultimately sedate them to inject a cure. It takes a heavily concentrated sedative, ordinarily lethal to humans, to slow them down. Moving about the ship has been difficult with multiple hull breaches, radiation, coolant leaks, and collapsed hallways.

"Additionally, the power and gravity spikes are getting worse, as is my condition. The entity must be building an immunity to the cure because I've had to inject myself again, and it's only been about twenty hours since the last time. The first dose lasted days. I've started running tests again, using the temporary cure as a basis, but I'll need something better to keep me going and help everyone else. One strange thing is I've spotted a cat watching me on multiple occasions. I think it belonged to an administrator."

That's where I recognize the cat from. It was with one admin who visited the medical labs when we first arrived. But what is it doing still wandering the ship?

5/19/909: "I finally gave the cure to someone who can help me, engineer Diana Joyce. She came around, and we've been discussing the issues on the ship. Together we're going to find a way to the engineering bay and put the reactor in lower output mode while she works on getting it stable again. Otherwise, it seems we're looking at a complete meltdown in the near future. So far, the bottom levels of the ship remain utterly inaccessible. I have to put off developing a better cure until the reactor is stable since the lab will lose all power when we shut it down. I've made a couple of backups of my data so far; one is on this tablet, the other is in lab number eight in the medical wing."

5/24/909: "I haven't recorded a log in a while because of the accident. During the reactor shutdown, there was a flair-up of some kind. I was above the core in main Engineering, monitoring the reactor's levels for Diana. She was in the reactor room when it happened. She got hit by a massive spike of radiation. It melted right through her protective suit. When I got to her, she was already unconscious. I put her into stasis, but she's in terrible shape. The reactor is currently down, and I don't know how to get it back online. I can't continue the research. I can't do anything…"

Beth pulled her eyes away from the exhausted and despair-riddled visage and put the tablet aside as sadness welled within her. She'd been alone and occasionally hopeless since she woke up, but it was nothing compared to the missing memory she now relieved. Watching herself talk like a vision of the past, a part of her felt glad the memories remained lost. She had been through something horrible.

Chapter 28

Will something in these logs help me understand why I can't remember anything?

She leaned back and thought about what she'd heard. It was unbelievable. If the words hadn't come from her own mouth, she wouldn't know what to make of them. Or maybe seeing herself is what made the whole thing seem like a lucid dream in the first place. Pride for her past self swelled up in her gut. The sorrow and strain in her voice broke her heart, but she had endured. Unimaginably, the situation had been worse when she recorded these, and the odds of survival slimmer. Yet, here she was, alive to relive her own tale. The infected still roamed the ship at that point, and she'd subdued them all. Beth started the logs back up.

5/27/909: "I've been in engineering for what feels like forever. I've got some good news. Diana made the necessary repairs before the accident, and I figured out how to get the reactor booted in low-power mode. I just hope it's stable. I know nothing about this department, but I'm out of options. The bad news is I took a lot of radiation when I charged in after Diana. Not as much as her, as it's taken longer for symptoms to manifest, but I've started getting sick.

"I could power up a few sections at a time, so I went back to my lab to continue the work as best I could. Unfortunately, in low-power mode, the computer won't run the samples. So, I've pulled out a microscope, dishes, and testing solutions to keep working the old-fashioned way. It's a pain in the ass, but I have to do something. Of course, I could always get a lucky breakthrough. Hope is a hard thing to give up on."

5/31/909: "This might be my last entry. The radiation is killing me. My only option is to go into stasis and hope someone from the colony returns or a rescue team arrives from the homeworld, but that's years away. The last several hours have been productive, though. I've secured all the crew I could find into stasis. As far as I can tell, no infected are running around the ship anymore. Well, except for me, that is. One of the last people I found was the head of security. He was pretty coherent for a few hours after giving him the vaccine. Before going into stasis, he showed me how to access the administration deck. I'll need to enter from outside the ship at their private airlock, but I've got the door code. I'm going to check one last time for any remaining crew.

"The other positive thing is the radiation hinders the spreading infection. Turns out the organism doesn't like it at all. So, that's a revelation. It's unfortunate I won't be able to test it. I went to the bridge and established a warning beacon for any ships coming to rescue us. I've also found several nearly decomposed bodies in the places I hadn't gotten to yet. The only theory I have is the infection breaks down the body after a while. I saw none of the infected eat. Perhaps, when the virus needs energy, it consumes the only thing left, its host. There's no way for me to test my theory, though. I'm going to hope someone finds this and can save us all."

Her past self had said that would be the last entry, but one more, with the same date, sat curiously underneath it. Beth played it with worried anticipation.

5/31/909: "I have to do something. I think the admins are behind this whole outbreak. I found a series of conversations in their restricted section between them and company headquarters. They're sending a ship to retrieve us, but it's not what I thought. The company declared the Celestus destroyed. As far as anyone outside the company is concerned, we don't exist anymore. They've been watching us this whole time. The cat is not a cat. It's robotic. It's been recording everything happening on the ship, including the outbreak and me trying to save everyone. If I can find it, I'm going to blow it out an airlock. We're an experiment to them now and they're coming to take us for study. The admins said it clear as the galaxy at night. We're all expendable. Everyone's life on this ship depends on me.

"I'm too sick to do much more, but I've got a plan. I don't like it at all, but I'm out of options. If I go into stasis, it's all over. I may never wake up. It's an insane risk, but I figure I'm dead either way. I found all the notes from Devin's virtual reality experimentations. His entire setup is still in his room. I'm going to transfer my consciousness and my memories into Devin's robot assistant. It's the only shot I have... We have... My body will not last long enough to power the ship up, find a cure, and get out of this system. I guess I'm desperate. Fuck! I hate this..." Her voice caught, and the image of Beth looked away and wiped her face. "If I can save everyone. If I can help Devin and everyone else in stasis and on the planet, I'm going to try.

"The cat seems to have access to the entire ship. It must be able to transmit override codes. I'll have to seal myself away so it can't see what I'm doing and can't interfere. If I suit up the robot, the company won't realize it's not me. I'm not sure how long I'll be out or if my memories will transfer at all. I might never wake up again. But I now know who these logs are for. They're for me. Beth, all the information I've gathered, the door codes, paths I've discovered around the ship, the cure, everything is on this tablet. I'm encoding it in case it's discovered by the company. I hope you remember the passcode. If you're reading this, it must mean you did. I'm counting on you, girl. I know this is a lot to take in, but look at all I... we've already done. You can do this."

The last log ended. Beth stared back at the menu screen, the last words echoing in her mind. It was a lie. It had to be.

I... I don't know what to think. I don't want to think about it. Her head twisted back and forth, a pendulum of denial. *It's a nightmare. I'm afraid to take off my helmet and look. It can't be true. It's just not possible...* Her hands moved toward the helmet release latch, then stopped.

Chapter 29

Beth held out her hands, palms up. She inspected her motor control with delicate precision. Her fingers rolled in repetition, as she would expect. Nothing mechanical about them.

It can't be true. She placed her hands on her chest, her eyes drifting past them. She hadn't taken the time to examine her suit for hours, maybe days. The front appeared normal, but curls of melted material had peeled forward at its sides. She leaned around further—a metallic leg showed through a charred gap where the pants had burned away during the hull breach caused by atmospheric reentry.

Fear and panic flooded in, and Beth rushed out of the control room toward one of the administrative quarters. The door refused to open, so she kicked it until it buckled inward. With her gloved hand, she grabbed hold of where it separated from the edge and wrenched it open. Inside, she stopped in front of a mirror, unclipped her helmet in a flurry, and then hesitated.

I already know what I'm going to see. Why even bother? I know what I am.

Beth heaved in a huge breath, then let it out slowly. *Wait... I'm breathing.* She pulled the helmet off, unsure of what she would see— hoping her past-self had found another way. A faceless head, smooth and silver, stared back at her. Mind racing, she shook her head, the silver shape mimicking the movement. Then she tried taking a breath. The robotic figure in the mirror puffed out its chest in an intake motion, then slumped slightly forward as she "exhaled." It was all in her mind. Every breath, every time she ground her teeth in frustration, even now with fear welling up in her chest, it was all her psyche simulating the sensation. She felt like crying but couldn't and never would again. So many things made more sense now. Her suit hadn't been malfunctioning. It couldn't read vitals because there were no vitals to read. It wasn't using up oxygen because she didn't need to breathe. Hunger hadn't bothered her because she didn't need to eat or relieve herself.

"Who are you?" she asked. Her voice sounded right, but was it an auditory illusion? She was a mind trapped in a body not her own, an artificial construct.

The radiation wasn't dangerous, and while the flames of planetary reentry had burned and melted the back of her suit, she hadn't felt a thing because she couldn't. She possessed the strength to force her way into this room and climb the lift tubes with ease. Gravity and inertial momentum had thrown and battered her body against floors and walls. She had thought it was the suit protecting her, but in reality, she was no longer fragile flesh and bone but hard metal and circuits.

Beth stared at her new visage for what might have been an eternity. She studied the smooth, eyeless face and wondered how its vision worked, all the while wanting to feel something, anything, real. The swirling thoughts and emotions melded into a numbness that sucked all the motivation and urgency from her. Was everything she felt a matter of programming? Was she even herself or a copy?

A horrific thought slammed its way through her circuitry.

The bones in the room—they're mine. That's... That's what's left of me. Should I...? Oh, stars...What do I do with them? Give myself a funeral? Say some words? It all seemed pointless. She choked back a sob but shook her head, knowing it was only a programmed response. "What do I do now?" she said to the stranger in the mirror.

Has this really changed anything? I laid out a plan, but now I don't know... She turned to the door. The cat sat there, watching her silently and licking its paw vigorously. Beth stood motionless and watched it go through a series of motions for several minutes. She could see it had the mannerisms of a cat, but it wasn't perfect. Its actions appeared slightly mechanical, ever so much unnatural. *Its movements are too repetitive, too perfect. It always licked its paw in the same way. It always tilted its head to the left afterward and flicked its tail.*

How long has it been watching me? My past-self thought it was spying on me. There's one way to find out.

Emotion burst through the dam of numbness in the form of rage. Beth rushed toward the cat, her arms outstretched to snatch it. The creature twisted around, contorting its body unnaturally, and dashed away. Beth's mechanical body was fast, much faster than her human one. Still, the cat, being of equal construction, proved even more rapid.

Its four legs worked in perfect unison. In seconds, it had put several more meters between itself and Beth. She'd never catch it.

There was one thing Beth possessed the feline didn't—the helmet gripped tightly in her hand. She hurled it with all her might, its target unaware of its flight. Glass shattered in a flickering burst as the protective face mask smashed into the fleeing creature. The helmet had struck it directly, but the force of the blow sent the headpiece and cat careening further down the hallway. The feline didn't stay down long and moved almost immediately. This time, it wasn't quick; it wasn't even peppy. Its rear legs had broken in the attack. Metallic joints stuck out from its fur at odd angles. It attempted to hobble away, but Beth scooped it up and stared at the thing. It hissed and raked its claws, though the artificial nails did little more than skitter off Beth's smooth metal face.

Her anger boiled over, and she dug her fingers into the tiny beast. She ripped at its artificial fur, which came off in chunks, exposing machinery beneath. Then, grabbing a handful of knotted wires, she yanked them free. The creature ceased to struggle, and the mangled body went limp in her hands. Beth's helmet had crippled its delicate frame. Designed for speed and agility, the cat couldn't withstand much physical force.

It probably needed to be the approximate weight of an actual cat to maintain its disguise.

Luckily, she found its memory chip buried deep in its torso. When Beth pulled it free, it appeared undamaged.

I don't have time to look at this now, but I'm guessing it contains a lot. Everything. She pocketed the chip in her suit's chest pouch, dropped the robotic beast's remains, then stepped back down the hall the way she'd chased it. But she stopped almost immediately.

Where am I headed? What am I going to do now? The information she'd heard herself say on the tablet and the revelations from the admin's transmission meant the company had orchestrated the horrible events on the ship.

The one thing which had thrown their plan off course was the gravitational wave. Now agents were coming to seize the Celestus and rescue the administrators who caused this disaster. What was their goal? The human rights violations would sink the company, undoubtedly. They had knowingly infected one of the crew and allowed the infection to spread, opting to save themselves and leaving everyone else to face certain death. The crew wouldn't see home again, not if the company had anything to do with it. There was still a ship of people to save. Beth knew what she needed to do.

The open airlock had cleared most of the admin rooms, so she looked for ones with closed doors and forced her way inside, one at a time. Finally, after a few intrusions, she found something she needed, an admin pass chip. With it, she would have access all over the ship. She inserted the chip into a slot near her suit's forearm screen.

Beth went back to the area with the administration airlock. To her delight, she found a blast door control to isolate the handful of rooms near the exit. That way, she could override the inner airlock door without blasting all the atmosphere out of the entire level again. The thick barrier slid shut, and Beth gripped a hold-bar before punching the cycle airlock override. It required authorization, so she brought her arm near enough to the device to read the chip inside. Lights in the hall flashed red, and the inner airlock doors parted slightly after a few seconds. Air sucked out in a violent torrent, the gap growing until Beth stood in the vacuum of space.

Activating her boots, she stepped out ninety degrees onto the vessel's hull. The distant planet brought an unexpected peace she hadn't felt in a long while. Someone could be down there hoping for rescue. That person could be Devin or any of her friends. Someone needed her, and the thought helped her push past her own existential crisis. It remained surreal she wasn't in her own body. She still felt like herself, with all the same emotions and insecurities she'd had before.

The whole thing couldn't be real. She wanted it to be a dream, to wake up, look down and see every wrinkle of skin covering her fingers, to feel the muscle, tendons, and bone underneath. The fleeting fancies didn't stick. She knew she would never be the same person. Maybe her mind was intact, which was something, perhaps enough to save her crew and find her missing friends. She'd deal with what she'd become and what it meant after everyone was safe. *Compartmentalizing your trauma, Beth. I'm sure you won't suffer any consequences for that later.*

Beth picked up her pace along the surface of the ship, her legs stretching out, extending her strides. The boots sucked her feet down to the hull with each step.

All the people aboard in stasis are safe for the moment. She reminded herself of what she'd accomplished and what she knew. The vessel coasted in a stable orbit with power restored to cryo-storage. Any company agents en route to pick up the administrators at point alpha were, at the very least, several years away. There would be ample time to deal with them. For now, the discreet distress call from the planetary colony haunted her mind. She had no way of knowing how long it had been since someone sent the message. It might've been days or years, but if there was any chance to rescue the crew trapped planet-side, she'd give it everything.

From her vantage point running along the outside of the Celestus, she glimpsed further damage to the hull. Jagged sections of silver-worn metal plating stuck out like frozen flames in the void. Countless tasks remained for when she got back. She wasn't sure where to begin after rescuing any would-be survivors on the colony. The damage left doubt in her mind the vessel could safely make the extended deep-space journey home. By herself, working around the clock with the help of the augmentation, finding and completing the repairs felt impossibly daunting.

I need to save as many people as possible. One step at a time, Beth. Just focus, and you'll get through this.

She cut a wide path around a deep gouge in the ship's skin. While skirting the edge, she recognized the spot where she'd initially been sucked into open space. The first of many times she'd almost died. But she was already dead. At least her organic body was.

So, what am I now? Dead or alive? She felt alive in all the ways that typically mattered, but by technical definition, she was deceased.

If she'd been sucked into the void, she'd have figured out her new body much sooner. With no need to breathe, her oxygen supply wouldn't budge, and in endless drifting hours without the constant distraction of a crippled ship on the verge of disaster, she'd have time to notice a lack of hunger. How long would it take for her internal batteries to run down? She didn't know how long the ship robots operated, but figured it was significant.

I'd probably go mad way before my body stopped functioning. Or the planet's gravity would pull me down to disintegrate during atmospheric reentry.

Around the bottom of the ship, Beth came to the shuttle bay airlock. Using the pass chip from the administration area, she gained easy access.

I hope a lack of gravity hasn't wrecked every single thing in here. After the air cycled and the inner door opened, Beth stepped out to utter disaster. Her head and shoulders slumped as fresh despair added weight to her fragile mental state.

Not only had gravity fled the bay, but it looked like it had ignited a bomb on its way out. Piles of mangled ships clustered in different sections, while broken glass and fragments of hulls lay strewn across every segment of the deck. The shuttles had magnetic struts to keep them from moving while docked, but they all had failed. Or at least enough of them came loose and crashed around the bay that nothing appeared usable anymore.

I can't leave the system if there's a chance someone is alive. But how do I get down to the planet now?

Chapter 30

The heaps of former shuttles rose like ransacked burial mounds. Glancing about, Beth hoped something flyable lay within the forgotten tomb. With a sigh, which wasn't a real sigh, Beth focused her resolve and climbed over the small debris hills in search of at least one vessel that might've survived the cataclysm. The ships most likely crashed together shortly after the wave hit; however, something about the carnage looked fresh. According to all the logs she found, she hadn't reached this part of the ship as a human. Nor had it been a priority to do so.

Beth scuttled over to an immense pile in the closest part of the room and began pulling the scraps of metal away.

If a ship survived, it would be hidden under one of these. After only a few minutes, she hit a snag. The smaller pieces of debris proved easy enough to remove, especially with her mechanical strength; however, below those first layers, she found a partially intact and unmovable shuttle. Clearing away all the debris would take time, and afterward, she had no guarantee the ship underneath would be operational. Dozens of daunting junk mountains rose within the dock. It might take weeks to sift through them all.

Stepping back from the task, she considered another option.

If I'm not strong enough to move these, maybe I just need to make them lighter. Beth traversed the scrap-scattered bay, making her way to a staircase leading to the control booth. She passed through a door into a room with several consoles designed to facilitate the landing and take-off of all the bay's traffic. "Computer, show me how to open the launch doors."

She no longer had her helmet, but a series of instructions appeared over the displays in her vision. Without the helm to reroute the signal, the module interfaced directly with her robotic circuitry. Beth followed the instructions, using the administration card to override safety protocols and open the doors without venting the atmosphere first. All the ship husks and scrap needed to eject with the atmosphere rather than becoming merely weightless, which would make them almost as challenging to move without leverage.

All the loose parts rumbled and shifted as the doors opened, sliding along the floor toward the widening gap. The doorway became clogged with metallic fragments and damaged craft in less than a minute. The gateway widened, allowing the blockage to soar into the void. As Beth hoped, the opening expelled the air and the smaller scrap at high speed while the larger craft drifted languidly out of the portal.

Once cleared, Beth shut the bay door, restored gravity, cycled the atmosphere, and left the control center for the small personnel airlock beside the main bay door. She exited and stood on the outside surface of the Celestus, gazing over the field of ship husks as they meandered apart. After a few seconds, she spotted precisely what she'd been looking for: a shuttle with minimal damage at first glance, floating amongst its ruined brethren. Beth walked along the hull of the colony ship until she felt she had a good angle on the shuttle. She bent her knees, keeping a focused eye on her destination, then released the magnets on her boots and pushed off with all her might.

Gliding through open space still sent all-too-real-feeling chills down her artificial spine. A part of her wished her miraculous transformation had toned down her anxiety. Still, she'd have to settle for inhuman strength and agility along with the entirety of her personality intact, insecurities included. Beth's trajectory proved right on target, though it was easy with the slow-moving landing zone. With a slam, her body rammed the side of the vessel harder than she wanted. Her arms lashed out, snagging the wing before her momentum could bounce her off into the endless void.

You don't know your own strength, even after all this time. She gained access to the shuttle's interior through the rear ramp entrance. Once inside, she closed it up and headed for the cockpit. "Computer, take me through the shuttle startup sequence." As before, instructions appeared, and she followed the startup sequence until the vessel roared to life. Once the main console came online, Beth ran a diagnostic of all the shuttle's systems. If anything went wrong, she needed to know now before attempting atmospheric entry to land on the planet. One by one, the checks came back in the green. The hull held atmosphere, ninety percent of the maneuvering thrusters fully operated, and the mini reactor functioned within normal parameters. "Well, I never thought I'd be a shuttle pilot, but here goes nothing."

Maneuvering the craft toward the colonial planet, Janis IV, Beth pushed the throttle forward. Within half an hour, she felt the shudder of the ship hitting the thin planetary atmosphere. "Computer, take me through the reentry sequence." She adhered to the directions, maintaining an appropriate angle to push through air friction without burning up her ride. As the ship shook and rattled, Beth's grip on the flight controls tightened. She never imagined herself doing something like this, which sent her nerves into overdrive.

How do cargo pilots get used to this? "Hold together, girl." She peered back at the ship's interior as if it might tear apart at any moment.

While reentry only lasted a few minutes, the gyrations and visions of fire around the ship felt like much longer, leaving her feeling tingles all over her body. When she looked at her still gloved hands, they twitched as if pumping with adrenaline, although she knew that to be impossible. "I would've never guessed that an artificial body would still react in such a way when given a consciousness. If I even see Devin again, he'll...."

She let the words drift away. What were the chances she'd see him again? None of her friends had been in her initial scan of the cryotubes. They'd escaped planetside, been infected, and died in stasis, or been blown out an airlock during the initial chaos.

He could still be alive down here. They all could. She had to tell herself and believe it fully. Considering the alternative even momentarily, that Devin and everyone she'd been close to had died, threatened to send her fragile psyche over the edge. Beth focused on the flying, pushing everything else out of her mind.

Her flight path took her across a landscape of endless, stubby, and worn hills. As she visually scanned the surface, it occurred to her she didn't know the outpost's location. Initially, the Celestus was in a geosynchronous orbit with its colony. But between the decay and her rushed rescue, it could be anywhere.

Wasn't there a location beacon or something?

"Computer, show me how to locate any active beacons." Beth glanced over the highlighted menu and activated a rolling scan for any repeated signals. One popped up immediately, and she recognized it as the emergency message picked up on the bridge from the colony.

"Computer, is there any way to trace the source of that signal?"

In her vision, an option called "Signal Trace" brightened in the menu already open. "Oh, well, that was obvious."

I'm relying on this augment so much I've stopped using my brain.

She selected it with her finger, and a topographical map appeared on the shuttle's main viewscreen. It showed repeating concentric circles emanating from a source a few thousand miles distant.

Beth set a course toward the origin, using the ship's autopilot system. Several hours later, she crested a slight rise, and the colony domes came into view. Three small, half-sphere shelters sprawled out from an immense centralized enclosure. The more massive one spread roughly four hundred meters in diameter, with the lesser domes about a third the size. Even from this distance, she identified the damage on two smaller shelters, giant gaping holes in their outer structure, and a darkened, large primary dome. With each passing minute, her hopes dwindled as she saw no evidence of activity among the ruins, no sign of repairs in progress, operating lights, or indications someone may still be alive.

A field, made level for landing modest-sized craft, sat near one of the damaged domes. After asking the computer for landing instructions, Beth switched over to manual control, then brought the shuttle in, setting it roughly on the ground with a heavy thump. She unstrapped herself and went to the back, opening the rear loading ramp using the control panel near the exit. After a couple of steps, she turned back, retreating inside. Searching through the various lockers near the entrance, she located another envirosuit.

Probably better if I don't look like a robot if I run into survivors.

She spent ten minutes pulling off the damaged suit that had carried her through all the trials and tribulations on the Celestus and slipping into the new outfit. Once satisfied, she transferred both the administration-pass circuit and the experimental learning mod to her updated ensemble. Then she placed the blood-sample vials, taken from those in cryostasis, in a secure locker in the shuttle. Last, she ran a check over the suit's systems. It showed a topped-off oxygen supply and a partial battery at sixty percent.

If this suit is anything like the other, my internal power source will refill the battery.

Beth approached a double door on one of the smaller, damaged domes about fifty yards from the landing zone. The entrance lay partially open, with one door sticking halfway out of its housing at a diagonal angle. Ducking through the gap this created, she passed through an open airlock and entered the structure. Inside, a vast expanse stretched ahead, with a few empty crates scattered about on the plastic tiled floor. It looked like a receiving area for goods brought down from the Celestus. Thick dust, blown through the cracks and holes in the half-sphere ceiling, covered the area and gathered in small drifts against the western wall. Partially filled-in boot tracks crisscrossed the space.

Looks like someone came here and removed all the supplies from these crates. But not recently.

She moved through the area, pushed open the doors at the far side, and stepped into the tunnel connecting to the central dome. Following the trail of imprints made by onetime survivors, she exited the tunnel and entered the main dome area. A pile of dismantled robots beyond the entrance told her she'd made the right decision about disguising her identity.

So, even planetside, the wave wreaked havoc on the robots.

The massive zone consisted of several short, half-built buildings, a few stacks of construction materials meant for further expansions, and ransacked storage crates. Movement caught her eye from across the area where a door obscured the tunnel to another small dome. Beth jerked her head in that direction and pulled the stun pistol from her belt.

Would the infected survive longer than the colonists on the planet?

Chapter 31

A laser zipped by Beth's head from her left. Dropping to a crouch, she turned and fired the stun pistol at someone in an envirosuit brandishing an energy rifle. Her shot missed, scoring the metal crates above them. Beth instinctively ducked further behind some storage containers as a flurry of light beams from other attackers pelted the makeshift fortifications. Seconds later, she popped back up from a different angle, her weapon at the ready. Her immediate assailant had moved out of cover to assault her position and froze like a child caught red-handed. Beth didn't know why they had attacked her, but getting shot wasn't part of saving the colonists. Squeezing the trigger, her stun pistol blasted the person directly in the chest. They convulsed before dropping to the ground as the incapacitating energy wreaked havoc on their muscle control. Hunched over, Beth sprinted back the way she'd come, going into a slide on the smooth tile and slipping behind a stack of unused structural supports as more lasers streaked by her.

Who do these people think I am? Who do they think would attack them? Footsteps on the floor echoed in the high dome.

"I'm not here to hurt anyone. Please stop shooting at me," Beth yelled over the suit's speakers, then waited for a reply. When none came, she didn't give up. "I'm from the Celestus. I've come to help." She peeked her head around the barrier and saw four individuals dressed in environment suits advancing cautiously on her position.

Maybe they can't hear me? Returning to cover, she tapped on her suit's interface and scanned for any active com channels. Beth stuck her gun past the barricade and blindly fired off a couple of stun bolts while the scan continued. She didn't care if they hit any targets as long as it made the team take cover and bought her time.

If I can't communicate with them, they'll kill me before knowing I'm here to help.

An indicator across her vision showed one active voice channel. However, when she switched to it, a male voice was already speaking "… around the other side. See if you can get a better angle."

Beth stayed quiet. She wanted to know who was in charge and why they attacked her before speaking up.

"I'm on my way. But who do you think it is? Harper has been gone for weeks," a female voice said.

"It can't be Harper. No one can survive outside the colony for that long. And besides, Harper took a heavy suit. This isn't her," the first voice said.

"Maybe they're from the ship," a third person said.

"That might be, but why did he shoot at us?" a fourth one asked.

They're just scared colonists. She'd heard enough. Besides, she didn't want to give them any more time to surround her. "This is Dr. Adler. Please cease-fire. I am friendly. Repeat, I am friendly."

"What? Really?" the third voice asked.

"Shut up, Gerard. She can hear you," the female voice said.

"How do we know you're who you say you are? We've heard no word from the Celestus in over a year." The first voice asked.

"I came down in a shuttle. What more proof do you need?"

"Is that what we heard?" the third voice asked.

"I guess it could've been a shuttle," the female said.

"I'm here to take you back to the ship and get us the hell out of the system unless you'd rather stay."

"Bullshit, you shot Felix." The first voice seemed like the leader.

"I'm using a stun gun. Felix will be fine." Beth once again popped her head over her fortification. Her assailants had stopped moving forward and had gathered near one another, having apparently given up speaking to each other over coms in favor of direct conversation. Beth stood up and raised her hands in the air, her finger clear of the pistol's trigger. "Look, I just want to talk. I'm here to help. Who did you expect was coming here to attack you?"

The group glanced at one another, fingering their weapons like nervous musicians before a concert, then looked to their apparent leader. Taking their cue, he spoke. "If you're from the ship, then you know about the madness and disease that's been taking over everyone."

"Yeah, I'm familiar."

He nodded his helmeted head. "It ran rampant down here as well.

166

Many colonists got infected, started killing the others, and wrecking the colony structures, which compromised our ability to survive on this planet. We killed as many as we could and burned the bodies, but plenty of them ran off. Occasionally, some of them show up and attack us again, but we've seen none in several weeks. It doesn't mean they're not out there. Someone showing up out of nowhere is something we're familiar with."

"Have you known any of them to carry on a conversation?" Beth asked.

"Well, at first, there's no way to tell who has it and who doesn't. But sure, after a while, they lose all sense of humanity."

"I think it's fair to say if I came here from somewhere other than the Celestus, I would've been infected a long time ago, and we would not be having this conversation," Beth said.

"You must be a doctor because your bedside manner sucks," the leader said.

"Complain to me about it when we're back on the ship and on our way home. What's your name? You seem to be in charge." Beth asked.

"Yeah, I'm in charge around here. I'm Nicoles."

Beth stepped from around the laser-scarred barrier and approached the group. Slowly and deliberately, she placed her pistol back in its holster. The leader motioned for his group to do the same. They complied with hesitant actions, slinging rifles over shoulders or slipping pistols back into belts. Two of them went to help their stunned companion get to his feet.

"I thought you'd be happier to have someone come to your aid." Beth rested her hands on her hips.

The leader shrugged. "Sure, but you're a little late. We got a message from the homeworld. A rescue transport is on its way from the company as we speak."

You contacted the homeworld but didn't attempt to reach the Celestus beyond setting up a beacon? If Beth had had a jaw, it would be resting on the ground. "That's a relief," she lied. "Maybe you can help me then. I'm looking for some people." Beth asked the question she wanted the answer to and dreaded more than anything. "Do you know a Devin Landis or Sophie Wilkes?" Everyone she loved and cared about could be dead. Maybe they were up in cryo, infected with the virus, and under the name Alice Bright. But from the sound of Devin's message, they'd been part of the group evacuated to the planet.

"Yeah, they're here…"

Beth stopped listening. The man continued, but the rest of the words never reached her ears. Devin was alive. Sophie was alive. That meant maybe Liam and Alan, too. It was what she'd hoped for since the moment she woke up on the derelict ship. The man was still talking when Beth spoke again. "Can you take me to them?"

Chapter 32

Silence hung past comfortable. The four gathered people looked at each other before the leader spoke again. "Yeah, come on back." The man waved as he turned toward the far tunnel.

I'm glad people are alive, but this isn't exactly the welcome I had envisioned. Still, Devin is alive. He's alive and here. Oh stars, what am I going to tell him? She'd spent hours thinking about this conversation, but felt wholly unprepared for actually meeting Devin and the others. It had always been the goal, but now that she'd discovered her true nature, that she was a mind in a metallic body, how could she explain it?

"Are you really here from the ship?" one person asked as he stepped up and walked with Beth.

"Yeah. Why is that so hard to believe?"

The only woman of the four approached her opposite side. "Can you blame us? No word from the Celestus in over a year, repeated attacks by our former colleagues and friends. Then you show up out of nowhere. Wouldn't you be wary?"

"I guess none of us have had it easy." Beth did her best to soften her demeanor and sound more sympathetic. They walked out of the enormous dome and into one of the connecting tubes.

Beth jogged up to the leader, and he turned and spoke at her approach. "You've come at a critical time. Our food supplies are on strict rations, and these are our last four fully functional enviro suits. There are others, but they've either been rendered unusable from damage or malfunctioned with no explanation."

"You've had random equipment malfunctions?"

"Only with the envirosuits. The other gear sent down has been fine."

"That's interesting." Beth went quiet.

Did the admins sabotage more than one suit? Could it mean Morgan Sims wasn't chosen but simply picked up the wrong outfit? Still doesn't explain how he left the domes without authorization.

When they entered the smaller dome, the group passed through a series of airlocks designed to eliminate contaminants from coming inside the protected shelter. The leader called out Devin's name when they passed through the final gateway. Beth spotted him immediately as he raised his head and walked over to the group. Everyone else began taking off their helmets and removing the rest of their environmental protections, except for Beth.

"We have a visitor that wants to see you," the leader said.

"A visitor?" Devin cocked his head.

"Yeah, someone from the Celestus." The leader's announcement drew everyone's attention.

"Devin…" the word eked out from Beth's vocal projector at near a whisper. She didn't know what to say. She'd wanted this moment more than anything, and now that it had arrived, fear gripped every part of her.

I'm not the woman he loves anymore. I've become some mixture of his creation and my former self. His dreams of digital consciousness had manifested in her, but in a way, they'd taken her from him. Beth resisted the urge to shake her head as she warded off the self-doubt. She had to play the cards dealt, regardless of the consequences.

"Yeah, someone from the ship is here to talk to you," the leader said, almost as an offhand remark, as he walked over to a piece of machinery and inspected it. Beth didn't buy his act for one second. The leader had been incredibly standoffish since their encounter. Now, he'd positioned himself near enough to hear whatever it was she planned to say to Devin.

I need to watch what I say.

"You're from the ship? What's going on up there?" Devin rubbed his hands together with excited energy.

"Yes, I'm… my name is Heather. I worked with Beth."

"Worked?" Worry washed over his face like someone about to get the worst news of their life.

"She's ok. She's in cryostasis on the ship."

"Stars, that's so good to hear. After security evacuated us, I didn't know if I'd ever see her again. But she's really alright?"

"Yes, she's good, truly. Um, tell me." Beth glanced sideways toward Nicoles. He still hung around the same area, but another colonist had approached him and started a conversation. Beth lowered her voice. "Who's in charge here?"

Devin pointed a thumb at Nicoles. "That's Mr. Nicoles; he's one of the admins. Got evacuated with us when the infected cut off access to the admin section."

"None of the other admins are down here?"

"No."

That makes so much sense. He didn't send a message to the homeworld. He knows the other admins called a rescue team, which eventually will come to the colony. I'm sure it wasn't part of his plan to be caught down here, but he's wasted no time taking control. He can't be trusted. I need to speak to Devin alone. She glanced in Nicoles's direction again. He wasn't there. Scanning the central room, she didn't glimpse him anywhere, but noticed several open apertures to other dome sections.

Now's my chance.

"Miss?" Devin asked. He squinted his eyes and looked into her tinted helmet.

"I'm sorry. It's been a tough time for all of us." She said, returning her attention to him. He was so beautiful. It took all her willpower not to scoop him up and hold him until they both grew old. She wanted to tell him everything, the truth behind what she'd become, but she didn't have the time to explain it all. Not with an admin in charge, running his own agenda. She'd be able to fill him in later. "Look, we don't have a lot of time. Where's Sophie?"

"Sophie Wilkes? She's... She's being held in one of the other domes."

"Being held? Sounds like she's in prison."

"She was infected a few months ago in a raid. Rather than kill her, I convinced Mr. Nicoles to hold her for study. We have her in an emergency cryotube."

That's not great. At least she's alive, and I can get a temporary cure for her, eventually. "What about Liam and Alan?"

"Liam never made it off the ship, and Alan, well, he..." Devin looked confused, cocking his head at her. "How do you know them?"

"Beth and I are good friends. I need to get everyone off this planet and out of the system. The admins—"

"Heather, was it?" Devin crossed his arms and narrowed his eyes. "Beth never mentioned you to me, but somehow you know all her other friends."

"Devin, I don't have time to explain right now. I just need you to trust me." Beth reached out a hand toward him.

Devin took a step backward. "I'm going to need more of a reason than that. Why are you still wearing your envirosuit?"

Panic and urgency surged up Beth's spine.

I'm blowing this. Stars, Devin, just trust me.

"What are you not telling me?" Devin glanced toward the rack of weapons near the dome entrance.

Beth's mind raced. How would he trust her? Only one thing came to mind. Something that only the two of them would know. "We're… We're just two binary stars, held in endless orbit."

"What did you say? How do you know about that?" Devin's mouth hung open as his arms dropped to his sides.

"Beth told me before going into stasis. She needed you to know you can trust me."

"But she wouldn't have told anyone…." Devin's voice trailed off as his hand unconsciously scratched at his chest.

"I know. Not unless it was life and death. Now, will you please listen to me?"

Devin's head lifted. Sharp determination and conviction reflected in his eyes. "Tell me what's going on and how I can help."

Chapter 33

Beth stepped forward, put her gloved hand on the small of Devin's back, and guided him to the side of the dome near the entrance. She wanted to be as far from prying ears as possible. Shifting her gaze around one last time for any sign of Nicoles, she launched into her story when the coast appeared clear.

"The admins orchestrated the infection. Morgan Sims or some other victim was meant to encounter the organism and be brought back for study."

"That's..." Devin's mouth worked as he tried to find the right words.

"I know. Please let me finish." Beth shot a glance over her shoulder before continuing. "They sabotaged a bunch of the envirosuits, including the one Morgan wore. It's why there are only a few working ones down here."

Devin pressed his lips tightly together as Beth kept speaking. "The wave caused the Celestus outbreak and wasn't part of their plan; however, it became the plan when the ship became compromised. Right now, the rest of the admins are safe aboard some vessel out in the system, waiting to be picked up. They've deemed everyone expendable, according to the company's official accounts. The Celestus has already been reported as lost, and the ones coming are not here to rescue anyone except the people in charge who set it all in motion."

Beth stopped speaking and stared at him, waiting for a reply. Devin looked away and seemed to digest all the info. Then, after a few long seconds, he turned back and nodded. "Ok, let's say I believe you. What do we do?" He licked his lips before pressing them into a thin line again. Beth recognized the nervous habit. She completely understood how he felt, but didn't have the luxury of certainty to comfort him.

"Do you know about the Grove?" Beth asked.

"Yeah. It's quite a few miles away. We've been able to get some intel suggesting the infected are living there."

Nodding her helmeted head, Beth continued. "That's good. I want to start by rescuing them."

"I think we'd all like that. The problem is, we don't have the people or resources. Besides, they kill anyone they come in contact with."

"You have the resources now that I'm here. I have a temporary cure Beth developed. It won't last forever, and I don't know how well it will affect someone who's had the parasite in them for months or years, but it worked on all those aboard the Celestus. I want to sedate all the remaining infected, give them the cure, and secure them in cryostorage. Does the colony have enough emergency medical stasis chambers for all the missing people?"

"As a matter of fact, we do. We considered using them on rotation to reduce the wait time on rescue; however, the solar array needs to expand to keep them running full time," Devin said. "We've been on rationed power after an attack damaged it several months ago."

"Alright, they will be fine on batteries until we have them plugged in back on the ship. The next part is going to be more difficult." Beth glanced around again for Nicoles and spoke when she didn't spot him. "We need to destroy the Grove and all traces of the organism."

"Ok, but why?"

"The company used illegal human trials to develop the organism into an uncontrollable bioweapon. I have no doubt they will come back and continue working if any of it remains. I've been able to quell everyone on the ship long enough to freeze them. Mostly because it's a confined space. Imagine this getting loose on the homeworld. It would infiltrate everyone on the planet, and then there would be no going back. The admins only see their bottom line. They're missing the fact this is an alien parasite we know nothing about. And it's deadly."

"I see. It'll be difficult to convince Nicoles to go along with this if what you said is true," Devin said.

"I figured as much. How loyal is everyone to him?"

"Well, he's pretty much been in charge since we arrived. He's fought the infected when they attacked us. He's well-liked, to say the least."

"Damn. It's going to be impossible if he doesn't go along with the plan."

"What plan?" Nicoles casually strolled over to Devin and Beth.

Shit, how long has he been listening? "I want to capture the remaining infected. I've developed a temporary cure that will—"

"A temporary cure?" Nicoles interrupted. "What's the point if it's temporary?"

"The point is, they are friends and colleagues. They're still people, just sick," Beth shot back. She noticed several people in the dome had stopped what they were doing and approached to hear the conversation.

"And what then? When your 'cure' wears off, they'll attack us again? I don't know what you've been doing on the Celestus, but we've been stuck down here losing people the whole time." Nicoles crossed his arms and stood firm, like an unmovable monument.

Beth put her hands on her hips. She did her best to keep the anger out of her voice, yet inside she seethed. The admins had done the unthinkable, human experimentation, and this guy was one of them. "We've all lost friends; I'm trying to get some of them back. Once the cure takes effect, we get them into stasis and back to the Celestus, where I can start working on a way to purge the parasite permanently."

"Adler, you said your name was...? I remember where I heard that name before." Nicoles rubbed his chin.

"What?" Devin jerked his head toward Beth. She cringed and cursed herself for using her real name when she first met Nicoles.

Nicoles kept talking. "You were one of the first infected after the quarantine break. I remember your name on the list. So, are you taking this cure right now? Will it wear off?"

"No, I..." Beth muttered, not knowing how to answer.

"Huh?" Nicoles kept up the barrage of questions. "Is that why you're still wearing a suit? Are you contagious?"

"No. I'm not infected," she said with more force than she meant to.

"Who are you?" Devin asked.

"Your story isn't adding up. I think we'd all like to know exactly who you are and why you've only now come to rescue us." Nicoles stepped forward and jabbed a thick finger into her chest.

Beth brushed his hand away, refusing to back down. Showing weakness now might undermine her arguments, and with everyone watching, she had to look like a leader; she had to be strong. "It doesn't matter what my name is. I'm here to save the people out there, and all of you too—"

"Help is on the way. We don't need your saving," Nicoles said on top of her.

Beth shot glances at those gathered. Some of them nodded their agreement, while others seemed to wait to hear more. Devin had stepped away and looked at her with a worried face and arms crossed.

"Look, we've all lost people up there, down here, but we can save some of them. I've done it on the Celestus. Here, I can't do it alone. Help me save as many of our infected friends as possible. That's all I'm asking. Afterward, anyone who wants to go back to the ship can. And anyone who wants to stay, well, that's up to them."

The crowd murmured. Beth heard many of them mention lost companions and a desire to do something besides wait. Nicoles opened his mouth to speak, then hesitated as he seemed to take in their general desire to save everyone they could. He rubbed absently at the salt and pepper stubble on his chin. "Alright, we'll hear your plan. Though first, we need to establish some trust. Don't you agree, Devin?" Nicoles focused his attention on Beth's only ally.

"Yes, of course." Devin nodded curtly, not taking his eyes from Beth.

Beth cringed. She felt so stupid. Of course, she would have to take off her suit at some point. Easing into the surprise had been the plan, but she didn't feel ready.

I should have been honest with Devin from the start. With so much going on, she'd figured leaving her true identity out of things would make the rescue smoother. Instead, it had complicated her effort, and now Devin's trust waned.

"Tell us who you really are, and take off your helmet so we can verify it. Unless, of course, you're a danger to everyone here. Are you?" Nicoles recrossed his arms, assuming his signature statuesque pose. The intimidation tactic must have worked frequently. His enormous frame and deep, commanding voice were real assets in these situations. Still, Beth didn't feel intimidated. She knew she was stronger, faster, and likely, more intelligent than the man before her; however, standing up to him directly didn't seem like a winning strategy. His leadership position held because these people let it. Though the majority liked her idea of saving people, and they both knew it.

Beth looked right at Devin, "I'm Dr. Beth Adler." Then she stepped right up to Nicoles, who didn't flinch. "I'm not a danger to anyone." She unclipped her helm with dramatic flicks and pulled it off. The gasps rang out like a detective unmasking the suspect at the end of a mystery vid.

Chapter 34

"You're... you're a robot?" Nicoles dropped his arms to his sides and even stepped backward. His whole macho persona melted away, replaced with shock bordering on fear.

"Yeah, I am, and I'm here to save everyone I can. I just need your help if our friends out there are going to have a chance." Beth's vision shifted to Devin's face. His eyes narrowed as he attempted to understand.

"Devin, it worked. Your project is an unmitigated success, and I'm the proof." She spread her arms out, then let them drop to her sides. His jaw hung open, eyes wide, as the realization of what had occurred bloomed in his mind.

"I've got no reason to trust this thing and plenty not to." Nicoles drew the pistol from his hip and glanced around at those gathered, as if looking for approval from the crowd to proceed with an execution.

"Wait." Devin stepped in front of Beth, blocking Nicoles's approach.

"Get out of the way, Devin." Nicoles waved his gun to the side in a move-it-or-lose-it motion. "For all we know, this thing killed the doctor before assuming her identity."

"I know that isn't true. This robot is offering to help us rescue our fellow crew. I think we need to hear what she has to say."

Nicoles shook his head. "All the bots went haywire. You know that! Now, this one's claiming to be a crew member? We need to dismantle it before it harms us."

"Yes, some of the robots short-circuited, but you're assuming they all did. We disabled them as a precaution years ago, right after evacuation. Any still operating must have survived whatever affected the ones down here." Devin shifted his attention to those gathered. "I'm telling you, we can trust this one. She came here to help."

"Aw, that's all bullshit, and you know it!" Nicoles moved forward, but Devin pushed him back with a stiff arm to the chest. His lips curled back as if he might shoot Devin to get to Beth.

"I know Dr. Adler was working on a cure when everyone evacuated the ship. It sounds like she succeeded, and now the Celestus is free of infestation and safe to return to," Devin said.

"That's correct," Beth said. "I've given those infected a temporary cure that surpasses the parasite, and they're in cryostasis. I'd like to do the same for those from the colony."

Another wave of murmurs washed over the stranded colonists. Nicoles stood statuesque, glaring at Beth, ignoring Devin completely.

"Let's save our friends!" came a cry from the crowd. Other voices join, a few in protest, not wanting to trust the stranger. Still, most supported Beth, calling for the rescue of their compatriots.

"What's it going to be?" Beth stared, eyeless, at Nicoles.

Nicoles shifted his gaze back and forth, and his jaw tightened. He'd lost this battle. "Alright, alright." He threw his hands up in the air. "We'll hear out this plan of yours, but I'm making no promises. I have a duty to protect the people who aren't lost. And don't think for one second I trust you."

Devin stepped aside as Beth put a hand on his shoulder and came forward. "You have anti-riot gear with injection guns down here, I presume?"

"I uh… sure, though no sedatives," Nicoles said.

"That's not a problem. I have more than enough of the cure back at my shuttle. How about ground transport? We will need to head to the Grove."

A woman dressed in dirty coveralls stepped forward. "We haven't tried any of the gadabouts in months, but they should work. If it's alright, I'll go start 'em up, make sure they aren't gonna quit on us halfway out there."

Nicoles gave a curt nod to her, then readdressed Beth. "Even with this cure of yours, how are we going to subdue all of them long enough to get them back to cryo?"

"A powerful sedative is in the mixture. Unfortunately, it will take some minutes to work, so I propose a strike and retreat tactic. I'm hoping someone from security will handle the tactical details."

Nicoles cleared his throat. "That's all well and good, but 'some minutes' is pretty vague. If you didn't know, those things are powerful. We've suffered devastating losses just defending ourselves here. To go on the offensive... I don't like it at all. We need concrete information."

"What do you suggest?" Beth asked.

"We have someone you can test your cure on."

"Sophie..." Beth whispered the name.

Devin must have heard and laid a hand on her back. She saw his eyes searching her face. She knew the seamless, oval, metallic head lacked features. Still, it made her feel like he was trying to meet her gaze.

"Take me to her."

* * *

Nicoles slipped his envirosuit back on with practiced ease. A few others followed his lead, including Devin. Then he led all those protected out of the habitation dome and back into the large central one. They passed through it and entered the tunnel to one of the other small domes. Beth remembered seeing the damage to its structure when she did a flyover.

How would they hold anything in here?

Inside, she got her answer. A box of welded metal plates and bars sat at the far side. She approached the cage and peered into the darkened interior. A form, humanoid, though otherwise unrecognizable, lay curled up in the back.

"Is she alive?" The words had barely left Beth's mouth when the figure lunged into motion like a coiled snake. Long, unkempt, bestial nails from a dirty human reached through the bars and raked across Beth's face. Forgetting little could easily hurt her metal body, she toppled backward onto her butt, scooting away as the prison rattled with the threat of collapse.

"I've never seen a robot get scared by anything. Interesting," Nicoles said. Beth could hear the sneer in his voice. "Don't worry, the cage will hold. This one has certainly tested it plenty."

Beth picked herself up. "I heard the same about the quarantine chamber." She let the comment sit and pulled out a syringe from her belt. Then she hesitated.

Oh, Sophie, I'm so sorry this happened. I'm going to take care of you. Don't worry. Steeling her resolve, she approached the writhing creature as it tried to force its body through the bars. Beth reached out with mechanical speed and strength, snatched Sophie's arm, and jabbed it with the needle. She released her grip just as quickly and stepped back before anyone in the room, Sophie included, could react. Beth whipped her head toward Nicoles. "There, she's been injected. Are you watching the time?"

Nicoles gaped for several seconds before pulling out his personal tablet and checking the time. Sophie recoiled and clawed at the spot where the needle entered, while Beth, with arms crossed, stood close enough to observe any behavioral change. Before she'd become one with her mechanical body, she'd apparently done this act dozens of times. It would have been much more dangerous as a flesh and blood human, but she'd had the advantage of being infected at the time and blending in as one of their kind. Unfortunately, she didn't remember any of it, and her recorded message had been vague on how she'd actually subdued all the infected aboard.

After just a couple of minutes, Sophie stopped thrashing against her prison, and her hyperventilating breaths settled. "How long?" Beth asked.

"Just over three minutes," Nicoles replied. "But she can't b—"

"The fight's gone from her. The sedative is taking effect and the parasite loosing its hold. It can't focus any real energy on manipulating its host." At best, it was an educated guess and, at worst, a blatant and dangerous lie. Still, Beth couldn't risk giving Nicoles any reason to doubt her plan. She had only the vaguest of ideas about what her cure was doing to the organism. All she knew was it kept the parasite in check for a time.

"How long until she's herself again?" Devin asked.

"It varies, but if she's been this way a while... I'm not sure. Still, I think it's worth monitoring her until she's coherent. Obviously, it's not a problem for the organism to keep its host alive in this environment. However, with it suppressed, I'm concerned Sophie will not live long without an envirosuit." Beth said.

"The atmosphere is breathable. You just won't want to be in it for very long, say, more than a few hours." Devin said.

"That's good to know." Beth turned to address Nicoles, who stood, arms crossed, in glaring observation of the proceedings. "Have your men move one of the mobile cryotubes here, so we don't have to transport her far."

A grunt met her request.

"Is there something else?" If she'd had eyebrows, they'd be raised in a questioning, do-something-about-it way. She wondered if she needed to adjust her tone to compensate for lack of body language, but decided against it. Her identity revelation had shaken something in

Nicoles. He still tried his hard-nosed approach to her, but there was a loss of confidence underneath it.

He might just be willing to go along with my plans, after all. I can't count on it, though.

Nicoles shook his head. "No, no. This will be fine. Anders, Celia, do as the robot says and bring a cryotube here. Make sure the rest of them are loaded on the transports. If that's alright with you, that is?" The last part he addressed directly to Beth. His tone came across as both cooperative and condescending at the same time.

"You've got the idea." Beth turned away from him dismissively and spoke to Devin. "I'd like to do a flyby of the Grove. Would you come with me?"

"Yeah. I'll do that." He didn't even glance in Nicoles's direction.

Beth didn't have to look at him to know he'd oppose the idea, but what could he say or do now, in front of other colonists?

I think his hold over them isn't as secure as he wishes.

Devin and Beth boarded the shuttle in silence and strapped into the two cockpit seats.

Once they settled, Devin put his hand on Beth's leg as he leaned in close to her. "Is it really you, Beth? Tell me this isn't a trick,"

"It's me, Dev. Your project made this all possible. Without it, I'd be..." Beth looked away and let the silence speak for itself.

Why is it so hard to face him?

"I... I'm so sorry. What you must have gone through... Beth... I don't..." He seemed to lose the words.

"I know... It's not how either of us imagined this going. Actually, I was running around the ship for a long time before I knew what became of me." Beth spotted a figure in a suit exit the small dome near the landing pad. It could only be Nicoles. He stopped just outside the airlock and gawked at the shuttle. "Time to go." Booting up the starting sequence and activating the lift-thrusters sent dust swirling upward, obscuring the figure near the structure.

Chapter 35

As the vessel lifted into the air, Devin stared into Beth's face and took her hand. She felt the pressure of his touch, but could only imagine the peel of the small calluses on his engineer's hands. "You really didn't know? How is that possible?" he asked.

Beth shrugged. "Admittedly, I ignored some obvious signs and chalked them up to a malfunctioning envirosuit and the idea I'd been given some serious drugs to stop the parasite in me. Still, it's strange how much I feel like myself. I feel like I'm breathing, smiling, blinking, and even smelling the artificial materials in this cockpit, but none of the sensation is real. It's all in my head."

"That's incredible!" He pulled away as he slapped his forehead with an open palm. "I noticed the mice in my experiment smelled and tasted the digital food I placed in their simulation, but it seemed too unbelievable. I'd been so preoccupied with getting the transference bugs worked out I'd done almost no experimentation on the fully digital ones. It makes sense, though. Signals are signals whether they're running through a physical object like a processor or a brain, or a digital platform like a program—"

"Or a consciousness." Beth finished his thought.

He blinked, and his eyes softened. "Yeah…" One side of his mouth turned up in a smile of pure love and admiration.

"The mind is an incredible thing." Beth grew quiet as she focused her attention on the piloting instructions provided by her augment. She saw Devin's attention switch between her and the landscape outside.

"How long have you…" He let the question hang.

"Been legally dead? Or in this body?" She kept her eyes looking straight ahead, finding it difficult to look at him.

Am I ashamed of what I've become?

"Both, I suppose."

Beth's shoulders slumped as she let out a non-existent sigh. "When I woke up in your room, I found a skeleton next to me. I didn't know it was the last remains of my body until days later. The parasite breaks down all soft tissue over time. Likely faster after death."

"Oh, my stars, Beth. I'm so sorry. That... that had to be awful." He reached for her, placing his hand on her arm. She couldn't feel it, lacking pressure plates there, but in her mind, she sensed the warmth of his comfort. It meant everything.

"It *was* scary, but I had no idea it was me lying there. I thought I'd used the temporary cure until just a few days ago. I'm missing a lot of memories from the past couple years, but I've pieced most of it together through the various tablets I came across on the ship. Surprisingly, I accomplished quite a lot while suppressing the organism. I feel like I spent my entire robotic existence putting together the pieces of a puzzle I'd nearly finished before."

The shuttle rumbled and jerked as it encountered a clash of atmospheric temperatures. She compensated by ascending higher in elevation, giving her a long view of the area. The choppy, barren landscape passed like frozen ocean waves. Silence stretched for a couple of minutes before she spoke again. "So, what have you been up to since I last saw you?"

"Wow, where to begin..." he let out a small chuckle.

"Let's start from when security dragged you out of my room right in the middle of recording critical information."

"Right... Well, they took me and several others to one of the shuttle bays for evacuation to the colony. On our way, the things attacked us from behind. I didn't see much of what happened—a bunch of yelling. Someone said run, and I didn't ask questions. My group made it to a shuttle and left the ship."

"What did you mean in your message that I might be the only hope?"

"You were working on a cure, and the last time we spoke, you'd made some promising progress, but then you got infected."

"So, how did I get free? I don't remember anything after security stunned me. I woke up in this body in your room, and that's all I remember."

"It was Liam's doing. He picked up where you left off and found your serum suppressed the organism. With Sophie's help to get past security, we injected you with it. There were a few scattered infected at the time, but security had mostly confined them to isolated parts of the ship. We thought demonstrating a working suppressant would restore order."

"But it didn't."

"No, I'm not sure why, but right after, things went sideways fast. One minute we're told the situation is under control; the next, everyone is being evacuated."

"That sounds like a change of objectives by the admins."

"It might've been."

Beth nodded. She focused on the shuttle operations for the next few minutes, locating the Grove and setting the course into the autopilot. Devin remained quiet, seemingly aware she needed to process everything he'd said. She'd always appreciated his ability to pick up on her state of mind. Finally, when she'd finished locking in a direction, she spoke again. "What happened to the colony? When did Nicoles take charge?"

"Things were chaotic, to say the least. People didn't take well to being trapped on the planet, especially anyone who planned to spend the entire expedition on the Celestus. Nicoles came down on a transport about a day after I arrived. He was clearly pissed about being here, but no one was happy, so I didn't think too much of it. Anyway, he basically took charge within an hour of arriving. The timing was right. Everyone was scared, and no one knew what to do. So here comes someone who seemed to have a plan and assured us a rescue was already in the works."

"A few lies and an intimidating stance is all it takes, I suppose."

"To his credit, he took charge and fought at the front when we had an outbreak amongst us. A few people brought down from the ship had been unknowingly infected, and well, you can imagine how it went. Without his leadership, we might not have survived it."

"So, he's more than a guy in a suit used to sitting in a boardroom; he can actually back it up."

* * *

Over the next twenty minutes, Beth and Devin exchanged stories of the events on the ship and planet since they became separated. Eventually, Devin pointed to a discoloration tucked between two mountains near the distant horizon. "That's the Grove there." Beth made a slight course change and took the shuttle closer to the ground. A few minutes later, a lush jungle of purple and green flora came into clear view. Beth recognized some plants as those she saw in the bioengineering labs. Many of the growths resembled tentacled creatures sticking out of tumorous lumps.

After several flybys, each closer to the tops of the tree-like excrescence, they'd spotted no infected humans. "Do you think they're dead?" Beth asked.

"I don't think so. We had an attack just a couple of weeks ago. The self-disintegration you described doesn't seem to happen to them in this environment. I saw a report from an early geological survey showing some caves at the base of one of these mountains. They may be sheltering there."

"Then we'll have to draw them out. It's going to be risky, though."

"What's your plan?"

"I want to burn the whole Grove to the ground. Not only should it force them out of cover and toward our ground forces, but it will prevent Nicoles or anyone else from accessing these plants in the future."

"Wow, that's not like you. Wiping out entire species just like that?"

"You've seen what it leads to. If it's left here, someone from the company will be back, or someone else will come. The organism spreads too fast in humans to be effectively controlled. If some of it got loose, it could wipe out an entire planet."

"That's a lot of ifs," Devin said.

"Are you suggesting I should let it go? Hope for the best?"

"No. Like you said, we've both seen what comes from exposure. You have more first-hand experience than anyone. I just want to make sure you've thought it through." He gave her a reassuring squeeze of the hand.

She imagined it must feel weird to him, clutching the cold, stiff, metallic fingers of this new body of hers. Still, it showed what mattered was the person inside. "I have given it a lot of thought. The administrators, including Nicoles, purposely infected the first human. It was all calculated. The wave altered their plans, but that just means we're all expendable. I have the proof."

Beth watched Devin's gaze dance around her smooth, metallic face, searching for her eyes. He shook his head. "I can't believe they would *all* conspire against us. How would they get away with it?"

Chapter 36

Beth removed the data storage device she'd ripped from the cat's body and held it up. "They've been spying on us the whole time." She inserted the chip into the shuttle's console, then adjusted the ship to autopilot back towards the colony. With a few inputs on the playback controls, she accessed the recorded video logs. Thousands upon thousands of hours appeared. She selected the last one, then set it at ten minutes before the cat went offline. It felt a little weird watching the scene from the cat's perspective near the floor, but the shot was perfect. She and Devin observed herself access the last message transmitted from the homeworld.

"... set it in a stable orbit. All crew is considered expendable. We have already dispatched a team to infiltrate and take back the Celestus, secure the samples, and subdue any uninfected crew. The team will also retrieve your shuttle and stasis capsules at point Alpha. Good luck to you all. See you in eight years."

Beth let the video play up through the part where she caught the feline spy, then shut it off. "I haven't had time to look through any of this, but I do not doubt the things the cat recorded would shock us."

"The cat?" Devin raised an eyebrow.

"Oh, yeah, I'm sorry. Do you remember seeing a black cat around the ship belonging to an admin?"

"Yeah, I saw it a couple of times."

"It wasn't alive. It was a surveillance bot. Totally unassuming and able to get to places we wouldn't expect, to record conversations or immortalize what the breakout of a deadly infestation might look like," Beth said.

"Stars..."

"The admins had a sinister plot from the beginning. I don't think the

186

wave causing ship-wide failures factored into their plans, but they're running with it, and we're all casualties of progress."

Devin went quiet while he took in all the information. Beth gave him the time he needed to wrap his head around what she'd shown him and what she had proposed.

"I take it you have a plan for burning the Grove," Devin said after a few minutes.

"Yes, and I'm sure Nicoles won't like it." Beth reengaged control of the shuttle and continued to the colony. "How's the fuel supply back at the domes?"

"There's a lot of it. No one has been using any vehicles, and we've got no working shuttles."

"Good. I need the colonists to hook up some extra fuel tanks to this shuttle under the guise I'm taking an extended fly-around since we didn't see any infected. However, I'm going to dump all the extra fuel over the Grove instead."

"And torch the whole thing." Devin nodded.

"But not until the right moment. I'll light it up when the vehicles are in position near the perimeter. Hopefully, that will bring out our lost people, and it'll be up to everyone to secure them."

"Nicoles might go berserk when he sees it."

"No doubt, but I'm looking forward to his explanation of why we should preserve the outbreak's source." Beth took the shuttle down and landed on the pad she had before. She and Devin exited and returned to the dome to meet with everyone else.

Nicoles must have had someone watching for them because he approached the moment they entered the secure area past the airlocks. "So, did you spot them?"

"We didn't." Beth raised her voice so that others could hear her. "I need some engineers to attach a couple of extra fuel tanks to my shuttle. After that, I will do an extended search of the area to locate our missing people." Several volunteers raised their hands. Then, turning her attention away from Nicoles, Beth said, "Good, suit up, and we'll get started."

Nicoles stepped in front of her view. "Dr... whoever you are. I think you forget that I'm in charge of this entire operation and have a responsibility to everyone on this planet."

"Not at all. If you have a better plan to rescue everyone, I'd be the first one ready to try it." Beth did her best to stare him down. His eyes narrowed slightly, but his thin-lipped expression of cold indifference didn't betray his feelings.

"That's all well and good, but I think you'd better share this sound plan of yours with me and the rest of us. So far, it lacks details. I won't risk the lives of these survivors for one infinitesimal chance at rescuing a few lost crew members. Your serum might work fast, but it still gives those things plenty of time to ravage us."

"That's why the vehicles and my shuttle are important. Once we have their attention, we have to stay ahead of them long enough for the cure and sedative to take effect. Then, once they are all down, we seal them in stasis for transport back to the ship. Having some long-term infected in cryo will no doubt be of help in finding a cure, among other applications."

Nicoles's chin moved up and down as his tight mouth worked through his thoughts. He probably wanted nothing to do with her rescue, but handing over more specimens to the company might make him look impressive in their eyes. Beth could almost feel the conflict inside him, though he seemed intent on hiding it. "Fine, you can proceed, but only until I say differently."

"Of course, thank you." Beth turned from him to those around the dome. "Alright, let's get this shuttle some fuel." The engineers suited up, and she followed them outside to begin the work.

Nicoles doesn't like the plan and doesn't trust me, so he must want the infected crew for specimens particularly badly. If he had any idea how many were aboard the Celestus, already in cryo, he'd probably come up with an excuse to abandon the ones down here.

* * *

Several hours later, Beth took off in the modified shuttle and headed toward the Grove. Partway to her destination, out of view of the domes, she pulled back on the controls. The ship ascended out of the thin atmosphere into space. It took her a couple of minutes, following the guided instructions, to locate the Celestus with her scanners. Twenty minutes later, she coasted into the empty docking bay. She didn't stay aboard long, just enough time to load the shuttle with as many envirosuits as she could find from the adjacent sections. Then she took off and headed down to the planet.

She made her way to the Grove, then, flying low, engaged the fuel dump. A spray of yellow mist filled the air and settled gradually on the tropical expanse. Monitoring the levels, she left herself barely enough to return to the colony.

I've got to make sure every inch of this place burns. Nothing can be left.

When she landed a couple of hours later, night had fallen. Rather than go back in, she stayed on the ship and browsed the cat's recordings to pass the time.

Shortly after the sun broke the horizon, a group of five suited people approached her shuttle. She opened the back hatch and met them. When one stepped forward and spoke, she recognized Nicoles's voice.

"We've had a problem with repairing the remaining suits. These are all the working ones. I don't think we've enough people to mount a full rescue, but if we save a few—"

"I anticipated that, and brought down plenty of spare suits for everyone. Besides, we will need all of them when we evacuate to the ship afterward."

Nicoles didn't have a reply. Instead, he stood there like a statue, unmoving, while Beth took the initiative. "I could use some help unloading these while I refuel the shuttle. How many vehicles are ready to go?"

"Now, wait. I'm—"

Beth cut him off again. "You do want to rescue as many as possible, correct?"

Nicoles crossed his arms over his chest and stood back on his heels. "Of course, they are part of our crew and our friends."

Beth could hear the sugar-coated lie, even through his suit's speaker. He didn't want to do this. He'd be happy with a couple of samples and to oblivion with the rest of them. His mistake had been to bring other people out here with him who wouldn't take kindly to him backing down without sound reasoning.

"Good. Once everyone is suited and armed, I'll distribute the cure to those with the inoculators. Then we can leave on your orders." She was just submissive enough to give orders without looking like she was in charge. At least, she hoped that was the case.

An hour later, Devin joined her in the shuttle. "You've got everyone pretty excited about this operation. We've had little to hope for since arriving. I'd just be careful with how much authority you throw around. There are a few people completely loyal to Nicoles. I'd expect some serious trouble after this is all over," he said as he strapped in.

"I've hopefully got a plan for that too, but yeah, for now, everyone seems eager to go along with what I'm suggesting, since I think most of them have lost friends. But in the end... I don't know."

"I hate to say it, but being in a robot's body gives them some ammunition. With all the robots going haywire after the wave, it will be difficult for them to trust you. I'm honestly surprised how quickly they've accepted your plan. I expect Nicoles to turn the tables the moment this is over, maybe sooner."

"If it comes to that, I don't want you in the crossfire."

"Ha! Nice try, Beth. I've been wracked with guilt ever since they forced me off the station and away from you. I feel like I abandoned you even still. It won't happen this time. I don't care what Nicoles tries. I love you, Beth."

Beth nodded, and her shoulders slumped as she went through the motions of a sigh. "I love you too, Devin." She wanted to cry. The tears felt just a breath away, but they would never come. They were light-years in the past and out of reach forever.

Chapter 37

As the shuttle lifted off, Beth observed five rectangular vehicles, each with four massive wheels, leave the largest dome. The front of the gadabouts sat lower than the rest, with a steeply curved window meeting where the main body began. The raised panels and bumped-out sections covered the body in a random pattern. She identified one as a top hatch and another as a reinforced side door with a small square window. As she'd hoped, the people inside could fire cure-filled darts from those openings with relative safety.

Flying ahead, Beth and Devin landed on a ridge overlooking the Grove and the lowland approach where the ground forces would appear. In the early morning light, the barrens, and verdant jungle lay in a hush; no breeze picked up dust nor rustled the viny, dark tendrils.

Soon, the shuttle's sensors picked up the approach of the gadabouts. When Beth spotted the first one, she maneuvered the shuttle to the far side of the Grove. The fire needed to start there to push the infected into the trap. Devin ran a final area scan to see if any infected lurked about in the foliage as they flew over.

"Things seem clear. They must still be underground. I'm concerned we've spotted no one between our two visits, though," Devin said.

"Me, too." Beth went quiet as she faced the ship toward the incoming gadabouts and set it to hover. She and Devin watched the vehicles approach through a narrow draw into the wide, flat barrens just beyond the sheltered valley of lush nightmares. She didn't wait for them to get into position, but started strafing the jungle with the shuttle's laser cannons. The landscape burst into flame, followed quickly by an echoing scream ringing through the air. A thousand other voices joined its haunting call as the fire spread.

"Oh, stars! The infected are in the jungle!" Beth turned to Devin, her

191

horror masked by her faceless visage.

"Impossible! They didn't appear on any of the sensors." he hunched closer to the sensor readouts, scrutinizing them. "Unless further mutations eliminate all heat from their body, it's not possible we missed them."

"I've made a huge mistake." Beth clenched her teeth and sucked in a deep breath; her chest rose to complete the imitated actions. Her head dropped into her hands.

I should have been more thorough. How could I...? Devin's hand found hers and pulled it down. She felt him squeeze it; the act calling her attention to him. His mouth sank, downcast with worried eyes.

"We couldn't have known." He shook his head. "You at least gave us hope. All these infected people were considered enemies to be killed on sight until you came along. You've been through so much already, but you shouldn't be hard on yourself, Beth. You're the smartest, hardest working person I know. Even when things go wrong, you always have a plan. If we don't save anyone today, we're no worse off than before. At least the Grove will be reduced to ash, and those who survive have a chance now. You've given me, all of us, that chance."

Seeing Devin's earnest face and hearing the love in his voice, Beth felt like she'd fallen into a dream state. She'd longed for those things for hours and days, as far back as she could remember, but the hurt and relief went deeper. She knew she'd been surrounded by things threatening to kill her for almost two years. Yet, even without the memories, something inside her felt her companion's absence for all that time. "Stars, I've missed you." She put her other hand on his. "Let's look for survivors and save everyone we can."

Devin nodded sharply.

She took the shuttle out of hover and strafed back and forth across the jungle. The high-pitched whines continued, though they originated from in front of them, near the fire's edge, and waned away in the charred landscape behind. "It's... It's the plants," Beth said, relief filling her voice.

"What?"

"The plants are making the sound. It's not our people."

"I... I think you're right. That's so creepy." Devin shuddered as the discordant screams of the flora echoed down the valley. Then, suddenly, his attention shifted to the sensors.

"What is it?" Beth asked, noticing his abrupt action.

"I've got movement on the infrared, coming from the caves."

"Thank the stars!" Beth's body stiffened as she threw her head back into the seat.

"They're holding position near the entrance. I'm transferring the image to your HUD."

"Alright, let's give them a little push." Adjusting the shuttle's course, Beth flew it in low toward the signatures. The fire hadn't reached the cave, but the horrific screams had alerted the infected to the danger. Taking careful aim, several dozen yards away from the people, she fired the ship's turret, laying down a new scorching line.

"Uh oh, they're coming this way."

"Shit, yeah, I can see it." Beth pulled back on the stick, taking the shuttle higher. Something bumped up against the bottom of the vessel, rocking it. Devin and Beth exchanged looks. "Okay, that was too close to the ground. Where are they now? I'm not seeing them anymore."

"Behind us. They're following." Devin said.

"That's better than expected. Now let's just hope Nicoles doesn't call the whole thing off after seeing the fire. You should get in position to help inoculate them."

"Okay. Wish me luck. I haven't fired a gun in a decade." Devin unstrapped himself, leaned over, kissed Beth on the head, then moved to the back of the ship. Beth felt the pressure of his lips, but the warmth and authentic feel were missing. Still, he'd shown little hesitation with her new form, which meant everything.

After a couple of minutes, the shuttle crossed over the line between the Grove and the lifeless wastes. Ahead, five vehicles waited patiently. Beth overshot them, then came around in a wide bank. Activating the universal communication channel, she made an announcement. "Alright, we're in position, and they are right behind us."

"You lit the entire place on fire!" the strained voice of Nicoles hissed over her headset.

"Unfortunately necessary," Beth replied. "Repeated attempts to draw their attention and rouse them from the caves failed. I needed something more persuasive." She waited for his angry reply or the whole thing to be called off, but the next voice came from one of the other crew.

"I've spotted them. They're exiting the trees now."

"Alright, everyone, keep moving and take your time with the shots," Nicoles said. "We've got limited ammo. We don't want those things catching us."

Beth switched over to the private channel between her and Devin.

"That was surprisingly cooperative."

"Overall, Nicoles has helped to keep us alive. He must be an ex-soldier and used his experience to gain everyone's confidence. He might stick with the plan now, but when this is all over... well, just be ready for anything."

The vehicles roared forward, then separated in five different directions. A swarm of over thirty individuals exited the Grove and tore across the flats. Beth punched the throttle. The charging mass stretched itself from a clumped pack into a crooked line as they ignored the airborne machine for the more vulnerable land-craft.

"Hold on to something," Beth said to Devin. The shuttle surged ahead, high over the top of their quarry. Beth pulled the controls to the left, sending the craft into a sideways air-slide, and dove low until they cruised just a few yards above the cracked surface. She set up a course parallel to the line of targets. Slam! The shuttle shook as it skipped off the ground. Beth's hands scrambled as she pulled the shuttle skyward. "I'm sorry, are you alright?"

"Shit, Beth, what happened?"

"I got too close to the ground. The mod works so well, I got a little cocky with the piloting."

"Yeah, okay. Let's keep some distance, anyway. We've seen how far those things can jump."

"You got it." Beth brought the shuttle back around for another flyby attempt, this time keeping the craft at least a dozen yards away from the surface. Devin's shots would be more challenging, but it meant a lower risk of unwanted boarders or a fatal piloting error. With the near-crash, they only had enough time for two passes before the infected would reach the retreating vehicles. Their speed stunned Beth.

The organism has continued to mutate them. Could being in the Grove accelerate it? Will the cure be enough now? Mostly, they still looked human, but inside both body and mind, they were drastically altered, more feral, aggressive, and sporadic in their movements.

Beth completed the first pass. "How did it go?" She asked Devin.

"No hits. They're too nimble."

"Damn, alright—one more pass. I'll swing in behind. That way, they won't be able to dodge as easily."

"Okay. I take it back. I think we need to be lower for me to have any chance."

Doing as instructed, Beth maneuvered the shuttle dangerously close to the ground, focusing all her attention on the surface variation. She also slowed their approach as shooting a moving target while flying at full speed would challenge a trained sniper, let alone a cybernetics engineer.

"Got one!" Devin called out.

"Nice!" The shuttle rocked suddenly. Beth knew immediately they'd been boarded.

Chapter 38

She threw the ship into auto-hover, not bothering to adjust their vulnerable height, then unclipped her straps and launched herself into the rear cabin. Devin ducked and dodged behind a bolted-down swivel chair while a feral human tore chunks of its padding away.

"Help!" he called out, but Beth was already in motion. She dove onto the creature, taking it to the floor. It lashed out, kicking her off. Beth flew backward; her balance lost as she stumbled toward the shuttle's open side. Her weight went down on a foot suspended in air. She tumbled out of the vehicle as her hand found a loose cargo strap flapping in the wind.

The strap snapped taut as it caught her weight. She swung underneath the vessel and back again as her momentum slowed. Hand over hand, she started climbing back up when something latched onto her left leg. An infected bit down on her calf, its teeth cutting right through the envirosuit. Beth saw the surprise in its face as its maw found a solid metal limb. She kicked with all her might, flinging the attacker off. It landed on the ground in a puff of loose, dry soil. Their presence had attracted plenty of attention already, as more of the infected turned their gaze on the low-hanging vehicle. "Take us up!" Beth yelled into her com, hoping Devin could get away from his attacker long enough to lock himself in the cockpit.

With haste, Beth pulled herself up the strap until her head popped over the edge of the shuttle floor. Right before her, the infected swung at Devin as he shot it with the inoculation gun. It knocked the weapon from his hand and lunged forward at the same time Beth heaved herself forward and reached out. She latched onto its ankle, stopping its attack. Devin met Beth's eyeless gaze and charged at the suddenly distracted creature, slamming into it with his shoulder. The act offset

196

its only solid foot enough that Beth's simultaneous tug sent the thing out into the open air. Seconds later, Devin had her hands as he helped haul her back inside.

"That was too close." Beth pulled Devin in tight. She might be difficult to injure, but any of these things would tear him apart with ease.

"I'm alright," he said. "You?"

"Fine. I'm pretty indestructible at this point." However, she recalled what Morgan Sims had done to M.E.R.C.Y, the medical robot, back at the beginning of this whole thing. Her strength, speed, and durability might be enhanced, but the infected could boast similar improvements. Still, she didn't want him to worry about her.

The two of them entered the cockpit together. Beth sat down and took the shuttle to a much higher hover.

"This doesn't look good." Devin pointed to an overturned vehicle in the middle of the swarm. Other cars circled far outside their disabled comrade as the gunners took shots at the mass of attackers.

"Strap in." Beth ignored her own advice as she drove the craft toward the action, and Devin secured his belt with a moment of panicked fumbling. The ship cut low, barreling through a small group of the infected at a controlled speed. They bounced off the front like electron particles off a ray shield. Cutting the throttle, she put the shuttle down with a rough slam next to the tipped gadabout. "Come with me, but keep your distance from those things." She handed him her inoculation gun as they exited the cockpit.

If I can keep them busy, it'll give everyone else a chance to take them down. Devin held his position in the doorway while Beth jumped out and ran the short distance to the disabled land-craft.

Four infected lashed out at the gadabout, trying to gain entry. A dart flew past Beth, landing in the butt of one attacker. It turned, noticed her, and charged.

Good, come at me. She waved a mocking hand its way. The mutant leaped, and she met it with a fist to the face, laying it out. "Didn't expect that, did ya?" Beth switched her attention to the others ripping their way into the vehicle. Then, picking up a hefty stone from the ground, she hurled it. The rock struck dead on, flinging the target onto the other side of the car, out of sight.

The remaining two snarled with gaping mouths and wild eyes as they surged at her in a berserker rage. Another dart zipped by, but the intended target flinched sideways, avoiding its sting.

Devin wasn't kidding; these things are fast. She barely had time to think before the first one lunged in, leading the way with all four limbs. Beth did her own sidestep. The infected's momentum took it past her as its flailing arms and legs swung madly. Beth brought her foot around, clocking it in the back of the head. Its body somersaulted in the air before landing face-first in the dirt. In her peripheral vision, she spotted Devin's approach. From point-blank range, he sank a dart into the prone creature.

Beth nodded to him as a massive weight slammed into her leg, taking her down. The remaining attacker bashed its fists into her side as it tore away at her suit. A dart sprouted from its shoulder, then another from the top of its head. The thing lashed out with unchained fury. As Beth tried pushing it off, it grabbed hold of the helmet attachment-ring around her neck. It wrenched her up by the neck with uncanny strength and speed, then repeatedly slammed her head down. Beth felt no pain, but that didn't mean no damage. Her vision blurred. Devin's voice rang out in her ears from nearby. She could just make out a figure beside her, kicking at the creature threatening to tear her apart.

Beth pulled her legs up as far as possible, then pushed out with her shins and feet. The maneuver partially dislodged her attacker. She couldn't tell precisely what Devin was doing, but it looked like he bashed the thing with the butt of his rifle. Regardless, the infected's attack subsided enough for her to sit up. She tried standing but only got to her knees before falling over. Her right leg, the one initially struck by the creature, refused to straighten.

"I need help. I can't see or stand," she called out. A blur of motion told her Devin had his hands full with fending off the creature's attacks. The crunch of tires from behind came as a welcome relief. The next thing she knew, two more blurry figures joined Devin, and together they laid the infected still.

"Are you alright?" Devin asked as his silhouette knelt beside her.

"That thing messed up my vision when it slammed my head, and I think my knee joint is busted."

"Damn, let me see if I can fix your eyes. Lay back." Devin opened a compartment on the side of Beth's head after she settled down.

"Maybe you should just get out of here. This is not safe."

"We're okay for the moment. Reinforcements have arrived, and your serum is kicking in on the first ones injected." Devin turned his face away from her and spoke to someone else. "Hey, get me a tool kit from out of that vehicle."

Someone did as he asked because Devin went to work on Beth's open head a few seconds later. "Okay, this isn't a big deal. I was worried it cracked your lens reflectors, but I see a loose connection here." Suddenly, Beth's vision snapped back, clear as the sky.

"That did it," she said. "Here, help me up."

Devin closed up her skull access panel and put her arm over his shoulders. Together, they got her to a standing position. She looked down at her right leg with clear vision. The snug but pliable suit showed the drastic bend at her knee. "It looks like the hit locked my knee in this position. I can't move it at all."

"Damn, probably clipped the motor connectors as well," Devin said. "Can you keep yourself up?"

"Yeah, now that I know I can't put my full weight on this leg."

Devin bent down and felt her knee through the material. From the corner of her vision, she glimpsed three people approaching the shuttle. She didn't need to look closely to know one of them was Nicoles. "Devin! Nicoles is after the shuttle!" He and Beth both started toward the ship, but Devin stopped immediately, as Beth could only hobble or hop on one foot. She'd never make it in time.

"You can't catch him like this. I'll go," Devin said, turning away from her.

He has no chance alone. Damnit, Beth, think! Beth glanced around. The two soldiers who had come to their aid still stood guard, their vehicle sitting nearby. "No, help get me on top of that transport."

Devin glanced to where she pointed and picked up on her plan right away. "You two, help me get her up here." He pointed to the vehicle. "We need to stop the shuttle."

The men looked at him, a little confused, but moved in their direction.

"Come on! We're going to be stuck down here!" Devin yelled. His warning whipped the crew to action as they rushed to join Devin and Beth at the side of the gadabout and heaved her up on top. Thankfully, the guards had left it running, and a few seconds later, the tires spun to motion, kicking up dirt and loose rocks. The gadabout barreled toward the shuttle as it rose off the ground.

Chapter 39

The gadabout jerked and rocked as it raced across the barren surface of Janis IV. Beth pushed herself to a hunched-over standing position, hands gripping a circular hatch. Ahead, the shuttle bobbed and swayed, not gaining much altitude.

None of them are experienced pilots. Beth thanked her lucky stars. If one of them had any skill flying, they'd be far out of reach by now. At the moment, the shuttle hovered about two yards above the ground, low enough that the land vehicle would scrap its bottom if it drove under. Beth readied herself to grab hold of a bar fastened next to the ship's side door. But as the moment of impact arrived, the shuttle suddenly shot upward.

"Shit!" With a desperate push-off, Beth launched herself skyward. Arms outstretched, she caught hold of a storage panel, her fingers narrowly gripping the raised edge. Above her sat the hollow of an atmospheric exhaust port. Bending her elbows, she hauled herself closer, then reached up with one hand, curling her fingers around the indented cove. Her other hand followed as she clenched to the rapidly ascending ship.

The thin atmosphere meant less air battered her body; nevertheless, the rushing wind made a go of flinging her loose. The acceleration whipped her around like a tree growing next to a launchpad. Finally, the ship entered the weightless void, and her body went still. Beth didn't dare relax, though. The constant thrust threatened to leave her floating behind if her grip failed.

After a few minutes, she realized the shuttle wasn't heading for the Celestus.

Maybe they don't know where it is since I moved it. But the scanners should find it easily. As the shuttle continued away from the planet, it became clear they had no intention of going back to the tragic vessel.

They're going directly to Point Alpha. As if in direct answer to her realization, a small, distant object caught a band of sunlight and gleamed among the vast spray of stars. The thing appeared as a rectangle with angled edges, more like a cargo cube than an escape ship. But the inactive thrusters on one of the long sides couldn't be mistaken.

The shuttle orbited the vessel once before approaching a set of large double doors at one of the smaller ends. During the pass, Beth noticed control center windows in the vessel's middle, opposite the thrusters. Moments later, the entrance opened wide, and the shuttle set down within the transport. She observed another shuttle sharing the area with room for a third. As the bay doors closed, Beth pushed off in the zero gravity as quietly as possible. A bang on the transport's hull would alert them to her presence, and she needed the element of surprise.

Soaring weightlessly, she caught the top of the other vessel just as gravity snapped on. The sudden change dropped her body onto the hull with a clang. She barely noticed the impact, and even the noise took a backseat as she slid immediately off the side. Beth pressed herself flat against the craft, trying to slow her descent enough to find a hold. As she slipped further, her eyes fell on a rung built into the side for top access. She loosened her grip and pushed off with her good leg. The ill-conceived maneuver was enough as her hands latched onto one bar. Her body swung briefly like a pendulum. Once she felt secure, she climbed partway up to observe the other shuttle without being easily spotted.

Did the noise alert them?

After a brief wait, the shuttle's ramp descended, and Nicoles and two other people exited. They all carried assault blasters and glanced about as if they expected an ambush.

Must have brought those from the domes. There were no guns on the shuttle.

"Look around. I definitely heard something on the ship after we took off," Nicoles said. One soldier nodded and walked a slow circle around their craft, keeping their rifle poised to fire. Nicoles and the remaining guard took a few steps away and watched the proceedings. Beth eased back behind the cover of the other shuttle and listened. With the weapons they carried, being spotted before she surprised them was the last thing she wanted.

"All clear," the soldier said after a few minutes. "Looks like if she boarded, we shook her off in the atmosphere."

"She *was* on board, though. Look at where the hull is bent in."

Beth couldn't see any of them, but knew what they had found. She hadn't had a choice. It was all she could do to keep hold when they took off.

"You're right, but she's not here now," the first person said.

"We'll lock down the ship when we get to the bridge. I'll set a program to move us away from Point Alpha until nearer the rendezvous time, in case she's out there somewhere," Nicoles said.

"Seems unnecessary; we took the only shuttle. She's trapped on the planet with everyone else if she even survived the fall," the second one said.

"We can't be too careful, especially once we're in cryo."

Beth heard a distant door sliding shut. Still, she waited for several more minutes before making a move. The three would put themselves into the cryo-chambers to await a retrieval team sent by the Ortelius corp. She surmised there wasn't an abundant supply of food and water on this ship, so they'd want to settle down sooner rather than later.

I should wait a couple of hours to be sure they're asleep—no point in making this any harder than necessary.

Over the next few hours, the bay remained silent. Neither Nicoles nor anyone else had reentered since leaving, and Beth decided it was time to make her move. She could have stayed in her hiding spot on the top of the shuttle for a full day or more, but it seemed unnecessary. What could her opponents do besides settle in for a long wait? With a thud louder than she liked, Beth dropped from the rungs built into the craft and landed on the floor. She made her way over to the doors and accessed the keypad. At first, the entrance rejected her open command, but after producing the admin access card, the barrier slid upward, revealing a hallway. Two open doorways stood about halfway down the passage, and a gateway similar to the one she just opened lay at the far end.

Beth waited, listening for any activity. The low hum of an idle vessel resonated in her mechanical receptors.

Seems like I made the right call. Moving up to the opposite-facing entryways, she stopped to take a quick peek around each corner. One opened onto the small bridge, while the other looked like an engineering section. Out the bridge window, Beth saw the faint movement of stars.

They must be relocating the transport, as Nicoles suggested. Let me take care of that right now. She entered the bridge and approached the center console. "Computer, show me navigation control for this ship."

"Unfamiliar design. Analyzing," the module replied. "Analysis complete." A series of familiar instructions appeared before her vision. Beth got right to work, first shutting off the autopilot, then inputting an alternative course to take them back to the Celestus. However, every time she tried to implement the course correction, an error flashed on the console.

From behind, the brief sound of something soft brushing across metal caught Beth's attention. She turned just in time for a metal rod to slam into her faceplate. The force spun her back into the bridge controls, then onto the ground.

What's—? She didn't have time to think before another blow scrambled her vision. Everything went black as her eye sensors failed. Beth kicked out and caught something solid with her boots as the rod struck her shoulder off-target. The thud, immediately followed by a metallic clang on the floor, told her she'd laid the assailant prone and disarmed them, at least briefly. Grabbing the edge of the console, Beth pulled herself to her feet.

"Shit," a familiar voice said. Beth recognized it, even with only a single word, Nicoles.

"Give up," Beth said, doing her best to face where she'd heard the man fall. He didn't know she was blind and might give up now that he'd lost the element of surprise.

"Fuck you, machine. You think you can take on the entire Ortelius corporation. You'd have been better off staying on the colony."

Beth followed the sound of the words as the man seemed to stand, then she lunged forward, arms outstretched. Quick footsteps rang out, and she caught only air, then rolled to the floor—the metal rod dragged along with a tink, tink, tink. "You think I'm outmatched? You seem to have some coordination problems," Nicoles said.

As Beth pushed herself up, the rod came down on her back, laying her out flat.

"I knew you'd followed us. You just don't know when to give up." Nicoles bashed her across the back of the shoulders. Thankfully, her head must have been out of his reach. She couldn't afford any more strikes to her sensory systems. She'd placed her consciousness in the only available body. An assistant bot. It was built sound enough for any strenuous task and resistant to most hostile environments, but she wasn't a combat model. Her body could only accept so much punishment before failing. With her vision gone, and her left leg locked at the knee, Nicoles had an advantage. If other systems received similar damage, she'd have no chance.

Beth rolled over and threw up a hand. Predictably, the rod crashed down onto her arm with brutal force. Despite the impact, she snatched it with her instant reflexes, then immediately jabbed it backward. The weapon contacted some part of Nicoles at the far end, and she heard stumbling footsteps. Beth got to her feet, steadying herself with the console, as the sound of an assault rifle charging up echoed in the room. Desperately, she swung the rod in the space. It clattered against a wall, missing her intended target. A blast of force cut into her chest as alarms rang in her head. He'd shot her!

She swung the rod again as her other hand reached for something to stabilize her balance. Her body jerked out of control, and her head spun with dizziness. Something solid met her hand as she fell. It caught her weight, and she kept her footing. Another shot is coming any second.

What can I do? Panic swelled within her. She felt sick, even though she had no bile to vomit up. She didn't feel any pain, but disorientation and failure assaulted her mind, as she knew her last moments had come. Everything she'd done was all for nothing. She'd survived infection from the organism, lethal radiation, falls, explosions, and having her mind separated from her body. And none of it mattered. In the end, the admins, the company, would triumph. All the survivors of the Celestus disaster would be nothing more than experiments for some future scientists to observe and dissect as the parasite experiments began anew.

The shots didn't come, seconds ticked by, and death didn't arrive. Instead, Beth heard cautious footsteps sliding closer.

What stopped him? Beth's steadying hand readjusted, and suddenly she suspected the answer. Though she couldn't see, she knew she stood next to the ship's navigational control and in front of the bridge window. One poorly aimed shot could destroy the ability to steer the transport or pierce the window and suck out all the atmosphere; two things Nicoles desperately didn't want. It was likely the reason he'd attacked her with the rod and not risked shooting at her when he'd had the opportunity. She could tell he approached to eliminate the chances of a miss.

"One more move, and I'll smash the controls." Beth raised the rod over the console.

"You wouldn't dare. You need this ship," Nicoles replied.

"You think so? It matters little to me whether you all face justice back on the homeworld for what you did here or drift into a star and burn alive. I've had enough." If Beth had had teeth, her words would've seethed through them in oily disdain. "Put down your weapon or seal your fate today."

Silence filled the space. She tried to determine his position from all the information she had. His voice put him near the entryway, a couple of yards off at most. He likely had the rifle against his shoulder, pointed at her body or head.

He's considering his options. Time to force this asshole's hand. "Fine." Beth lifted the rod, then brought it downward. At the same time, she dodged to the side. The rifle went off. A loud crack echoed, followed by a high-pitched whistling sound as the shot blasted the window, compromising its integrity. Beth released the rod at full strength toward the glass as she lost balance and fell. The preceding whoosh of air let her know she'd hit her target, opening the bridge to the void. Nicoles screamed something unintelligible as his voice flew across the room, chasing his body through the gap.

Beth held on to the base of a bolted-down chair until all the atmosphere evacuated. After, she heaved herself up and into the seat. In the silent stillness of space, her mind worked.

How do I get back to the Celestus and get everyone up from the planet? I can't fly a shuttle if I can't see. In the utter black of sensory deprivation, something bright lit up in one corner. Beth turned her head and saw the module instructions floating in the blank void. They weren't really there to be seen with eyes or sensors, but projected directly into her processor from the augment. "Computer, show me how to stop the ship." An additional set of directions appeared, and Beth pressed at the hanging lights, her fingers finding the buttons.

"Ok, but can I use this to get back down to the planet?" She felt at an impasse. Could she leave the ship here and take a shuttle down to Devin, where he might restore her sight? Getting this transport to the Celestus felt like a secondary objective compared to that. Still, she'd like to find it again after leaving. "Computer, does this vessel have a signal beacon?"

"Analyzing... Affirmative." A new light bloomed in the endless night. Beth pressed it, though nothing indicated anything had changed. Perhaps a light on the console showed the beacon active, but was no use to her dead eyes. Beth shuffled her way across the room despite her head feeling like she'd spent an hour in a launch simulator. When she exited into the hall, she found the door button and closed off the bridge. As oxygen filled the space, the breach alarm rang into existence. She ignored it and felt her way to the docking bay. Inside, she conjured up an image of the area, recreating the positions of the two ships in her mind. It worked surprisingly well. As she crossed the room, her fingers felt the side of a shuttle almost exactly where she expected to find it.

When she got inside and sealed the hatch, she took a seat in the cockpit and brought up the flight instructions. Luckily, the shuttle had an autopilot capable of undocking and flying toward the planet. However, finding the colony and landing would be a different matter.

Chapter 40

I don't know enough about robots to even begin to restore my sight. She hesitated, lost for what to do next, then settled back and brought her hands up to her face. Her fingers traced a concave indentation, the impact point of Nicoles' first attack. It lay directly where her forehead and nose would be. Next, she felt at her side, where the shot had pierced her metal skin. A crater-like hole marred her smooth carapace. It wasn't a large hole, and while it seemed to mess with her mobility, she hadn't become disabled. The wounds would have been fatal to her human body, and the blindness may still prove lethal, but for now, she felt able to push them down on the priority list.

The shuttle cruised on autopilot in what Beth hoped was the direction of the planet. "Computer, I need to open a communication channel with the colony on Janis IV." The familiar highlighting appeared like beacons on a starless night. She already knew how to contact the colony using the shuttle, but having the bright instructions over the controls meant she didn't have to attempt the process entirely by feel. Pressing the proper inputs, she heard the soft static of an open line. "Attention, Janis IV colony, this is Dr. Beth Adler. Does anyone receive me?"

The dead line whispered hollow static back at her. Beth waited a full minute before repeating her message. Again, no response.

Damnit! I know they abandoned their communications array, but with the infected subdued, they should have free access again unless something happened with the roundup. She shivered at the thought of the infected gaining the upper hand in the confusion of Nicoles stealing the shuttle and abandoning the mission. The battle seemed somewhat in hand when she left to chase after him, but things certainly weren't over.

What if the infected turned the tide and overwhelmed everyone? What if

Devin was killed because I left? Helplessness washed over her. She'd had no choice but to follow Nicoles; he'd taken the only shuttle. If she'd stayed to finish capturing the infected crew, they'd all be stuck on the planet.

I should have waited longer for Nicoles to get into cryo. Was he really so paranoid as to wait around hours for me? She knew the answer, though.

Beth slumped her shoulders. She needed to find the colony and land the craft, all without using her eyes. "Computer, show me how to locate all beacons in the area." She didn't know if the ship had the capability, but this was the way to find out. To her relief, instructions bloomed bright, and she activated the console. Then nothing. "Ugh! Of course, I can't see the beacons. This doesn't help..." Her fists clenched and her hydraulics tightened throughout her body.

How in the galaxy do I do this? I need to see or have something guide me. The ship has sensors, but I can't read them. If only I could use the module to somehow see with the ship's eyes.

An idea struck. "Computer, show me how to interface a robot with the ship's systems." The directions flared to life, and Beth leaped from her seat. "Yes!" She pumped her fist in the air, then wobbled on her locked knee before plunging back into the chair. "Ok, let's see what this looks like." Using her arm's access port, she extended a retractable cable. After fumbling around for the socket, she plugged into the console's interface where the module instructed, then punched the commands to link her processor to the ship.

A buzzing sound hummed inside her head as an uneasy and invasive feeling crept over her. She struggled to describe it, but it felt like when she first woke up in Devin's room in her new body. Dizziness and disorientation threw the space into a spin of sensations, even without sight.

After a few seconds, however, the disorientation subsided, and Beth tried to decipher her senses. Beyond her body, she could "see" a three-hundred-and-sixty-degree spherical field. Still, it wasn't a vision of the galaxy as she'd expected. No pinhole stars twinkled in the void. Scattered fields of red, like liquid spilled in Zero-G, washed amongst the black. Four objects stood out: a large blotch which seemed the most distant and scattered, a medium, somewhat circular spot, and a couple of nearer angular shapes.

These must be heat signatures from the sun, Janis IV, the Celestus, and the admin's transport. Though the sensor's infrared detection showed her the general location of those nearby objects, she didn't feel confident it gave her enough clarity to locate the colony or even land successfully.

"Computer, show me how to lock onto the colony beacon with the shuttle sensors." Across the red and black void, the directions came to life. Beth saw a pulsating dome of light expand outward from a spot on the planet and fade away into deep space. This phenomenon repeated every few seconds. "Perfect." Taking the flight controls, she maneuvered the vessel toward the signal's origin.

Minutes later, she felt the atmosphere hitting the ship as friction sent vibrations through the craft. In her sensor-guided vision, she made out the vague definition of the ground. Areas touched by the sun bloomed bright red, while regions in shadow appeared purple. Despite the view, she kept the craft high in case a mountain, which looked like a valley, appeared between her and her destination.

Another idea formed in her mind. She could activate the radar sensors, which should show the definition of solid objects for a significant distance. No sooner had she considered asking the computer for directions than her sight filled with the region's topography. Mixed with the infrared, it made for a maddening picture. Beth attempted to look away from the mass of geographic information but had no eyes to close; the data pumped directly into her visual processor. *Ah! Turn it all off.* Suddenly, her vision went blank.

Beth panicked. She frantically hit several controls on the flight console, trying to find the auto-hover feature. The ship went into a brief dive before leveling out and holding position.

This is crazy! I just think something, and the shuttle does it. Alright, activate radar.

The mountains and valleys, with all the terrain in between, appeared, though only as a tightly woven green grid against a black background. Still, the detail was good enough that she should be able to spot the colony compared to the landscape.

She took to the controls again and set a course for the source of the beacon. After about forty minutes, Beth swooped over a tall ridge and spotted four domes poking up from a flat plain. Her shoulders rose and fell as she went through the motions of relief. "I'm almost back to you, Devin." She saw several parked vehicles outside the structures, marking the capture force had already returned. Beth maneuvered the ship above the pad she'd landed on previously and put it in hover. Then, after silently asking for instruction, she initiated the auto-landing sequence.

The shuttle set down with a dull thud, and she cut the engines but left the sensors running. Once she disconnected, she'd be just as blind as before. After a couple of minutes, the radar picked up people moving out of the nearest dome and in her direction. Beth disconnected and felt her way blindly to the vessel's rear, where she engaged the ramp and opened the cargo door.

"Beth, you're back!" Devin's voice rang out. "Stars! What happened to you?"

It was the sweetest sound Beth could imagine. Finally, she'd made it back from her crazy mission, and Devin had survived the assault on the infected.

"I ran into some trouble. I need your help." She took one step and collapsed.

Chapter 41

From a walkway overlooking the cargo bay, Beth and Devin watched the crew load the remaining stasis chambers containing the colony's infected onto the Celestus. The ground crew had taken care of shuttling all the subdued people and supplies up from the planet over several trips. Devin worked diligently on repairing Beth's robotic body and restoring her sight. Once she felt capable, Beth insisted on overseeing the last of the evacuation.

"Looks like they're just about done abandoning the colony. How are your eyes?" Devin asked for the third time in the last hour since finishing the repairs.

Beth laughed. "You are so worried about me. You did a great job; I'm not having any trouble."

"I *am* worried! File corruption is an actual concern."

"So, my entire consciousness is just a file to you?"

"What, no... I—"

Beth smiled an unseeable smile. "I'm just messing with you."

Devin let out a short laugh and shook his head. "It's impossible to tell with A.R.I.A.'s lack of expression. But seriously, this is unfamiliar territory I'm dealing with. I didn't know if shutting down your processor would kill you or not."

Beth stood straight from the rail she'd been leaning on. "But you didn't have to. I was awake for the entire procedure."

"Not entirely. I put your processor on backup power, and did the fix to your optics, then reattached everything. You might have noticed some time dilation."

"Huh... So many things have felt weird in this body that not feeling myself has become the norm."

"Hopefully not forever." Devin took her hand in his. She couldn't feel his warmth or calluses, but the pressure of his touch sent a surge of heat from her fingers, across her chest, to her extremities. Despite knowing she had no organs, blood, muscles, or tissue, it still amazed her at how much she felt like herself in that metallic shell.

"What do you mean, not forever?" she asked.

"Well, it will be a long trip back to the homeworld. More than the usual eight years since we're hoping to avoid the company retrieval team en route. Which means I've got a lot of time to work on this experiment."

"Surely you won't stay awake the whole time?"

"Maybe not, but I can set up a series of experiments, then take some rest in cryo until they're complete. Though I'd like to keep you company for the trip."

"I would appreciate the company, but I think you'd get bored with the journey." Beth shrugged.

Devin laughed. "Are you kidding me? You transferring your consciousness is just the breakthrough I needed. All that has to happen now is find a way to put you back into living tissue, something I never accomplished with the mice. But with no company admins or directors dictating my workload, I can attack this problem full-force."

Beth tilted her head and smiled, though Devin would only see a smooth, blank, robot face. "I've got no body to go back into, and I don't wish to live the rest of my days as a mouse."

"Hey, mice have it pretty great, eating, sleeping all the time, and all the other mice-tail they care to chase."

They both laughed, then Beth embraced Devin, taking care not to use her full strength. When they parted, Devin spoke again. "Anyway, I'm excited about what's ahead. Depending on how it works out, I'll need your help."

"Of course, but I've got to work on a permanent cure and test everyone still in cryo. If some bio-scientists and research doctors are clean, I can have them thawed to assist in the cause. But, it'll be much easier to make progress myself with no need for sleep. Most of all, I want Sophie and Liam cured as soon as I have a counter agent. I've really missed everyone."

"I understand." He gave her hand another squeeze. Together, they observed the crew lock in the final cryo-chamber, suspending an infected colonist. "Is the ship ready to take us home?"

"Almost. There's one thing I want to do to throw off anyone coming to retrieve the admins. The Celestus is pretty damaged and will be slower on her return trip, at least at first. I don't want anyone out there looking for us."

"That's a good idea."

"I'll take care of it right after we bring in the admins' ship."

"Already on it. The shuttle crew is towing it back as we speak." Devin put his hand up to his mouth as he yawned.

"I don't even know what time it is. How long have you been up?"

He chuckled. "Too long. No offense, but working inside your head was pretty strenuous."

"Why don't you get some sleep in my room? Yours is a little messy. I'll join you after we're underway." Beth stepped down the hallway and beckoned Devin with a wave.

"You sure?" He followed.

"Yeah, I'll check in on you in a bit."

"Alright, no argument here." The two of them walked to her room, with Beth escorting him along a safe path with no depressurized areas, fluctuating gravity, or toxic environments. She made a mental note to distribute a digital map of all the dangerous sections and safe passages she'd logged for the rest of the crew. They'd have their hands full with all the needed repairs. The best she could do for them was diagnose any uninfected people still in cryo, get them awake, and put them to work. At her door, she and Devin embraced again before parting ways.

She left the crew quarters section and headed to the bridge. Once there, she canceled the emergency beacon she'd set while still human, then recorded a new message: "This is Dr. Beth Adler of the Celestus, calling for anyone who can hear. We've been caught in the gravity of the star, Janis. Our engines are shot, and maneuvering thrusters only have enough power to keep us in a slowly decaying orbit. We desperately need aid. We have over eight hundred crew aboard, including those in cryostasis."

She transferred the message to an external beacon and launched it into the system to broadcast.

I'll take the ship on a flyby of the sun. Any debris that comes off will help with the deception. With the first task done, she began prepping the colony ship to leave the orbit of Janis IV.

On the sensors, she spotted the shuttle approaching the massive colony ship. Behind, it towed the rectangular transport, holding the admins frozen in cryostasis. Beth opened a channel to the vessel and spoke, "Cargo shuttle, this is the Celestus. Redirect course to the main shuttle bay. We can store the transport there, separate from the rest of the crew in the cryo bay. Let me know when your cargo is secure."

"Roger that, Celestus. Adjusting course."

Beth watched the vessel on the external cameras. Once it docked, she shut the bay door. A few minutes later, the pilot called the bridge to inform her they had locked the shuttle and admin transport down. Using the module to assist, Beth moved from the communications console, took a seat at the helm controls, and steered toward the star at the system's center. She programmed in a gravity slingshot maneuver, taking in the computer's recommendations on the condition of the vessel and the available power to the engines.

The best thing she could do for now was to get everyone as far from this system as possible. She couldn't risk letting any agents sent by the company discover the Celestus and its survivors. Given some time, she would develop a counter to the parasite, and then it would be safe to wake up the entire crew. Things were going to get better, eventually.

The Celestus cut a broad curve around the sun. It kept a prudent distance to avoid becoming a victim to the star's insistent pull. Still, a few indicators lit up on the bridge. Their flashing red language let Beth know the exposed parts of the ship were taking heavy radiation. Finally, an alarm rang out as weakened elements tore from the craft, leaving a sparse trail of debris. The vessel wouldn't be in danger for much longer. Still, Beth manually piloted it a little farther from the blazing star to ease the strain on its already mutilated hull.

A few hours later, the last survivors of the Celestus disaster cruised out of the Janis system and away from the abandoned colony, silently racing for the safety of the infinite void.

Epilog

With a metallic clang, Beth sat down opposite Devin just as a loud argument erupted. Liam, Sophie, and Alan rounded out the group as they ate in one of the many mess halls of the Celestus research and colony starship. Dented and scarred metal enclosures with white cracked-ceramic edging bulged out in the corners of the walls and ceiling encircling the room. No other crew members occupied the many tables. Due to the ship's sheer size and the small number of workers awake on the return journey, most people kept to their sections.

Beth greeted the group with an invisible smile and a nod. However, they paid her little attention, as Liam was in the middle of another one of his rants.

"The problem with only having a skeleton crew awake is with all the work that needs to be done; there's no time between shifts to hit the debrik court." Liam jerked a thumb in the general direction of the mess hall entrance.

Alan nodded. "I hear what you're saying—"

"Liam, I'm going to thaw more people next week. We're officially less than a year from the homeworld, and we'll want everyone awake for the arrival," Beth said.

The gathered group looked in her direction, but Liam spoke up. "That's ahead of schedule. Are you sure the supplies will last?"

"Wow, we're that close?" Sophie said, her fingers scratching at the lines of gray that had appeared in her hair. "I haven't been paying enough attention."

Beth nodded. "I've just come from Requisitions. Alex and Cynthia have another water recycler up and running, and the hydroponics in the bio lab show significant promise. Anyway, I'm only thawing a few people at a time, so we can ensure the life support systems can handle the extra strain."

"Who knew you'd be so good at running a ship?" Sophie chuckled.

"Have you contacted anyone on the homeworld yet?" Alan asked.

"Not yet. We've got some time before we appear on any long-range sensors."

"All hell is going to break loose when we show up. The company will have a lot of explaining to do," Liam said.

Devin nodded and crossed his arms. "They'll feign ignorance, but we have a few hundred witnesses on our side."

The group laughed.

"I have one more announcement," Beth said. "Today, I plan to destroy the last of the organism."

"What? Really?" Liam's mouth dropped open.

"Yes. The antigen has successfully removed any trace of it from all crew members. The only way to be sure it never affects anyone ever again is to destroy my last remaining samples."

"I know the damage it caused, but are you sure it isn't worth further study? As a doctor and a scien—"

Beth cut Liam off. "I've had more time to think about this than anyone. If we keep it, we're no different from the company that used this ship as its petri dish. After seeing its effects and studying it for the last several years, I can confidently say the consequences of failing to contain it immensely outweigh any benefits gained by its continued research. Besides, we won't be able to control how it's used once it leaves this ship. Eventually, the wrong people will get hold of some. Then it's the Celestus incident all over again, except this time, it's an entire planet that's infected."

Liam's shoulders slumped, but he nodded his agreement. "It's difficult throwing away a discovery, dangerous or not. But I understand your logic."

When they all finished eating, Beth and Devin excused themselves and headed for her lab. "You don't have to come if you have something to do," Beth said.

"And miss this historic moment? No way. Besides, I haven't visited your lab in forever, and I want to see how your half of our project is coming along."

"I think you'll be pleased." Beth wiped her hands together as if they were sweaty, but gazed past them at the metal-plated floor as they walked. A lot was about to change again. They were still a year out from reaching home, but as soon as she alerted the homeworld of their existence, chaos might erupt. That, combined with completing the organism research and the project with Devin, reminded her of the ever-forward march of time. She'd had plenty of quiet time on the multi-year journey, unending days spent in silent research and days conversing with Devin and her friends when they were out of stasis.

I'll miss the solitude, I think.

"What is it?" Devin asked, breaking her daydream.

"What is what?"

"You seem distracted or... well, something."

"Oh... I guess I just have a lot on my mind." Beth wanted to say more, but they reached the lab and entered at that moment.

"Look, we don't have to go through with anything. I'm fine with the status quo."

"We both know that's not true. I'm not satisfied, but then again, I can't place my apprehension."

Devin approached a sizable cylindrical chamber lying on its side in the back of the room and looked down through the oval window spanning the top. Beth hesitated, then joined him. Her gaze fell upon the naked form of her younger self, though not far off from when she'd lost her body.

"The growth accelerants are looking good," Devin said. "Any mutations?"

Beth shook her head. "Nothing the gene editors couldn't clean up. All markers are clear. It helps that I'm not accelerating cell growth much, just above double the normal aging. Most enhanced clone experiments run at three or four times the standard rate. I've heard of successful subjects grown at ten times, with only slight anomalies. Course, this lab isn't set up for that level of acceleration or the resulting mutations."

"We're lucky the company included cloning as a backup plan for populating the colony in case of disaster."

"They'll have my eternal gratitude," Beth said, her words slick with sarcasm. "Anyway, I think by the time we reach the homeworld, my clone will be close to the age I was when my body died. Unless you're looking for a younger version of me?"

Devin laughed. "I'll take you any way you want, even if you decide to stay as you are now."

Beth kept her gaze on the clone but shook her head. "There are advantages, but I don't think I want this forever. It's fine on this ship.

Everyone has accepted what I am, but back home... There's no precedent for a human consciousness in an artificial life form. Things would only get more complicated. Still, I can't deny the advantages of this body." She stepped away from her living doll and glanced around the rest of the lab. "I'm scared."

"Beth—"

"How are things on your end?" she turned back, interrupting him, hoping to move on from the decision she'd eventually have to make.

Devin sighed but didn't press her. "Great, actually. My team has successfully conducted multiple transfers back-and-forth between the mice and hardware. Of course, there are some issues with repeated transfers of the same subject, but the survival rate has been steadily improving. I think when your new-old body is ready, there will be little chance of complications. I will be one-hundred percent sure of the process before we even discuss it again."

Beth smiled and nodded, though she knew there was no smile for Devin to see. The reflex and sensation of being human had never gone away.

Maybe I do need to be back in my body or the next closest thing.

She moved in silence to a console near a glass case of vials held by metal claws. Devin followed. With a few inputs on the keys, the cylinders rotated, most empty. Finally, the motion stopped, with four vials facing her, each a little over half full of blood. "Here we go." She shot a glance back at Devin.

"I'm proud of you. I'm proud of everything you did for all of us."

Beth smiled at him once again. She felt like he could almost see it. Turning to the console, she entered the commands to purge the samples. One by one, the claws moved the capsules into another enclosure within the larger housing. A sheet of lasers passed up and down, then back-and-forth over the vials, vaporizing all the contents and sterilizing the vessel. When the last one finished, Beth stepped back and let her body slump in a mimicked sigh.

It's done. "Let's go to astrophysics and sit in their observation lounge. I think I want to watch the stars go by for a while."

Devin took her hand, and together they walked out of the lab. A significant event had come to a close with a simple action, and yet, Beth still had plenty on her mind. Along with deciding to transfer her consciousness to a body cloned from her bones came the inevitable court battle with the company upon returning to the homeworld.

As if reading her mind, Devin spoke. "What are we going to do about the company when we come sailing back into the starport? They will not roll over easily."

"They'll play dumb, but they don't know I have all the recordings from the cat. I've also had Sophie and some of the other security members taking testimonials from the crew. It's all amounting to a cosmic pile of evidence."

"That's great, but why am I sensing some hesitation in your voice?"

Beth stopped walking and faced him. "Their crimes were so brazen, so callously bold. They were willing to sacrifice an entire ship of people, some of them well-known researchers, to retrieve samples from the planet. There had to be a contingency plan in the event things didn't go as planned. They won't go down without a fight. I just hope we're three moves ahead and not the other way around."

"I don't think they'll be expecting us."

Beth took Devin's hand and started walking again. Around a corner, they arrived at a lift. She pressed the call button, and the two stepped in when the transport arrived. "I hope you're right. You know, there's a part of me that wants to avoid the whole thing, take the ship into the galaxy's far reaches, and set up on a distant world unlikely to be discovered for generations."

"Yeah, you've mentioned it once or twice. That's a huge decision to make, Captain."

She shook her head. "Well, it's on my mind. Once they're all awake, I think I'll put it to the crew to vote. That's at least one decision I don't have to make. In any case, it's still a few months away."

They arrived at the observation deck and moved to one of the many couches, then sat in an entangled embrace. Beth pushed the weight of her new responsibilities and the consequences of her actions to the back of her mind. For now, a little alone time with the man she loved, watching the endless void drift by, sounded like bliss.

Note from the Author

Thank you so much for reading Orbital Strain! It's the first novel I've chosen to self-publish and I sincerely hope you enjoyed it. The process of writing and editing a book, then putting it out in the world, is a long and very surreal undertaking. If you enjoyed reading Orbital Strain, you'd be doing me a huge favor by leaving a review. Your feedback will go a long way in helping this and future books reach new readers. Thanks again for reading!

Made in the USA
Las Vegas, NV
29 December 2024

15592664R00125